WATCH AND PREY

HIDDEN NORFOLK
BOOK 15

J M DALGLIESH

First published by Hamilton Press in 2024

Copyright © J M Dalgliesh, 2024

ISBN (Trade Paperback) 978-1-80080-633-7
ISBN (Hardback) 978-1-80080-766-2
ISBN (Large Print) 978-1-80080-644-3

EXCLUSIVE OFFER

Look out for the link at the end of this book or visit my website at **www.jmdalgliesh.com** to sign up to my no-spam VIP Club and receive a FREE Hidden Norfolk novella plus news and previews of forthcoming works.

Never miss a new release.

No spam, ever, guaranteed. You can unsubscribe at any time.

To Jason, whose generosity is unmatched
on the north Norfolk coast

WATCH AND PREY

PROLOGUE

THE HINGES on the door protested as it closed with a heavy thud, the latch clicking into place, an echo reverberating throughout the lobby. Shaking the water from his coat, he hung it on the rack to the right of the entrance, shivering against the cold. This building never felt warm, although he was used to that by now. The winter in these parts was nothing like those he knew growing up.

The drawing room was aglow with flickering firelight, burning in the hearth and spitting the occasional ember. The leaded windows blocked what little daylight there was from passing through them and the wood panelling lining the interior walls and the shelving, crammed with dusty old books, felt oppressive and yet strangely comforting. Following the sound of voices coming from the rear, he shuffled past the door to the drawing room and on towards the kitchen, finding pans steaming away on the stove and a small transistor radio atop the kitchen table.

The hosts were discussing the day's events, momentous in recent years but not surprising to anyone who followed what had preceded last night's news and what had occurred in the months running up to it. The door to the cellar was open and he walked to the cellar head, peering down the stone steps into the gloomy basement, lit by a single bulb, seeing shadows move.

"Have you been listening?" he asked, knowing full well what the answer was. The BBC's analysis was on the radio, after all.

"Yes. It is happening just as you said it would."

"Is it just you down there?"

"Yes. I'll be up in a minute."

Nodding approvingly, he turned away from the cellar, tuning his ear to the broadcast. *The new Prime Minister is expected to return from the Palace within the hour, officially forming the new government following a week of uncertainty…*

"A week of uncertainty," he muttered to himself, pulling out a chair and sitting down at the kitchen table. Heaving a sigh, he stretched out his right leg, wincing as he did so. The winters may not be very cold here, but they were much wetter and the damp played havoc with his joints.

"Are you all right?"

He turned and nodded curtly. "It's this accursed country. It feels like it's always raining, forever damp, cold… and set in its ways."

"You're a fine one to talk!"

He frowned then. *Set in his ways?* He knew what was expected of him, and that meant no deviation. Maintain the standards. Remain well above suspicion, and then aim to achieve the goals set out for him. They had all worked so hard to reach this point but now, with everything happening in the country, there was change in the air.

It's not that change wasn't expected. It was. Planned for even. But this… this was something different altogether. The polls had the opposition party in excess of twenty percentage points ahead with talk of election fever brewing. The collapse of the government brought such change closer, potentially. Would they dare to go to the country now?

Change wasn't necessarily a bad thing. Change could bring about renewal. A fresh approach. Different goals. The direction of travel was such that forecasts predicted a shift to the left after such a lengthy period of dominance by the incumbent party. A party with a leader more successful than any of her predecessors in modern history, at least this century. History wasn't his strong suit, to be fair. This was a government which had arguably squandered its own popularity in recent years.

The events of this week, though... changes things. Forecasts would need to be remodelled. The incoming figure, the youngest serving Prime Minister this century, was something of an unknown. He was taking on a fractured party but one still with a significant majority. He had risen rapidly, making few enemies along the way, as far as could be seen anyway.

What would he do? Could he win the party a fourth election? Could he turn the tide of public opinion? Possibly. Possibly not. Either way, the analysis needed to be revisited. We may need to chart a different course entirely.

"Any chance of a pot of tea?" he asked, over his shoulder, opening a notebook and jotting down some immediate thoughts on possible scenarios. The back door opens and a cold draught brushed against his skin.

"I just need to get something from the garage."

"Hmm... okay," he replied, gnawing thoughtfully on his thumbnail and twiddling the pen in the other hand, keeping half an ear on the radio. As it turns out, he would never hear the broadcaster announce the departure of the new Prime Minister from the Palace, beginning the short drive across London to Downing Street. Nor would he witness the mass of camera shutters clicking as the PM stepped away from the cavalcade and approached the entrance to Number 10, offering a short address before the triumphal wave signalled his passing through the famous black door and into the heart of government.

He didn't even feel the first strike to the back of his head, let alone those that followed, or see the blood flowing before him on the kitchen table, pooling around his cheek as he lay face down on the surface, eyes open.

The kitchen was empty now, and the only sounds come from the disembodied voice carrying through the radio and the almost hypnotic sound of dripping blood from the table's edge to the stone floor beneath.

Good morning to you all. May I say firstly that I am extremely grateful for the trust that my Parliamentary colleagues have put in me…

CHAPTER ONE

APPREHENSION HUNG over the operations room when Tom Janssen entered, hanging up his coat beside the entrance. Eric was trading text messages with Becca, much as he had been doing since his arrival half an hour earlier. DC Danny Wilson had his feet up on a desk in the corner, stifling a yawn with his arms folded across his chest.

Cassie approached Tom before anyone else could address him.

"What's all this about, sir?" She had lowered her voice, and he could feel the tension in it. It had been a hell of a few days and the bruising to Cassie's face showed her role at the heart of those events. She was lucky to escape with only a severe beating, rather than forfeiting her life.

"That's a good question, Cass." Tom frowned, lowering his own voice to a conspiratorial tone. "I'm just as much in the dark as you are on this one."

"That's never a good sign," Cassie said, stepping away.

"Can you speak up a bit?" Danny asked from across the room. "I can't hear you if you drop your voice." Cassie hefted a stapler in the air and Danny threw his feet off the table and planted them on the floor, ready to dodge the throw but Cassie merely smiled and put the stapler back on the desk.

"Sometimes it's just too easy with you, Daniel."

Danny exaggerated a hiss in her direction. "My mum calls me Daniel. I hate it."

"Thanks for the tip," Cassie said, taking her seat and lifting the mug of tea to her lips. She caught Eric's eye and he nervously looked towards Tom who had entered his office.

"Any idea how long we'll be here, Cass?" he asked. "Becca is bathing George and she's a bit on edge… with, you know, everything that's happened. She wasn't very happy about me coming back tonight."

Cassie arched her eyebrows. "I hear you, Eric. I really do. At least you have someone who's missing you."

"So?"

"No idea," she said, nursing the mug in her hand. "Sorry."

Eric frowned and returned to his mobile, typing out another response. Danny came to stand over him. "I see you're still on the single finger typing, Eric. I thought you'd be two handed, like the other kids do these days."

Cassie snorted. "Danny, you're about five seconds older than Eric yourself!" The detective constable shot her a sideways look.

"At least ten seconds, maybe twelve."

The team had been put through the wringer on this case. DS Cassandra Knight had been abducted, along with her partner and another friend, and it had come very close to ending badly. Despite having an awful lot of paperwork to do, they were keen to explore some well-earned downtime. That changed less than an hour ago when they were summoned back into CID by DCI Greave. However, no one had any idea why.

They heard a phone ring and Tom immediately answered

it from his office, glancing through the window into the ops room as he spoke. Everyone's eyes turned towards him, although they all did their best to be subtle about it. Tom nodded glumly and hung up. The three detectives waited, and none of them spoke.

Tom slowly got up from his desk and came through to them.

"The DCI is just coming down," he said.

"And?" Cassie asked, speaking for all of those present. Tom shrugged.

"We'll soon see." Tom crossed the room and cracked the blinds with the fingers of his right hand, peering down into the car park at the front of Hunstanton Police Station. "Well, that's interesting."

"What's interesting?" the three detectives asked in unison.

"DCS Cole is leaving," Tom said quietly, taking his hand away and allowing the blinds to drop, as he turned to face the room, "and he does not look happy."

Cassie blew out her cheeks. They all knew what that meant. It was never a good omen for the team. They didn't have long to wait. Tamara Greave walked into the room a couple of minutes later and all eyes turned to her expectantly.

"Well, don't you all look full of the joys this evening. Thanks for coming back in. I thought you'd want to hear this from me rather than on the vine tomorrow."

Tom smiled, perching himself on the edge of a nearby unoccupied desk, and folding his arms. "We are all on tenterhooks to see what we're doing here."

Tamara sighed, cocking her head. "I'll cut straight to it then." Eric put his mobile down under Cassie's instructive eye and Danny Wilson pulled out a chair. Cassie kept nursing her mug of tea, as nonchalant as she could be, but it was clear she was just as keen to know what this was all about. "Our investigation has been referred to the IOPC—"

"What?" Cassie exclaimed, sitting forward and slamming her mug down onto the table. Eric sat open-mouthed and Danny shook his head in disbelief. It was only Tom whose demeanour didn't shift in the slightest.

"Hold on," Tamara said, raising her hands. "No one should be surprised by that. The involvement of the Major Crimes Unit with their informant, particularly regarding their behaviour in both theirs, and our, investigation has muddied the waters."

"But that's not us!" Eric complained bitterly, momentarily forgetting protocol. Tamara didn't seem fazed. It had been a tough week, and none of them had had time to decompress following the culmination of the investigation.

"No, Eric," Tamara said calmly. "That wasn't us, and for what it's worth, I don't think there is any suggestion that we are in any way tainted by their actions." Eric settled, nodding. "However," she said, looking at Cassie, "one of our officers was abducted and almost killed by an informant... and there was always going to be an investigation into our conduct, that of Major Crimes and... the levels of oversight we have above us."

Her gaze shifted to Tom, and he read the implication in her expression. That would explain DCS Cole's manner in the car park just before. He was only too happy to stand shoulder to shoulder with his Major Crimes counterpart, and that allegiance appears to have backfired. Dramatically.

"Ma'am," Tom said, "who is carrying out the inquiry?"

"No names yet, Tom," she said, "but it will be headed up by West Midlands Constabulary."

Cassie snorted with derision. "Like they have a decent track record when it comes to being dodgy!"

"A long time ago," Tamara said, locking eyes with Cassie and something unsaid passed between them. Cassie took the hint and didn't say anything further.

"And what does this mean for us?" Tom asked. "Operationally, I mean."

Tamara swallowed hard and cleared her throat. "Detective Chief Superintendent Cole has been suspended. Effective immediately." There was a sharp intake of breath around the room, and looks were exchanged. "I know. I'm surprised by that, but the chief constable has made that call."

"What about Major Crimes?" Tom asked.

Tamara tilted her head to one side. "I'm not in that particular loop, but I should imagine the same has occurred there too."

Tom heaved a sigh. "There's going to be some fallout from this."

"That, Tom," Tamara said, arching her eyebrows, "is an understatement. In the meantime, we will carry on as usual."

"Under whose watchful eye, Ma'am?" Cassie asked.

"For now," Tamara said, "mine."

"Ooo… promotion!" Cassie whispered.

Tamara looked uncomfortable but she nodded. "I am acting superintendent, for now." Cassie gave a brief round of genuine applause but when no one else took it up, and Tamara stared at her, she let it drop away.

"I was just saying congratulations," Cassie argued. A trace of a smile crossed Tom's lips. Tamara looked around the room.

"Does anyone have any questions?" No one did, and so she glanced at Tom, nodding towards his office. "Tom, a word?"

The two of them left the room, entering Tom's office and he closed the door behind them. Cassie, Eric and Danny formed their own little huddle to digest the information. Tamara rounded on Tom, and he could see the tension in her face.

"Am I right that you're not too happy about this turn of events?" he asked.

"You are the master of understatement tonight, aren't you Tom?"

He laughed. "I try not to get emotional. What's the problem?" Tamara paced the room, running a hand through her hair. Eventually, she stopped, took a breath and looked at him, lips pursed.

"There's a lot of scrutiny coming our way."

Tom shrugged. "Let it come. We have nothing to hide."

"I wish I had your confidence." Tamara shook her head.

"We acted above board. Cole and Major Crimes have questions to answer—"

"And they'll try to push it aside onto others."

"That's to be expected, particularly when it comes to a man like Cole."

"Don't underestimate them, Tom. I know Major Crimes, and people like Cole. They'll fling…" she hesitated, steadying herself. "They'll throw mud in every direction, and sometimes—"

"It sticks," Tom said.

"Even when it doesn't stick, it flows down," Tamara said, knowingly. "And we are beneath."

"You worry too much," Tom said, smiling. He glanced through the window into the ops room. "They're a good team. It will be fine." He then looked back at Tamara, his smile broadening into a grin. "And you get to be Superintendent. Auditioning for the role—"

"One that I will never be confirmed in." He cocked his head quizzically towards her. "We exposed some shady practices being carried out by Major Crimes, Tom."

"Inadvertently," he countered. "If we hadn't, Cassie would likely be dead by now, and things a lot worse."

Tamara waved that comment away. "I don't disagree, but my point is more about where we are now."

"You've lost me."

"They can try to minimise what they did, the possible outcomes that may have occurred. You and I both know they were willing to sacrifice Cassie to maintain their informant's cover, and keep their investigation going. Everyone will see that, even if the IOPC and the senior brass manage to white-wash it."

Tom understood, biting his bottom lip. "We did what we had to do. And it was the right course of action."

"That won't mean anything to the rest of the rank and file, let alone those above us. We will all have to make statements on the record. And we cannot lie." She closed her eyes, her tone taking on a bitter edge to it. "We did the right thing, and they will likely be destroyed. If not in the eyes of the public but certainly heads will roll, and careers will be ended." She shook her head. "Mine included."

"You did nothing wrong—"

"I will still be the DCI who brought about the collapse of a major investigation into organised crime and ended the careers of – at least – two colleagues. No one will ever trust me again. This will be the shortest promotion in history."

"I'm sorry," Tom said.

"I'll probably end up in charge of a neighbourhood watch liaison team once this all pans out."

"That's a depressing thought."

"Well," Tamara said, forcing herself to sound cheery, even if it was clearly artificial, "if I'm going down, you're coming with me."

Tom chuckled. "What's that?"

"Congratulations, Tom. You just made DCI."

"I did?"

"In an acting capacity, obviously."

"Okay," he said, expressing consternation. "So…"

"What?"

"When you get punted to neighbourhood watch, can I keep your job?"

Tamara laughed, and her tension appeared to ease. "I'll need someone to put the signs up on lampposts."

"I'll give you Cassie?" Tom asked. Tamara followed his gaze out to where the DS was laughing with the other two. "How is she?"

Tamara inhaled deeply. The climax of the case had almost seen Cassie's partner suffer the same fate as her. This had tested the strength of their relationship which was already coming upon rocky ground. Cassie was staying with Tamara for the time being until things calmed down. "She's masking it. You know Cassie."

"I do," Tom said. "Do you think she'll be all right?"

"In time, yes," Tamara said. "We could all use a bit of R and R after this lot."

The phone on Tom's desk rang and he leaned over, lifting the receiver. He looked sternly at Tamara, thanked the caller and hung up.

"Problem?"

"A suspicious death," he replied. "Over at West Acre."

Tamara rolled her eyes. "So much for rest and relaxation."

Tom walked out into the ops room and the conversation stopped. "A suspicious death," he said, looking between them. "I'm taking it, but I'm feeling charitable. Who's coming with me?"

Cassie smiled. "Since when does a detective inspector

attend a suspicious death?" she asked, glancing at the clock. "Especially at this time of the night."

"I'll go one further, Cassandra. Since when does a DCI attend a suspicious death at this time of night?"

"Well, well, well," Cassie said, beaming. "Congratulations, sir. Does this mean I get to be Inspector for a week?"

"Er… no, DS Knight," Tom grinned, "but you do get to accompany me to West Acre."

"But you said we could choose who—"

"The moment passed," Tom said, setting off for the door. "Don't forget your coat. It's gone a bit chilly outside."

CHAPTER TWO

THE VILLAGE of West Acre lay in the heart of the Nar Valley. The narrow lanes approaching the village green were silent. Tom easily spotted the patrol car parked on the verge before the All Saints Church beside the ruined gatehouse that once led to the West Acre Abbey. The abbey had long since perished, but at one time was incredibly influential to the region.

PC Marshall, standing at the gated entrance to the church, peered into the car as they drew alongside him. Recognising both Tom and Cassie, he smiled and nodded.

"Good evening, sir," he said to Tom, who greeted him and pulled his car into the verge behind the liveried patrol car. Getting out, Tom noted a couple of nearby bystanders watching proceedings, suspecting word was getting around the small village.

"What do you have for us?" Tom asked. The constable seemed nervous, his eyes flitting between the two of them.

"What is it?" Cassie asked him.

"I... um... wasn't sure, but I didn't expect the two of you to come out tonight." Tom understood. The officer had reported the suspicious death, and was clearly surprised to see a detective inspector and detective sergeant attend.

"Don't worry, Sheriff," Cassie said with a smile, using the constable's nickname, "you've struck lucky and got the dream team tonight."

"He's inside," Marshall said, thumbing over his shoulder towards the church. The bystanders were edging closer and the constable lowered his voice. "I'll be honest, I'm not sure but… it doesn't feel right."

"What doesn't?" Tom asked.

Marshall shrugged. "It might be nothing, but I had a really strong sense that it was all wrong."

"A sense?" Cassie asked, amused.

"Yeah… a sense," the PC replied.

"Are you channelling your medium abilities now?"

"No," Marshall said indignantly. "Don't you ever – I don't know – get a feeling?"

"Usually it's down to something I ate," Cassie said. The constable was about to respond but seeing Tom's expression, he thought better of it.

"Why don't you show us," Tom said.

Marshall opened the gate which shrieked on its hinges, holding it for them to follow. Cassie took the lead and Tom entered last. The gravel-lined path leading up to the doors of the church was flanked by large conifers which had been topped off since Tom had last been here, although he wasn't sure when that had been. It was likely a decade or more since he'd last visited the area, and the trees had been almost as tall as the bell tower back then. Now, though, they were only a little taller than he was.

Despite the rapidly descending darkness of nightfall, Tom paused as Marshall opened the door to the church and he and Cassie entered. Tom craned his neck, looking up at the clock mounted on the knapped flint exterior wall of the bell tower.

"Sir?" Tom lowered his gaze, seeing Cassie standing in the doorway. He resumed his walk, gesturing for her to continue with a flick of his hand and she turned, leading him inside.

All Saints Church wasn't very large. Just inside the entrance was the baptismal font, with an organ behind it. To the right of this were a drawn set of burgundy curtains, beyond the ornately recessed archway, shrouding the entrance to the bell tower. Casting an eye around the interior, across the pews to the pulpit and the chancel beyond the communion rail, the church was much as Tom remembered. His eye was drawn to the Barkham family coat of arms, mounted upon the west face, acknowledging the role of Sir Edmund Barkham in the restoration of the church that begun back in the 1600s.

"It's just here," PC Marshall said, standing to one side and taking hold of the drape but hesitating momentarily before moving the curtain aside, revealing the ropes connected to the ring of bells above in the tower. There were six ropes, five of which looped down and were tied off at the wall. However, the sixth was taut. The weight of a man's body, suspended halfway down from the floor of the belfry, ensured that was the case.

Cassie exhaled loudly whereas Tom took out a torch, angling the beam up to illuminate the body. PC Marshall did the same with his, and the two beams cast shadows across a man's pale face. His face held a tortured expression, set in place by his death. The body was swaying ever so slightly, probably due to the draught they'd created by opening the door.

The man was elderly, possibly in his mid-eighties, Tom guessed but, from ground-floor level and in this light, it wasn't easy to tell. He was dressed in a black coat and trousers, his white hair, receding from his forehead, sprouted from each side catching the torchlight and casting macabre patterns on the knapped flint wall behind him.

"Who found him?" Tom asked.

"One of the villagers," PC Marshall replied, still looking up at the body. "The church is unlocked every morning and left open for parishioners and visitors alike to come inside. The warden locks up each night."

"The warden found him?" Cassie asked.

"This is the warden," Marshall said quietly. He glanced sideways at her. "Someone out walking their dog passed by and saw the door was ajar, and came to investigate thinking the warden hadn't come by." Marshall sniffed. "Found him like this."

Tom moved his beam, studying the rope. At ground level, the rope sallies were coloured and made from wool to protect the hands of the bell-ringers. Above this, perhaps three feet higher, the rope of twisted woven flax rose up to the belfry. At the centre of the belfry level was a trapdoor. This was open and, presumably, it was from here where the warden fell, the rope wrapped around his neck.

"Well, it beats hanging yourself from a wardrobe door, I suppose," Cassie whispered. Tom looked at her.

"You're thinking suicide then?" he asked. Cassie cocked her head.

"More interesting than the usual method."

"What about you, David?" Tom asked, addressing the constable. Marshall looked at him. "You called us out. What do you think?"

"My first thought was the same as Cassie's," he said.

"But then?"

Marshall wrinkled his nose. "I'm not sure. The lady who found him," he glanced through the archway into the church, "couldn't believe he would do himself in. She was shocked. Didn't see him as the sort—"

"They never are," Cassie said drily.

"No, I mean she was more certain than what we usually get," Marshall said, leading Cassie to roll her eyes. "And then there's the rope." Tom looked again at the rope hanging from the belfry.

"What about it?"

"The thickness for one," Marshall said. "It will weigh a tonne. Okay, maybe not a tonne, but it hangs down, and for him to wrap it around his neck like that, he'd first have to haul it all the way up there, through the hatch. It'd take some effort."

"Fair point," Tom said quietly. He realised they were all keeping their voices down. People often would inside a church. It must be the reverence for churches that society instils. "How old do you think he is?"

"Mid-eighties?" Marshall said. "Do you think you could lift that rope all the way up there? I'm not sure I could at that age."

"I'm not sure you could do it now," Cassie said.

"The point is," Marshall continued, undeterred by Cassie's barbed sarcasm, "it takes some doing. A lot of effort for someone looking to off themselves. Usually, they'll do it at home or—"

"Step in front of a train," Tom whispered.

"Exactly."

"Any signs of disturbance?" Tom asked. "A break in, robbery?"

"Nothing that I could see, sir," Marshall said. "There's a donation box inside the porch, collecting for the ongoing restoration works, but as far as I can see it's not been touched. Other than that," he said, moving his torch around the interior, "there isn't anything of value. Culturally significant, yes, but nothing financially valuable."

"What about the man himself?"

"Martin Odiham," Marshall said. "He lives locally. He's been the warden for All Saints for the last ten years or so, took on the role from the incumbent when he passed away." He shrugged. "The villager who found him, Angela Gibbons, describes him as the salt of the earth. Always cheerful, and very passionate about the church and its place in the community."

"Not depressed or suicidal then?" Tom asked.

"She says not. She's waiting around the corner in the pub, gone for a stiff drink."

Tom cast his eye up to the belfry. "How do we get up there?"

"Stairs up are this way," Marshall said, indicating to their left.

"Okay, stay down here and make sure no one comes in. Cassie?" Tom inclined his head towards the narrow steps winding their way up the side of the tower. The two of them began the climb. The steps were only wide enough to walk single breast, and Tom took the lead.

They were both breathing heavily as they walked onto the timber floor of the mid-level. The bells were mounted at the centre of the tower, and Tom looked down from the trap door, seeing the warden suspended a few metres below them. His head was angled in such a way as to make it obvious his neck was broken, the head stuck at an acute angle, vacant eyes staring up at them.

The tension in the rope made it creak under the weight of the warden. Cassie also peered down into the gloom below. Now that PC Marshall had gone outside, there was no artificial light for them to see by. It was as if Martin Odiham was suspended in mid-air and, but for the visible rope around his neck, he could almost be floating.

"What a way to go," Cassie said. Tom turned the light of his torch to the immediate area around them. Scanning the floor, made from centuries old timber, he sought anything that stood out, signs of a struggle, any loose planks that could have seen him trip and fall in an unlikely but plausible accident.

There was nothing. The beam highlighted the dust in the air, disturbed by their presence.

"I doubt many people come up here very often," Tom said. Cassie was beside the wall, looking through a slatted covering of an exterior opening. A metal mesh cover was fixed to the inside, protecting the belfry from nesting birds.

"You get a great view of the village and the surrounding lands from up here," she said absently. Turning back to Tom, hands in her pockets, she walked back to where he was standing. "But I can think of better places to top myself."

"Have you given it much thought?" Tom asked, continuing his search.

"From time to time," she said, drawing a glance from Tom. She shrugged. "You know me, I like to keep my options open."

A fleeting thought crossed his mind. Cassie had almost been killed in their most recent case and, although she was prone to dark humour, he found himself wondering how well she was coping with what happened to her. Particularly, when put into the context of her relationship collapsing as a result, too.

He was about to say something to her when a glint of reflected light from his torch caught his eye. He moved to investigate, finding a piece of paper, green and white, with a sliver of foil attached to it, wedged between two planks close to the stairs that brought them up. Tom knelt beside it, holding the torch over it.

"What's that?" Cassie asked. Tom studied it from another angle.

"Chewing gum wrapper or something similar," Tom said. Taking a pen from his pocket, he used the tip to tease the sliver of paper out of the crack to see it better. There was a little bit of print on the paper, small, but Tom could just about read it in the light. He didn't recognise the language though. "What is that? Polish?"

Cassie leaned closer. "I don't know. It certainly looks Slavic. East European, almost certainly." Tom frowned, lifting his eyes and scanning the belfry.

"What are the chances?" he asked.

"Weird," Cassie agreed. The sound of vehicles pulling up came to them and Cassie returned to her viewpoint, looking across the church yard to the road where PC Marshall was now speaking to the arrivals, another patrol car and a civilian. "The FME has arrived."

"Well, we'd better get onto the scenes-of-crime guys and have them come out to bring the poor chap down. Fiona," Tom said, referring to the forensic medical examiner, Doctor Fiona Williams, "will have her work cut out for her unless we get him down."

"We could always get her up a ladder," Cassie said. Tom arched an eyebrow and Cassie winced. "Sorry. I'll make the call."

CHAPTER THREE

TOM DESCENDED the stairs to the ground floor, Cassie following on. Meeting Doctor Williams, accompanied by PC Marshall, in the porch, they stopped.

"Hello, Fiona. Sorry for the call-out, but I think this is one we need to look into."

"Tom," she said by way of greeting, then looked past him to Cassie, smiling at her. "You and your team seem hell-bent on keeping me in work."

"We do try," Tom said, responding with a smile of his own.

"A possible suicide," Dr Williams said, then looked side-ways at Marshall. "Albeit one that has given young David here the heebie-jeebies."

"I think you should come at it as if PC Marshall is onto something." The constable's ears pricked at that and looked between Tom and Cassie. Tom allayed his excitement with a raised hand. "We'll not get ahead of ourselves, but scenes of crime will be along in due course." He looked back towards the church's interior, as if he could see through the walls and into the tower. "But it is a strange one."

"Aye, there's definitely a sense around it, for sure," Cassie said, winking at the constable who bridled but didn't say anything.

"The witness," Tom said to Marshall. "The one who found the body. Where did you say she went?"

"Angela Gibbons, sir. She's just along at the pub," Marshall said, directing them off to the right. "The Stag, it's only a hundred metres or so down there, on the bend."

"We'll be back," Tom said to both of then, directing Cassie to come with him. Outside, they found another constable who'd arrived to support PC Marshall. They exchanged a nod before Tom and Cassie walked along the road into the darkness in search of the pub.

The Stag Inn was a traditional free house, located right on the road with a knapped flint exterior and a parking area to the rear. Two eight-seater wooden picnic tables were out front beside the road, but there was so little through traffic that patrons using them would never be at risk of being hit. Flower baskets hung from the exterior walls of the building and the wooden window frames were painted green.

No one was sitting outside, and Tom pushed the door open and entered the tap room. There were half a dozen people socialising and a couple of others behind the bar. All eyes turned to them and conversation ceased as they entered. Looking around Tom approached the bar, taking out his warrant card.

"DI Janssen. We're looking for Angela—"

"Just through there," the man said, pointing into the adjacent room. Tom judged he was the landlord. "In a right state, she is. And who could blame her," he added glumly.

"Thanks," Tom said, and he and Cassie walked through to the next room. It was clear which of the four people, seated on brightly coloured chairs, was Angela. Her eyes were bloodshot and swollen. The others sitting with her were offering her their moral support. Seeing Tom and Cassie standing over them, the small group parted ways and made room for them. "Hello, Angela. My name is Tom and this is DS Cassandra Knight. Do you think we could speak to you about earlier?"

"Yes, of course," she said, nodding and her friends moved aside, leaving the three of them alone.

"May we sit down?" Tom asked and again, she nodded and they both took seats around the table. "Can you talk us through what happened, please."

"I–I was out walking my dog, Trix," she said, indicating the dog lying at her feet beneath the table. It had its head down on its paws, looking dejected, almost as if it'd picked up on its owner's mood. "I was coming back past the church, I take the same route most nights, and I saw the door was ajar. That was very odd because Martin is so good at locking up. He's never missed a day, unless he's been away visiting family or sick, of course."

"Had you seen him today? Earlier, I mean?" Tom asked. Angela shook her head.

"His car was parked out front, and I found that odd because of how late it was, and seeing the church still unlocked was surprising."

"He drives here? So, he doesn't live in the village?"

"No, he lives in Castle Acre. He used to cycle over to us, but I know he was finding that quite hard recently and took to driving instead."

"What car does he drive?"

Angela thought about it. "It's a little Fiat hatchback. Sorry, cars aren't my thing."

"That's okay, don't worry. He's been unwell then, Martin?" Tom asked.

"Getting old," Angela said, inclining her head. "Aren't we all?"

Tom smiled sympathetically. "So… you saw the church was open?"

"Yes, and I went to check. I was going to close up and then give Martin a call… and…" she put a hand to her mouth, closing her eyes.

"Take your time," Tom said. "It's okay."

She swallowed hard, slowly taking deep breaths to steady herself. "I went into the porch and I poked my head through the door. I wasn't planning to go inside but…"

"But what?" Tom asked.

Her forehead creased. "I saw something." She shook her head and winced, almost as if seeing something in her mind's eye.

"Did you see Martin?"

"No, no… I was at the door. It was the curtain, through the arch to the tower. It hides the bell ropes"

"What about it?"

"One side was drawn back. It was open." She looked at Tom and then Cassie. "*It's never open.* The church is for the community, and we let people come and go, visiting as they please, but no one has access to the tower. Ever! Only… the warden or those of us who are involved in the running of the church."

"Would Martin have drawn the curtain back?"

"I don't see why he should have, no," she said, thoughtfully. "Anyway, that struck me as odd and I went through looking for Martin, expecting to see him tinkering with something or other. He's like that, you know. He is so very focussed once he sets his mind to something. And… I found him… like that."

She lowered her gaze, her hand shaking as she reached for her drink. A gin and tonic, by the look of it. Tom gave her a moment to take a sip and gather herself.

"Did you see anyone else hanging around while you were out walking Trixie?" Tom asked. At mention of her name, the little cockapoo stood up and moved over to inspect Tom. He stroked her head, scratching behind her ears.

"No, I didn't," she said. "I didn't see anyone at all. I would usually see some of the other villagers out with their own dogs, but I was out later myself tonight."

"What time does Martin usually close up the church?" Cassie asked.

"Between five and six." Angela shrugged. "If people are around then maybe later but most visitors are away by that time."

"How well do you know Martin?" Tom asked.

Her face lit up. "He's such a lovely man. I've known him for years, ever since he came to the area. He used to live here in the village, but when the house started to get a little too much for him, he downsized and moved to Castle Acre."

"Is he married?"

"Widowed." His wife passed away before I knew him. It's such a shame... for his life to end that way. I never would have thought he was one of those types."

"Those types?" Tom asked.

"Yes, one to take his own life. Especially in the house of the Lord as well."

"You think it was a suicide then?"

"Well..." she looked at Tom and then nervously towards Cassie, both of whom kept a straight face. "That's what your constable said. W-What else could it be?"

"Was he unhappy? Depressed?"

"No, I wouldn't say so..." she looked past them and into the other room of the pub. "I guess you never really know what's going on with some people, do you?"

"That's true," Tom said. "Tell me, has Martin been travelling recently as far as you know?"

"Travelling?"

"Yes, a holiday abroad, visiting friends? Anything like that?" Angela concentrated hard, her lips pursed.

"No, I don't think so. I believe he went to Vienna in the summer, but that was for a long weekend. He'd always wanted to go there. A bucket-list trip, to see the architecture." Her expression took on a faraway look. "That was one of Martin's passions, architecture. Church architecture, specifically."

"And does he know people abroad?" Tom asked.

Angela shrugged. "Not that I know of, but… maybe. Why do you ask?"

"It's just to get some background," Tom said, smiling. "We look to build up a picture of what's been happening in the lead up to someone passing away."

"You're a detective, aren't you?" Angela asked him and Tom nodded. She then looked at Cassie, her expression darkening. "What do you think happened here tonight?"

"It's just routine, Angela," Tom said. "Nothing for you to be concerned about. You said Martin was a widower. Does he have any children or other family living nearby?"

"No, he doesn't have any children that I'm aware of. He certainly never speaks about them – spoke about them – if he does. He lives alone. Not that he's ever been short of visitors. He's always been welcome here in the village. I've not heard anyone say a bad word about him."

"Where did he live before he came to West Acre?" Tom asked. Angela's brow furrowed.

"Come to think of it, I've no idea. He wasn't one to speak about his past very much, and I'm not one to pry."

"Why do you think he didn't speak about it?"

"I don't know. I figured… he found his past too painful. I know he would have been in his seventies when he first moved here, and perhaps he'd recently lost his wife, because he moved here alone. Some people always want to speak about their partners, you know, once they've passed, and others choose not to. I assumed he was the latter."

Tom nodded. He looked at Cassie, silently asking if she had any questions but Cassie offered him an almost imperceptible shake of the head. "Thank you, Angela. You've been very helpful."

"What happens now?"

"We will make the necessary arrangements with the undertaker," Tom said. "First off, we will have to look at the scene and satisfy ourselves as to what we think occurred."

"Right. Yes, of course."

"DS Knight will take your details, if that's okay?" Angela nodded. "And one of my officers will come by to take a formal statement from you tomorrow."

Tom bade her goodbye and as they stepped away from her, the patrons returned to the table, no doubt curious to hear what was said. Neither Tom nor Cassie spoke until they were back outside, the latch on the door to the pub clicking into place.

"You're taking this very seriously," Cassie said, almost accusatory in tone.

"That's right, I am," he said, setting off up the road back towards the church. Cassie had to hurry to catch up with him, Tom taking broad strides.

"Why?" Cassie asked, coming alongside. "Because of a chewing gum wrapper?"

Tom glanced sideways at her, sporting a lopsided grin. "You could say I'm *sensing* something."

"Oh, don't you start, sir!" Cassie said, shaking her head.

"You'll be having voodoo sessions with Sheriff at this rate." Tom chuckled and they came upon the stone wall lining the church yard moments later. "What is it?" Cassie asked.

"What's what?"

"What is it that you saw, and I missed?"

Tom stopped on the path leading up to the porch. The forensic team's van was parked in the lane and Fiona Williams came out of the church, seeing them, she made a beeline for Tom.

"Good timing, Tom."

"What can you tell me?"

"Not much, at least not until your crime scene techs have brought the poor man down, but…"

"But?"

"There is an abrasion on the left cheek. I was able to inspect it with the zoom lens on my mobile – cameras are getting good, aren't they? – and it is quite substantial."

"Caught his cheek on the rope as he fell?" Cassie asked. "A friction burn?"

"I will reserve judgement until we can inspect it properly, but I think it is more of an impact abrasion than something to that effect, Cassie."

"He'd been struck?" Tom asked.

Fiona was noncommittal. "I think he was struck, yes, but what I can't tell you is the manner of it. It is possible that the force of his weight on the rope, plus the angle of his pitch may have led to a pendulum effect."

"English, please, Doc," Cassie said.

"He may well have swung against the wall of the tower, perhaps more than once. Such a connection would almost certainly leave its impression on his facial tissue, Cassandra."

"Smacked his face against the wall," Cassie said, with a

curt nod, turning the corners of her mouth down. "Much easier to understand."

"Indeed," Fiona said. "However, he could just as easily have been beaten. I dare say the postmortem will be able to determine the cause."

"Cause of death?"

"Impossible to say while he's still dangling twenty feet up in the air, Tom, but you know that."

"I do, but I thought I'd at least ask."

"I would expect nothing less." Dr Williams smiled to both of them. "If you will excuse me, I have to see my grand-daughter before she leaves to go back to her mother's house."

"Thanks again, Fiona," Tom said. It was an unusual call-out for the on-call doctor. They would have to wait to have what he suspected confirmed. Tom found Cassie analysing him with a searching expression. "What?" he asked.

"You haven't told me."

He smiled. "I know. I'm quite enjoying watching you squirm."

Cassie snorted, looking around. "Go on, I give up. Tell me now and I won't even complain when Eric and Danny make fun of me tomorrow. What have I missed? How could you suspect foul play before Fiona gave you that information?"

Tom swept the church yard with his gaze. Cassie followed. "What don't you see?" Tom asked her.

Cassie looked around, then rolled her eyes as her gaze fell upon the police vehicles parked in the lane. "It's not here," she said. "There's no Fiat parked out front."

"There's no Fiat," Tom said. "Which means either we have the most opportune car thief working in West Acre or—"

"Whoever killed him took his car," Cassie said. PC Marshall appeared at the entrance to the church and Tom beckoned him over.

"Sir?"

"When you arrived earlier, was there a car parked in the lane?"

PC Marshall looked over towards where the patrol cars and the forensic van were parked, biting his lower lip. "Yes, come to think of it, there was. A red Fiat was up on the verge," he said, pointing to where he remembered it being.

"You're sure?"

"Absolutely certain, sir."

Tom looked at Cassie. "Then, whoever was here was most likely still inside the church when Angela came out to raise the alarm." Cassie seemed horrified. "The car was outside when she went in, and still there when David arrived. Then it's logical they were still in the area, if not inside the church itself."

"If they were inside the church when Angela came out to raise the alarm—"

"Then they could have slipped out unseen but hung around for the police to arrive before taking the car."

"Damn, they took a hell of a risk," Cassie whispered. "You're good, sir."

"That's why I'm an inspector—"

"Acting chief inspector, sir."

Tom smiled briefly, turning his gaze upon the church. His eyes lifted to the clock. The dial was renowned in Norfolk, a black face with gold leaf lining the circumference matching the gilding of the letters positioned in place of the numerals around the face. The phrase taken from the book of Matthew, 26:41, upon the eve of Jesus's forthcoming betrayal, written in gold.

"Watch and pray," he whispered.

CHAPTER FOUR

CASTLE ACRE WAS LARGER than its namesake counterparts of West and South Acre, with the population living in the areas surrounding the old priory and the castle ruins which gave the village its name. The castle having fallen into ruin in the late 14th century and the imposing priory falling foul of the dissolution one hundred and fifty years later: now the village was a draw for tourists as opposed to the cultural centre of its heyday.

"It should be just along here on the right, next junction," Cassie said as Tom approached a narrow side road on the edge of the village high street. "This one," Cassie said, and Tom pulled the car over close to the verge. None of the roads around these parts were very wide, never having been planned for modern use.

At the meeting of Priory Road and South Acre Road, separated from an imposing medieval church by the latter, stood a traditional knapped flint cottage. The structure was a simple square, butting onto the lane on the east side and the main road on the north. The rear was enclosed by a tall wooden fence, and a large gate offered vehicular access. The gate was securely closed and even Tom, with his formidable height, couldn't see over it.

Cassie walked along the fence line, inspecting it. Tom took out his mobile phone and quickly tapped out a message to Alice, advising her not to wait up for him. A knot had fallen out of one of the planks and Cassie peered through the hole it had left. "The car is here," she said. Tom looked at the house. The windows were square, and very small. They would offer little natural light to the interior, but originally such small windows lost less heat than the grander glazing in the aristocratic or merchant stately homes. This was a workers' cottage.

The cottage was in darkness. There were no visible signs of movement coming from within. If Angela was right and Martin Odiham lived alone, then who brought the car back here and why?

"You go around to the front door, and I'll go over," Tom said, inclining his head towards the fence."

"Be careful," Cassie said, and Tom nodded. He tested the fence in several places and when he found an area he was certain could hold his weight, he hoisted himself up, lifted his leg over and gently lowered himself to the other side. Landing in soft shrubbery, he stood still in the darkness, studying the cottage.

It was a double-storey building with a rear entrance door and a set of narrow French doors from a rear-facing reception room. He approached cautiously, eyes fixed on the doors and windows for any sign of movement from within. As he got closer, he could see the French doors were open, merely pulled to. Coming alongside them, he put his back to the wall and chanced a look inside.

The reception room ran from front to back. It had a low, beamed ceiling, likely fabricated from the old deck joists from the shipping industry refits. The old timbers were often repurposed for floor joists in the period these properties were constructed. Despite the interior gloom, Tom could see that the room had been utterly ransacked. The floor was covered in detritus, paperwork and drawers taken from a writing bureau, rifled through and tossed aside. No quarter had been given.

He heard Cassie knocking at the front door and he listened keenly for any reaction, any sign of response from someone inside. However, he couldn't be sure, but he suspected whoever had been here was long gone. A professional burglar could ransack an entire house and be gone in less than five minutes. Granted, if someone was intent on finding something in particular, then it may take a little longer but, even so, it appeared as if this person hadn't been too fussed about being meticulous.

Tom eased the door open, craning his neck to hear anything. There was nothing but silence to greet him. He stepped inside, trying not to step on anything but there was nowhere he could put his feet to avoid treading on something. Ideally, he would call for a forensic team, but he had to make sure the house was clear. Moving on into the kitchen, he found the scene to be familiar.

The cupboards at base level and head height had all been emptied with no care as to where the contents ended up. There was dried food, tins and broken glass alongside utensils and cutlery everywhere. Even the fridge door was open, the interior light offering scant illumination of the room accompanied by the whirring of a fan as the fridge desperately sought to compensate for the open door.

From the kitchen, Tom made his way into a narrow hall leading to the front door. A staircase was to his left and Tom checked there was no one lying in wait for him before he crossed the hall to the door and opened it. Cassie nodded a greeting, and he stood aside, allowing her to enter. She glanced to her left into the reception room, eyes widening at the scene of devastation.

Tom put his forefinger to his lips, indicating for silence and then pointed up the stairs. Cassie nodded and Tom put a foot on the first tread which squeaked under his weight. It sounded like a car alarm in the silence, but if someone was upstairs then they knew they were there. Cassie had been knocking after all.

Tom slowly made his way upstairs, Cassie a few steps behind. At the top they found themselves on a small landing with only three doors off it. The first door was open and led into a bathroom. Tom poked his head in and had a quick look. There was an airing cupboard housing the hot-water cylinder, the door hanging off the top hinge. A small vanity unit was in the far corner above a basin, the contents of which were lying in the basin or had spilled into the bath.

Moving to the next door, it was closed and Tom took a deep breath before turning the handle and easing it open. This looked like a spare bedroom with a single bed pushed up against the far wall. A standalone wardrobe was located against one wall, the doors open. The clothing and boxes within had suffered the same fate as everything else in the cottage. The mattress on the bed had also been overturned and shoved aside. Beneath the bed were storage boxes, their contents strewn around. It looked like old paperwork and box files. The discolouration of the folders suggested they were very old.

Moving to the last room, Tom felt a flutter of anxiety. The look on Cassie's face suggested she too was feeling it. There was a sheen of perspiration on her face, and he wondered if she was feeling the manifestation of the after effects of her kidnap ordeal. He drew her attention and with a simple look he checked she was okay. She nodded and forced a fleeting smile.

They both braced themselves and Tom pushed the door open. They were greeted by silence. The rush of air from the door opening did draw a draught through an open window, the breeze rustling the lightweight curtains hanging across the window. However, the room was empty. It had also been trashed.

"What were they looking for?" Cassie said.

"Whatever it was, I'm thinking they struggled to find it, if they even did."

"I think we can put to bed the idea this was a suicide," Cassie said. A massive bang seemed to shake the room, startling them both and, reflexively, they ducked. A rush of air passed over them a few seconds later. "What the hell was that?" Cassie asked. Tom turned and ran back onto the landing, Cassie following on. A flickering glow was visible through the obscured glass of the bathroom window and Tom hurried back downstairs. Cassie paused, staring at the window, the smell of smoke carrying indoors and up the stairwell. She then ran after Tom.

Downstairs, Tom found the back door from the kitchen locked and they had to go back through the French doors to reach the garden. The red Fiat, parked on a concrete hard standing next to the rear of the house, was ablaze. The windows had shattered from the force of the explosion and the interior cabin was already a raging inferno. Bits of plastic trim, heated by the blaze melted or popped every few seconds.

Tom held his hands up to protect his face from the heat as he approached the car. "Damn," he said quietly. "We'll not be getting any trace evidence from inside there." He turned, surveying the rear garden, the trees running along the perimeter fence and the assorted bushes, trying to see signs of movement. His eyes were no longer adjusted to the darkness though, the fire having seen to that. Scanning the shadows, he was blind. "Get onto the station. Have some uniforms come out here as soon as possible. I want this building secured."

"Shall we try and close off the area?" Cassie asked. Tom would like to, but this was rural Norfolk. There really wasn't any easy way to close it down like you could in a built-up area. There were so many lanes crisscrossing the county, farm tracks and open fields that it was all but impossible. Besides, they had no idea who they were looking for.

"No, for now, let's focus on what we can do well. When you've called the cavalry in, get onto Eric and Danny. I want background on Martin Odiham. Who he is, what he's done in the past. Former job roles, where he lived. Everything. And I want it now."

"I'm on it," Cassie said, taking out her mobile. Tom walked around the burning car. He doubted there was a timed device fitted to detonate. It didn't have to be that complex. A can of petrol, a rag and lighter would be enough to lay waste to the car. It was quite possible that whoever set the fire was watching him right now. He scanned the garden once again, keeping his wits about him, but there were no signs of movement, no sound other than that coming from the burning vehicle.

Had they arrived here five minutes later, he wondered if the cottage would have met the same fate as Odiham's car. Then they'd have even less to work with.

"Okay… you've got my attention," Tom said under his breath, just as another crackle burst into life as something else inside the car ignited, "and now I'm going to make sure I have yours."

CHAPTER FIVE

IT WAS APPROACHING midnight by the time Tom pulled into the driveway of his home. The exterior lights were still on, but he could also see the lights were dimmed in the living room. He'd expected both Alice and Saffy to be asleep by now.

The police radio Tom had on the passenger seat crackled into life, a hit-and-run collision had just taken place. Tom turned the volume down, until the device switched off. Martin Odiham's cottage was now secure with a permanent police presence. Forensic teams were deployed at both All Saints Church and the cottage in Castle Acre. Tom didn't need to coordinate anything else until the results of the examinations began filtering through to the incident room the following day.

Bone weary, he got out of the car, feeling the chill of the night air on his skin. Unlocking the front door, he was greeted by Russell, their terrier, who plodded out of the living room into the hall, sat down and yawned.

"I hear you, little man," Tom said, dropping to his haunches and scratching the dog behind the ears. He must have picked up the scent from Angela Gibbon's dog because he suddenly became more interested and inspected Tom's sleeve, sniffing him, his stumpy tail wagging furiously. "Don't worry, she's not a patch on you."

Peering around the corner into the living room, he found Alice sitting on the sofa, a blanket pulled up over her with Saffy lying against her, head on Alice's chest. She was sound asleep whereas Alice herself must have only been dozing because she opened her eyes, whispering Tom a sleepy greeting.

"Hey there, DI Janssen," she said, smiling. Tom took his coat off, hanging it on the newel post at the foot of the stairs before walking through. He kept his voice low, keen not to wake Saffy. Cocking his head, he studied the little girl. She looked so angelic, far from the bundle of energy that wreaked havoc almost everywhere she went. He noticed streaks on her face. She'd been crying. Alice read his expression, gently moving the hair away from Saffy's face, gently stroking her cheek.

"What's going on?" Tom asked, keeping his voice low.

"One of the other children in her class has been upsetting her," Alice said, glumly. "She couldn't sleep, and so I let her stay here with me." Russell, who had been keeping close to Tom, decided he'd spent enough time gauging this new creature in Tom's life, and trotted over to an armchair, hopping up onto it and curling himself into a ball. However, he kept half an eye on proceedings, just in case.

"Which child?"

"William."

"Is that the entitled one with the wealthy mum and dad?"

Alice nodded. "Yes, that's him."

Tom was pensive. This wasn't the first time the boy had made his presence known, and he wasn't only targeting Saffy. He had a habit of working the room, so to speak. What was different though, was the effect it had clearly had on Saffy. She was one to take everything in her stride, and seldom allowed anyone else to derail her.

"That's not like Saffy to be troubled by him."

"It's different this time. He's brought it closer to home."

"Why, what has he been saying?" Tom asked, kneeling down and sitting back on his heels.

"Saffy was telling her classmates about what happened with Cassie," Alice said, stroking her daughter's hair. "You can't blame her, for children at this age it's one hell of a story. A real-life adventure on your doorstep."

"With a happy ending," Tom said.

"Of course," Alice agreed. "And that's why I don't mind her telling it but I – and I'm certain the other parents agree – am glad she isn't party to all of the gory details."

"Hey, I haven't said a word," Tom said, holding his hands up in supplication.

"I know, but it's the story of the moment. It's in the papers," she glanced at the television which was off, "and all over the telly."

"Yeah," Tom said, absently rubbing the back of his neck. "Not a lot tends to happen around here so when something does, it all gets a bit crazy."

"Yes. Anyway, William thought it would be fun to point out that what happened to Cassie could happen to you, at any time."

Tom heaved a sigh. "He's… a pleasant child." It was something Tom had considered in the past. His job brought him within touching distance of the worst people in society, and there was a level of risk when doing so. That was inarguable. He did his best to keep it away from his home life, shielding his family from it, especially Saffy. He thought he'd done a good job so far, although perhaps he was mistaken. "She knows I can take care of myself—"

"And she thinks Aunty Cassie is indestructible too, remember?"

"Cassie does like to convey that at every opportunity, yes," Tom said. "She's not low on self-esteem is Cassandra. Even so—"

"William also decided to remind her of..." Alice paused, taking a breath.

"Remind her of what?"

"That her father was murdered."

Tom exhaled heavily. Although Saffy had been a few years younger, therefore spared the full horror of understanding what had happened to her biological father, she knew he'd been killed. Together, he and Alice made the conscious decision not to hide reality from her, but at the same time treated it sensitively. Saffy had required a great deal of therapy to cope, and she had coped remarkably well. He was grateful and immensely proud of her for that, but the circumstances surrounding his death were common local knowledge.

"William is a little—"

"Ssh," Alice said, putting a finger to her lips just as Saffy stirred.

"Scrote," Tom said quietly. Saffy's eyelids flickered and she opened them, gazing upon Tom. As soon as she recognised him, she smiled and lifted her head from Alice's chest.

"Daddy," she said, sleepily.

"Hello, munchkin." Saffy pushed the blanket off her and moved towards him. Tom effortlessly scooped her up into his arms. Saffy leant into him, resting her cheek on his shoulder and wrapped her legs around his waist like a Koala bear. "How are you princess?"

"Fine," she whispered. Tom hadn't met a female yet who

was genuinely fine when she said so. It always meant the opposite.

"Shall we get you into bed?" Tom asked, angling his head away from her so he could see her face. She nodded, almost imperceptibly and Tom smiled at Alice who returned it. She stroked her daughter's back.

"I'll come and check in on you later, darling. Okay?" Saffy nodded again and Tom stood up, feeling the extra weight of his adopted daughter putting him off balance. Russell lifted his head from his paws and as soon as Tom made to leave the room, the terrier leapt down and ran ahead of them, leading the way upstairs. Russell would sleep on Saffy's bed until Tom and Alice retired themselves, and then he would sleep in the kitchen.

Tom silently mouthed the words *love you* to Alice as he backed out of the room. Alice stifled a yawn, and Tom made his way slowly upstairs.

Nudging open her bedroom door with his foot, he saw Saffy's night light was on beside her bed, casting the room in a soft blue tone. He lowered her onto the bed and she rolled off him. Tom pulled her duvet across her and Saffy drew it up to just beneath her chin. Her eyes remained closed and he was certain she'd be asleep in seconds. He waited beside the bed though, gently stroking her hair until he was sure she'd drifted off to sleep. Picking up Coges, the name of her current favourite soft toy, a furry, floppy stuffed dog, he laid it beside her. If she woke during the night, then he'd be right there for her to cuddle up to.

Satisfied she was asleep, he leaned over and kissed her forehead. She didn't stir. He looked down at Russell, sitting patiently on the floor beside him, and nodded towards the bed. Russell leapt up, did a couple of circles of the foot of the bed before finding his space and settling down. Tom stroked his head, but Russell had already closed his eyes. He wasn't going anywhere anytime soon.

Tom left the bedroom, pulling the door to but leaving enough of a gap for the light to permeate from the landing and also giving Russell the space to leave if he chose to. Then he made his way back downstairs. Alice was in the kitchen, removing clingfilm from a plate she'd taken from the fridge.

"I'm assuming you haven't eaten?" she asked.

Tom realised he hadn't eaten since breakfast and his stomach reminded him of that fact. He'd skipped lunch expecting to finish at a reasonable time and be home for a family meal. They were rare these days.

The entire team were going to get some of the extra time back they'd been working on during the last case. Overtime payments were, unofficially, largely a thing of the past for junior CID officers, having disappeared along with the dinosaurs, and time off in lieu was frowned upon, but Tamara gave them scope to take time off – unofficially – at the conclusion of a stressful investigation. This last one certainly qualified under that criterion. The developing events had changed things though.

"Thanks, I'm starving," Tom said.

"So… what's happened?" Alice asked, placing the plate in the microwave and heating the meal.

"Well… I got promoted."

"Sorry, what?" Alice smiled, shooting him an inquisitive look. He raised his hand.

"It's only temporary, so don't get too excited."

"Where's Tamara going?"

"She's still here but she's acting up as well." He sighed, rubbing his face with his palms. "There's going to be an investigation into the conduct during the last case. Reviewing everything that happened in light of the role of the informant," he winced, "what happened to Cassie… all of it."

"Is there anything for us to worry about?" Tom moved to her and pulled her towards him. Alice looped her arms around his neck and Tom encircled her waist with his, linking his hands at the small of her back.

"Nothing whatsoever."

"You're a terrible liar, Tom Janssen."

"Acting Detective Chief Inspector Janssen, if you don't mind," Tom said playfully.

"I like the sound of that," she said, smiling. The microwave pinged and Alice disengaged from him. He patted her back-side as she walked away from him.

"Don't get too used to it, because it can be gone as quickly as it is given."

"Does that mean you get a pay rise as well?"

"Probably," he said, taking a knife and fork from the cutlery drawer and pulling out a chair at the dining table. "It won't be much, but maybe I can get the boat back into the water."

"Hah!" Alice said, setting his plate down in front of him. "Saffy needs new school shoes first."

"Again? What are we feeding her?"

"She sleeps in a bag of fertiliser these days. That way she can get to full height faster, and then we won't need to buy her so many clothes."

Tom grinned, holding up his fork which had a mouthful of steaming lasagne on it. "What do you think we should do about William?" he asked, before blowing on the food and putting it into his mouth.

"Any chance you can plant some drugs on him and have him sent to borstal, or whatever they call it now? Juvenile detention, is it?"

Tom almost choked on his food, covering his mouth as he replied. "I would be shocked if I thought you were serious."

"I am serious. Horrible little child. He looks so sweet and innocent, but he's a nasty piece of work." Alice leant against the counter, folding her arms across her chest. "Now you're a DCI and everything, I—"

"Acting."

Alice shrugged. "It still counts. Can't you fit him up with something? It happens all the time. You see it on the telly."

"On the telly, yes," Tom said, "and that's not real life, as you well know."

"It's just a thought," she said innocently. "He is a scrote though. I'll speak to his parents."

"Maybe I should do that."

"Why?" Alice asked.

"Because I'm trained in conflict de-escalation techniques, and you…" he frowned, searching for the correct words, then gave up, "are not."

"I can be diplomatic."

"Really?" Tom said, smiling.

"I can!"

"How is your step-mum?"

"That's different."

"Is it?"

"Yes. She's pure evil and has brainwashed my father into thinking that spending his life savings on driving around Europe in a camper van is a sound strategy for life."

Tom's smile broadened into a grin. "They are having a good time though."

"I don't doubt it. He's knocking off – around – with someone half his age—"

"Not quite half," Tom said, "but I take your point."

"While she gets to do absolutely nothing!"

"Whilst spending your inheritance."

"That has nothing to do with it!" Tom knew she wasn't thinking that way about it, but it certainly got a rise out of her. His smile made sure she knew he was joking, and she simply tossed a tea towel at him which he caught deftly before setting it aside on the table.

"So you'll speak to William's parents tomorrow?" Tom asked.

"I'll try and catch her in the car park at drop off. She's a bit more approachable than he is."

"If that doesn't work, I'll send some mounted police around to their house, trample the garden or something."

"Promises, promises," Alice said. "How's the lasagne?"

"Lovely, thank you. And don't worry about Saffy. I'll speak to her tomorrow and reassure her that nothing is going to happen to me."

"The thing is, she's a smart girl. She knows you won't be able to guarantee that." Tom sighed. It's true, he couldn't. The risk came with the warrant card. "So what else happened to keep you out so late or were you off celebrating your respective promotions?"

"Drowning our sorrows would be more like it," he said, taking another bite of his meal. Alice offered him a quizzical look but he waved it away, setting his knife and fork down, and swallowing what he was chewing before speaking. "We caught another case this evening."

"Something serious?"

Tom considered his answer. He didn't know, but he suspected it was going to be anything but simple. In light of what was happening at school with Saffy, he thought it best not to elaborate. "We'll see, but it's early days."

"Then I know it's serious," Alice said sternly. "At this rate, you'll be chief constable by the end of the year."

Tom blew out his cheeks and shuddered at the thought.

CHAPTER SIX

THE HOME OFFICE pathologist was standing to the left of the entrance as Tom entered the morgue. "Good morning, Tom!" Dr Paxton said. "I gather congratulations are in order."

"Word travels fast, doesn't it?" Tom said.

"Well yes, it certainly does in these parts," Dr Paxton said. "The thing is there is so little going on that is actually worth talking about these days. I have to say I find discussions on the condition of the fairway approaching the sixteenth hole rather boring." He frowned, lifting the spectacles he had perched on his nose and cleaning them with the corner of his lab coat. "Not that I was ever particularly interested in the first place."

"I was surprised to get your message this morning," Tom said, glancing around the room. The pathologist had left him a note to say he'd already carried out the postmortem on Martin Odiham during the night.

"As I said, life has been growing rather dull of late. It's been a pleasure to have something interesting to really get my teeth into!" He swiped a closed fist through the air in front of him, pretty much celebrating the need of his services.

"When I was notified last night, I got on my bike, so to speak."

"I'm… pleased we've been able to accommodate you," Tom said drily. Paxton wasn't fazed by Tom's sarcasm, and he didn't appear to even register it. He looked over Tom's shoulder at the closed door and, seeing no one else following Tom inside, seemed glum. Tom looked round which broke Paxton's train of thought.

"I was just… um… wondering if Cassandra would be joining you?"

"Not this morning, no. She's back at the station on another task."

"Ah, I see," Paxton said, clearly disappointed. "Shame," he said absently. "She's very insightful, young Cassandra. For someone from the north, anyway."

"I'll be sure to pass on your best wishes," Tom said, with the trace of a smile. He would love to be able to deliver such a barbed comment in person, and Cassie would be just as happy to send him a cutting riposte. If Dr Paxton was happy with the offer, he didn't show it.

"Indeed." He cleared his throat, replaced his glasses, adjusting the looped temple tips, and snapped to attention before crossing the room to where the mortuary fridges were located. Opening the third one along, he pulled out the tray. The sound of the runners echoed in the tiled room. Presumably, this was Martin Odiham. Paxton moved to the side and unzipped the bag revealing the head and upper body.

Tom came alongside, casting an eye over the body. Odiham's skin had greyed as the colour had drained away from the surface of the skin. His veins were showing, and the skin was now almost transparent in many places. The man was slim, bordering on skeletal, Tom figured as he studied his frame. He had wispy white hair growing from his upper body and Tom noticed some discolouration around the abdomen. Paxton saw him looking.

"He was bashed around a bit prior to his death," he said, pursing his lips.

"Beaten?"

Paxton nodded. "I would say so, yes. I've seen worse, though. Much worse, but not in a man of this age. We bruise fairly easily once we pass a certain age, you know, Tom."

"Roughing him up rather than a severe beating?"

"Yes, that's it. Although, at his age," Paxton frowned, "even a light one would be extreme enough to cause significant damage." Paxton hurried back to his desk, producing several printouts, returning with them and passing them to Tom. "The X-rays showed multiple fractures to his rib cage, and the left forearm was also broken. I think the latter was not likely caused by an acute blunt force trauma—"

"So he didn't raise an arm in defence or anything like that?"

"No, I don't think so or, at least, that's not what caused the break in the radius here." He pointed to a clear break in the left arm a couple of inches from where it joined the wrist. "No, it was much more likely caused by him striking a flat surface – a hard surface, no doubt – but perhaps falling to the ground or even colliding with the wall while he was swinging back and forth on the rope." Paxton made a pendulum motion in the air with a flat palm.

"Fiona was thinking something similar."

"I'm not surprised. Now there's another bright lady, Fiona," Paxton said thoughtfully. Tom leaned in, inspecting the abrasions around the neck, without doubt the work of the rope. "Friction burns, abrasions and subcutaneous tissue contusions... all resulting from the rope being wrapped around his neck," Paxton said, arching his eyebrows. He produced a photograph of the rope, taken at the scene, holding it aloft and studying it. "The imprint on the soft tissue of the neck matches the weave pattern of the flax, you see?" He passed the photo to Tom and he gave it a cursory examination. "Now, it wasn't tied into a noose in the traditional manner, rather wrapped tightly enough that the man's weight would tighten it and constrict the throat. Simple, crude, but most certainly effective."

"Cause of death?" Tom asked.

"A broken neck," Paxton said, his eyebrows momentarily raising as he looked down at the body. "A blessed relief for the poor chap, I should imagine. The Lord acted mercifully upon this occasion." He frowned. "Rather a quick slip and a snap rather than the slow agony of suffocating due to the downward pressure of your own body weight killing you off."

"It happened quickly then?"

"Oh yes, death would have been instantaneous." Paxton looked at his notes. "That would probably have been something of a relief bearing in mind what must have gone before."

"What can you tell me?"

"Purely speculative, I should say but backed up by the evidence."

"Please, go on."

"Well, he took a beating, as you know already. There are splinters of wood that I managed to recover from multiple points on his body. They weren't hard to find, notably on his extremities," he held his free hand aloft and wiggled his fingers in the air. "I also found some more in the tissue of his face, both the left and right cheeks, and within the scalp above the hairline, too. I had a brief look under the microscope. The wood is aged and treated with what I presume will turn out to be a pesticide to kill off wood-boring beetles and the like. To ensure we are thorough, I've sent them away to your forensic chaps for a deeper analysis."

"He was thrown around in the belfry," Tom said.

"That's what the science would suggest, yes. I also think he would have had some time to consider what was about to happen to him, unless he lost consciousness."

"Explain, please?"

"My late brother was a keen campanologist, you know?"

"I didn't know that," Tom said. How would he?

"Yes, and our parents would take us to church every week without fail. Gerald would take his place every week. Loved it. Absolutely loved it." Paxton took on a distant expression, thinking hard. "Now, which church was it we would attend… you know, I don't recall. Anyway, one time we were taken up into the belfry to see the ring of bells. That was quite an experience. I was much more interested in the engineering required for the mechanism than the sound they made—"

"The rope?" Tom asked.

"Oh, yes of course." Disappointed by the interruption of his story, Dr Paxton took a moment to gather himself. "That's right, the weight of the ropes. They are rather heavy and as a result are quite taut. Obviously, there is some play in them, but that is more at the bottom rather than up in the belfry."

"Meaning?"

"The rope would need to be untied at ground-floor level and then hauled up to the middle level, where it could then be wrapped around this poor fellow's neck, and then," having placed the folder down, he gestured with both hands in an upward motion, "heaved him through the trapdoor. Believe me, pulling the rope up enough to give – pardon the phrase – enough rope to hang him with, would have taken some effort, and therefore time."

"Just to be clear, there's no way he could have hanged himself?"

"No, certainly not," Paxton, returning to the X-rays again, producing another and handing it to Tom. "You see there, the vertebrae in the upper spine between the shoulder blades?"

"Yes, but it looks foggy," Tom said, frowning.

"That's because he was suffering from advanced anky-losing spondylitis, an inflammatory condition affecting the joints and the tissue surrounding the spine. Over time it can cause stiffness and affect flexibility. In a worst-case scenario, the vertebra eventually fuse together – just as we see there – leading to the sufferer walking with a Quasimodo-esque hunched appearance. Rather painful and, I dare say, quite a debilitating disease when it reaches this point."

"He couldn't have pulled the rope up himself."

"Exactly," Paxton said triumphantly. "Similar thing happened with Rudolph Hess, you know?"

"The deputy Nazi leader?"

"Yes, died by suicide in his Spandau cell after all those years, but there's no way that chap could have tied the noose around his own neck without help." He shook his head defi-antly. "Physically impossible. Assisted suicide perhaps, but definitely more to tell than the official record would have us believe."

"I didn't have you down as a conspiracy theorist, Doctor Paxton," Tom said, smiling.

"Hah! I'm not, but I am a man of science. I can speculate, after all it can be rather entertaining to do so, on occasion, but when it comes to a medical opinion there are only evidence-based conclusions to draw."

"Is there anything else you think I should know?"

"No, sadly," Paxton said. "I rather hoped you'd brought

me something interesting to examine, but on this occasion, it has all been a little too straightforward."

"Sorry about that. I'll try harder next time."

"No rush," Paxton said, checking his watch. "I'm hoping to get nine holes in before it gets dark. I'll be sure to write up my findings and have them over to you before I tee off."

"Thank you. I appreciate it."

"No problem at all, Tom. Please do give my best to DS Knight."

Tom's mobile rang before he reached his car. He answered it, recognising the caller.

"Good morning, Debbie. What can I do for you?"

"Hello, Tom, I'm sorry to trouble you this early. I should probably just dial 999 but—"

"That's okay. What's up?"

"I'm down at the sailing club, and I think there's something here you should see. I know it's early, and I haven't had a cup of coffee yet, so maybe my mind is playing tricks on me but… I really think you should come down."

As Tom reached his car, turning his back to it, he leaned against the side listening as she explained. Debbie was quite right. He needed to go down to the sailing club. Assuring her that he would head straight there, Tom thanked her for calling him and hung up. Immediately, he called the ops room at Hunstanton station. Eric answered.

"Eric, it's Tom. Get your coat on, pick up a couple of uniforms as well, and meet me down at Snettisham Sailing Club, would you?"

"Er… yes, of course, sir," Eric said. "Why, what's going on down there?"

"Good question, Eric. That's what we are going to find out."

"I'm on my way," Eric said, hanging up.

CHAPTER SEVEN

Snettisham Sailing Club was located on a strip of coastline sandwiched between The Wash and a basin forming a perfect lake for sailing. The approach road, winding through a holiday park beside the lake, was pockmarked with massive potholes, disintegrating former repairs and lined with various materials. Tom had to steer his way through the worst of them, avoiding bottoming out as best he could.

The road picked its way through privately owned holiday cabins, many of which were in a dilapidated state but would still fetch a premium on the open market. Here, no one was paying for the views but for the storage and access to both the lake and the sea.

It was quite understandable that no one invested in these roads or even in their properties. Situated, as they were, on the sea-facing side of the tidal defence system, they were prone to flooding when the conditions were right. A tidal surge combining with a storm front would see the area underwater. The lake was saltwater as a result of this. The sailing club-house though was located on a ridge, standing proud of the surrounding buildings to compensate for the risk.

Tom drove past the clubhouse on his left, climbing the steep incline and coming over the blind crest before the route dropped down to sea level once more. It was in this open space that members stored their sailboats, only a short distance from the water's edge at high tide. At this time though, the tide had retreated leaving a vast expanse of mud flats with the water in the distance.

Eric was already there, standing on the club's terrace with two uniformed officers. Tom recognised Debbie, the lady who'd called and asked him to attend. She was at the heart of everything to do with the club, and the driving force behind many of the events. There wasn't much activity around, seeing as the tide was out and a strong wind was forecast, too strong to make sailing on the lake viable. Eric broke away from his conversation, walking down the ramp to meet him when Tom pulled up.

"Good morning, sir," Eric said.

"Hello, Eric." Tom cast an eye across the area. Besides the police cars, there was only one other vehicle he could see. It was parked in the centre of where members would usually leave their cars, the boats all resting on trailers around the perimeter, their masts tied up, sails wrapped. Tom focussed on the car, a burgundy Range Rover. It was old. If the licence plate was accurate then it was from the early nineties. "Is it that one?"

Eric nodded. "Yes, sir." Tom walked towards it, Eric falling into step alongside him. "It was here this morning, first thing. No one was seen in or near it, and there was no one else hanging around. At least, not when anyone arrived to open the sailing club."

Tom studied the car as they approached it. It wasn't in a good condition, there were many panels showing signs of rot and decay, rusting around the wheel arches and on the split tailgate at the rear. The paintwork was faded, showing its true age. It also appeared to have been parked without much consideration. The front wheels were turned out to the right, rather than straightened up.

Coming alongside, Tom saw the driver's side door was unlocked and only closed on the first catch. This added to the idea that the vehicle had been stopped abruptly and the engine switched off with the occupant disembarking quickly.

"Have you already looked?" Tom asked Eric.

"Only through the window, sir," Eric said. Both men walked around to the rear, stopping at the rear quarter window. Tom peered inside. There was a large sheet of tarpaulin, not a heavy gauge by the look of it, and it had also seen better days. There were rips and tears in the material, and the edges were also damaged. There was dried mud on the plastic, and the gaps gave way to reveal fabric material beneath.

At one corner, the tarpaulin wasn't quite covering what it was presumably supposed to conceal. A human hand extended from beneath, hanging limp. Dried blood was visible on the skin, having run from beneath the tarpaulin and dripped from the fingers, pooling on the plastic boot liner the body lay upon. Tom sighed, his lips pursed. Eric passed him a set of nitrile gloves and he donned them; Eric did the same.

Tom pressed the button for the boot release and, although there was some resistance from the mechanism, the glass lifted. They were not greeted by a foul odour, not foul enough to be indicative of the body having been present for several days. "You say the car was seen this morning?" Tom asked.

"Yes," Eric said. "It wasn't here at eight o'clock last night when they locked up. They had a fundraiser on in the club-house, so it was pretty busy up until then. Once everyone had gone home, the parking area was empty."

"They're sure?"

"Positive," Eric said. "This is a tight-knit community, as you know. Everyone knows everyone else, and their cars."

"Yes," Tom said, nodding as he took hold of the tarpaulin and gently lifted it to see the body beneath. He grimaced at the sight. It was a man, in his early to mid-forties, Tom guessed. He was dressed in blue jeans and a dark T-shirt, also wearing a black donkey jacket, a thick wool blend with the collar turned up. The body was curled up in the foetal position, his back facing them. A stain was visible on the back of the coat, and the wool was thick; a dark liquid. "I don't think it'll take too long to come up with the cause of death on this one," Tom said.

"No," Eric said softly. The staining was evident, but not as clear as the gaping hole in the coat. The diameter was easily twelve inches. The hole wasn't complete, though, the material looking like it had been shredded.

"Shotgun," Tom said.

"In the back," Eric said. "At close range, too, I reckon."

"Less than four feet away, I would say, based on the spread pattern of the shot."

"You don't get up from those," Eric said. Tom shook his head, slowly lowering the tarpaulin back down. "I've notified the scenes-of-crime team," Eric said. "They're not even through at Odiham's cottage yet. I suspect they'll have to send another unit up from Norwich for this one."

Tom was pensive. Stepping back from the vehicle, he examined the passenger side. There was some damage along the panels, impact points and scrapes visible in the paintwork. It was recent too. Making his way along to the front, he found the front bumper was distorted and had come away from its mount on the nearside. Tom dropped to his haunches, inspecting the damage. The rectangular cover for the fog light below the bumper was also missing. The light cluster housing was cracked and the bulb was broken, the wiring visible hanging down from above.

"It matches the description of a hit-and-run that happened late last night, sir," Eric said, consulting his notebook. Tom glanced up at him. "A Range Rover," Eric continued, reading from his notes, "dark in colour, collided with another vehicle driven by a pregnant woman who also had a toddler asleep in the back seat. Her car left the road and struck a tree."

Tom frowned. "Are they okay?"

"The toddler was taken home from hospital by the father, after a check-up. The driver is shaken up, has a concussion, and she's being kept in for observation, but as far as I know, both she and the baby are doing okay."

"Where did it happen?"

"Sandringham, sir."

"Any witnesses to the collision?"

Eric shook his head. "No one has come forward. It was another passing motorist who came across the scene and raised the alarm. The mother was found unconscious. The toddler in the back was in great distress when she was found, apparently."

"Have you run the plates?" Tom walked back along the vehicle's nearside inspecting the damage. He found some flecks of white paint in one of the more badly damaged panels.

"Yes, sir. I'd just called it through before you arrived. The vehicle is registered to Jason Law. He lives on a farm on the outskirts of Great Bircham."

Tom stood up, glancing beyond the car and out across the mud flats, feeling the breeze coming in off the sea. "What do we know about him?"

"No priors, no convictions at all. He's not on our radar," Eric said.

"We're some way from Great Bircham here."

"A good place to dump a car though," Eric said, looking around. "There's no through route this way, unless you count the path from Lynn along the sea front up past Heacham to Hunstanton. No security to speak of. No streetlights or cameras."

Tom also looked around, seeing Eric was right. If the weather was good, and at the right time of the year, then this place was teeming with tourists and locals alike making use of the water. If not, then it could stay empty for days on end. Over the winter this area was pretty much abandoned.

It was perhaps only down to the vigilance of people in the sailing club who noticed. Otherwise, the body could have lain undiscovered for weeks. There was an old Renault parked at the side of the approach road, the tyres were flat on one side, and it looked like it hadn't moved in months if not years.

"Whoever brought the car here could abandon it, leave on foot north or south along the coast and not be seen," Tom said. His gaze drifted in the direction of the holiday park and the cabins along the lake shore. None of them were visible from where they stood. "Or they never left at all," Tom said.

"Sir?"

"Have the uniforms going door to door, find out who is still in the area and whether they saw or heard anything. You never know."

"Will do, sir. I don't know how many residents are here, what with the weather the way it is, but I might need help."

"I'll get onto the station, see if I can rustle up a few more bodies to help you."

Eric nodded, turned away and beckoned the two constables over towards them. Tom continued his inspection of the vehicle. Touching as little of the passenger side door handle as possible, he opened the door and peered into the cabin. There was a distinct odour within. Nothing sinister, but a smell of age-old abandonment and a touch of damp. He noted the passenger window was cracked open about an inch, and the glass was lopsided in the frame. It was clearly broken, and he suspected it didn't close properly any more.

He noted a number of spider's webs inside the car, at the edge of the windscreen where it met the top of the dashboard, and also around the rear-view mirror. The interior was showing signs of wear, not surprising based on the vehicle's age. The seats were ripped in places with the padding protruding through the covering in places. The plastic switches had seen their markings worn away over time as well. Although, for a vehicle that was more than three decades' old, the fact it was still functioning was a testament to its build quality.

Walking back round to the driver side, he opened that door as well, careful not to touch anything that wasn't absolutely necessary. The keys were in the ignition which was something he did find odd. The driver's seat was also in such a position to suggest the driver wasn't as tall as Tom. Looking at the height of the seating position and the distance from the pedals, he figured the driver couldn't be much over five foot seven or eight. Perhaps not unusually short by any means, but not tall either.

He found none of the car litter one might expect to find. There were no food wrappers on the floor or discarded parking tickets screwed up in the door bins. There was nothing to indicate who had been in the car or where it may have been in recent days or weeks. Backing out of the car, he pushed the door to, closing it on the first catch. Retreating, he peeled off his gloves, and then looked into the boot once more.

62 J M DALGLIESH

Whoever this man was, someone had seen fit to dump him somewhere. He found it unlikely they were looking to leave him in the car, and not in such a public place as this. His working theory was that the collision with the other vehicle the previous night saw them panic. The car would be on the police radar for failing to stop, and the last thing the driver would have wanted was to be pulled over with a dead body in the back.

More than likely, it was the hit-and-run that saw them change their plans and abandon the car in a convenient and yet fairly deserted location. He doubted anyone would have seen the driver leave the vehicle. Where the car was left wasn't in the line of sight of any of the local cabins or caravans. Even if they were unlucky enough to have someone come upon them, a late-night dog walker for instance, there was no light with which to illuminate their face. They would simply be another shadow passing through the darkness.

It was smart, no doubt thinking on the fly, but the best scenario they could manage which would give them the best chance of escaping cleanly once they'd been involved in the accident. That got Tom thinking. The perpetrator was likely to be a local, or at least someone familiar with the area around the sailing club. Who else would know this place would work so well for them? Dumping the car here, along with the body, in an isolated spot such as this would allow them time to put as much distance as possible between them and the body.

After all, that was the first rule when planning how to dispose of a victim. Every person in between you and the body, once discovered, becomes a suspect before you do. That gives the killer precious time to cover their tracks or even to disappear completely if they felt the need. Without the collision last night, this body may well have found its way out into the North Sea on the receding tide somewhere along the coast. They may never have found it at all.

The thought did cross his mind though. Why didn't they put the body in the water last night anyway? Then all they would have to fear, if caught, would be committing the offence of failing to stop at the scene of an accident. He would have to check the high tide timings for last night. Perhaps that had been the plan, only to arrive here and find the water was already too far out for them to do so. Rather than drive some-where else, they took off on foot instead.

First off, he needed to pay Jason Law a visit and see what he had to say for himself.

CHAPTER EIGHT

Beech Farm lay south of the village of Great Bircham. No longer an operational agricultural concern, Tom drove past a recently constructed access road into an area of converted barns. The old access track to the farmhouse itself lay a little further along the road. When Tom pulled off the main highway and passed through two imposing brick pillars, they found themselves on an unmade road that wound its way around the barn development and up to an old farmhouse.

It wasn't a particularly large structure by the standards of modern detached properties. This area was pockmarked with old farmsteads who each managed landholding of various sizes. Once it had been commonplace to find two farms operating side by side, the farmhouses almost within a stone's throw of the other.

The farmhouse was unusual in the manner of its construction though. The majority of old buildings in the area were constructed from a mixture of red brick and knapped flint walls under a red clay pantile roof. The home of Jason Law, however, had mellow brick walls. Tom assumed it was a later addition to the area, possibly when a farm passed into the hands of more than one child and another residence was required to be constructed.

Tom had first driven back up to Hunstanton, collecting DC Danny Wilson from the station, and then set off across country to the village of Great Bircham. The closer they got to the house, the firmer the access road became, transitioning from baked earth to gravel.

Pulling up in front of the house, Tom cast an eye over the building. It was clearly old, and although showing significant signs of its age, it was fairly well maintained. The plants lining the garden to the front were well kept. Someone took pride in the appearance of the vegetation. However, the large sash windows had seen better days. There was rot visible in some of the frames. Some had been replaced with modern units, and these were brown whereas the older ones were white, and single glazed.

The detectives got out of the car and approached the front door. There was no doorbell as such, but a metal bell with a clapper was mounted from the wall to the right of the door. Tom rang it twice and felt his ears ringing for seconds after-wards. The sound of a passing vehicle carried to them on the breeze, but the farmhouse was well sheltered from neighbours and passers-by.

A figure came into view, visible through the obscured pane to the right of the door. At some point the original door must have been replaced with a smaller one, requiring a slim panel of glazing to fill in the gap. It would also present the benefit of more natural light permeating through to the interior.

The door creaked open and an elderly lady looked out at them, evidently surprised to see two unknown men at her door. Tom displayed his identification, and Danny Wilson did the same.

"DCI Janssen," Tom said, then gestured towards his

colleague, "and this is Detective Constable Wilson. I'm looking for Jason Law."

"Jason?" she asked, putting a hand flat against her chest.

"Does he live here?" Tom asked.

"Yes, of course," she replied. "I'm Natasha, Jason's wife."

"Mrs Law," Tom said, smiling. "May we come inside?"

"Certainly," she said, pulling the door wider and stepping aside to allow them to enter.

The reception hall was narrow with a steep flight of stairs against the wall to their left. A stair lift was in place. Tom smiled at the woman as she closed the door. He could hear a clock ticking loudly from the reception room behind him. There was a matching room mirrored on the other side of the entrance, and the hall itself stretched back towards the rear of the property. "What is all of this about?"

Tom heard the nervousness in her voice, and he took her measure. She was in her early to mid-eighties, he guessed. She seemed sprightly enough, walking with grace as she guided them through the farmhouse towards the kitchen at the rear. Her hair was almost white, tied up into a bun at the back of her head and she dressed well. Her face was made-up, but not overly so. She was probably responsible for the presentation of the garden, if her personal attention to detail was anything to go by. She didn't present herself in the way the wives of farmers he knew well would do. As a result, Tom was confident that she'd never been raised working the land.

"Perhaps we should wait to speak to your husband," Tom said, just as they entered a traditional farmhouse kitchen. It was a no-nonsense design. The cabinets were crafted from pine, stained a darker colour, and an old Aga stove was recessed into what was once the fireplace, giving access to the chimney.

If she was bothered by Tom's reluctance to explain their

presence, she didn't show it. Beyond the kitchen was a lean-to conservatory. It must have been added in the sixties because it had a very Scandinavian-inspired style to it. The walls were lined with strips of varnished pine, floor to ceiling, and indeed across some parts of the ceiling too. An old electric fan heater was mounted on one wall, the likes of which Tom didn't recall seeing even when he was a child. It must be freezing out here in the winter. Whereas in modern buildings exterior light would come via a roof lantern or similar, here they had used corrugated plastic sheets which probably made the room unusable in the summer.

In one corner two wing-back chairs were set out beside a single glazed picture window overlooking the rear garden. Between them was a small table and a tall floor lamp arced above the two chairs. In one chair a man was seated, a tartan blanket pulled up over his lap.

"Jason," Natasha said, brightly, "these gentlemen are here to see you."

"Mr Law," Tom said, walking across to him, Natasha by his side. Jason tilted his head and looked to his wife and then his gaze slowly drifted up to Tom. It was immediately clear that he wasn't focussed. "I'm DCI Janssen, from Norfolk Police." Jason stared at Tom with a blank expression, his lips parted slightly but there was no hint of acknowledgement, let alone recognition.

"He has good days and bad days," Natasha said, turning to Tom and smiling apologetically. She sighed. "And I'm afraid today is one of the worst he's had in weeks."

"I see," Tom said, pursing his lips. "Is he suffering from…"

"Alzheimer's, yes," she said, grimacing. "It began affecting him almost a decade ago now, but these past couple of years have been particularly brutal, I must say." She smiled nervously, forcing herself to appear relaxed about it but she was certainly emotional, absently twiddling with the pendant hanging on a delicate gold chain around her neck.

"I'm sorry," Tom said.

"Thank you," she said, exhaling deeply and looking at her husband wistfully. He turned his gaze back towards the garden, seeing two small birds land on the bird table planted in the ground a few metres away from where he was sitting. Natasha exhaled, turning away. "So… detectives, let me make you some tea and while I'm doing that, perhaps you could tell me what we can do for you?"

Tom's gaze lingered on her husband for a moment longer. He was thin, and one could consider him gaunt, the complexion of his face mottled by multiple occurrences of lentigo. He had a shock of almost white hair swept up and away from his forehead, and it gleamed with reflected light. His eyes were sunken and, despite the crystal blue of his irises, they were offset by dark patches around his eyes.

Sitting with his hands together in his lap, Tom saw he also suffered from arthritis, the bones of his fingers twisted at the joints into almost impossible angles. Tom doubted he would be capable of holding a shotgun, let alone discharging it. Tom stepped away, following Natasha back into the kitchen.

"We are actually here about a car that is registered to your husband, Mrs Law—"

"Natasha, please."

Danny looked at his notes. "A burgundy Range Rover, registration number L356—"

"Yes, that's Jason's," Natasha said, frowning with surprise. "Why ever would you be interested in that old thing?"

"You do still own the car then?" Tom asked.

"Yes, of course," she said, filling a kettle with water as she looked back at him over her shoulder. "But it isn't roadworthy."

"It's not?"

"No," she said, setting the kettle down and flicking the switch on. "The old thing hasn't run in years." She looked towards the conservatory as if she could see through the solid wall to her husband. "Jason hasn't driven for…" she thought hard, "at least the last two years. It might be even more than that. I was thankful that he saw that in himself after a couple of close calls."

"Accidents, you mean?"

"Yes, nothing too major. He scraped it on one of the gateposts out front, which is no great crime in the scheme of things, but when he missed a red light once at a junction, then we had to consider what we were doing."

"He gave up his licence?" Tom asked. Natasha winced.

"No, not officially, but he was responsible enough to leave the keys alone." She folded her arms casually across her chest. "He's always been like that, my Jason. He will always put others before himself." She shrugged. "We just had to make changes in our life, that's all."

"Such as?" Tom asked. "If you don't mind me asking?"

"No, not at all." She was thoughtful for a moment. "My eyesight isn't the best and I am plagued with diabetes these days, aren't we all when we reach a certain age? Anyway, I can't drive at night – the vision issue – and I have to admit I don't care to drive during the day much either."

"How do you get around?"

"Taxis, if the need is great. Although we do keep a little runaround for emergencies." The kettle boiled and she looked between Tom and Danny. "Tea or coffee?"

"Tea for me, please," Danny said.

"How do you take it, young man?"

"White with two sugars, please," Danny replied. "Thank

you." Natasha arched her eyebrows towards him and glanced at Tom.

"He'll be dealing with diabetes too, adding that much sugar to his tea," she said, shaking her head. "And for you, Mr… sorry, what did you say your name was?"

"Janssen, Tom Janssen."

"Tea or coffee?"

"Tea, if you're sure it's no trouble?" he asked, and she waved the comment away. "No sugar for me though."

"You're sweet enough," she said, smiling and reaching for a metal tea caddy from a nearby shelf. She took out two tea bags, dropping them into the mugs and then took a third herbal tea from a different box, tore open the wrapper and placed it in the last mug, dangling the string over the lip.

"Do you find not driving to be quite isolating?" Tom asked. "Living all the way out here, I mean."

"I suppose you could say that," she said, pouring water into three mugs. "But I don't feel the need to go anywhere these days. We can get around if we really need to. As I say, the local taxi companies are great, and you can have your weekly groceries delivered to your door these days." She turned around, leaning against the counter. "And we have the countryside on our doorstep if we feel the need to get some fresh air. There's no better place to be living at this time in our lives. Besides…" she gazed straight ahead at nothing in particular, "what else do we really need?"

"Do you have family nearby?"

She shook her head. "No, we don't have any children. Not for the lack of trying, I should say, but it never happened for us."

"I'm sorry."

"Don't be," she said. "If children had been in His plan for us, then we would be blessed. Jason was always focussed on his career anyway, so perhaps things worked out for the best." Natasha set about removing the teabags from the mugs, and then looked at Danny, pointing towards the fridge. "Please be a dear and pass me the milk from the fridge."

"Of course," Danny said, opening the door.

"What did your husband do?" Tom asked.

"He worked in the insurance business," she said. "It paid the bills. No," she said, dismissing her own comment. "It was much better than that. I can't complain, but he did work a lot, and it was stressful for him. I wasn't sad when he took early retirement and became a teacher for a little while."

"How did he cope with the stress?" Tom asked. It was easier making small-talk this way than firing detailed questions one after another.

"Oh, we had our community," she said, and seeing Tom's inquisitive look, she elaborated. "Jason was a Lay Preacher at our local church." This piqued Tom's interest.

"Locally? Here in Norfolk?"

"Oh no, in and around the West Midlands, near to where we used to live," she said. "We still attend church here, of course. Once we settled here Jason dabbled a little, but Norfolk is well served in that regard."

"True," Tom said. "Did you ever attend All Saints?"

"All Saints?"

"Yes, in West Acre."

She shook her head. "No, I can't say we ever have. Why do you ask?"

"Just curious," Tom said, hiding his disappointment. "Where were you from in the West Midlands?"

"We only lived there for Jason's work, in and around Worcester," she said. "Originally, we are both from elsewhere though."

"Quite a move," Danny said, "from the West Midlands to Norfolk. A bit of a culture shock, I should imagine."

"Worcester isn't in the West Midlands."

"It isn't?" Danny asked, frowning.

"No, it's in Worcestershire. The clue is in the name." Danny flushed, but Tom sensed she hadn't meant to belittle him. Natasha smiled warmly. "As for the culture shock, I don't know," she said. "It was all such a long time ago now. It's been years, and we're very much part of the community now."

"I found that," Danny said. "How long does it take for the locals to embrace outsiders?"

"How long have you been here?"

Danny thought on it. "A year or so."

She offered him a sympathetic smile. "Give it another fifteen years or so."

"Until I'm accepted?"

"Until you're welcome. It will be another decade on top to gain acceptance."

"Huh," Danny said, exhaling heavily. Tom smiled.

"What is it about Jason's car you're so interested in that would bring the two of you all the way out here to see it?" Natasha asked.

"We believe it was involved in a hit-and-run incident late last night," Tom said, acccepting the mug of tea from her. Natasha was startled and scoffed at the notion.

"I doubt that, Mr Janssen," she said, shaking her head and smiling. "I doubt that very much."

Tom remained straight-faced. "Where do you keep the car?" he asked, glancing out of the window overlooking the side of the house.

"As I said, it's off the road," Natasha explained. She gestured towards a barn a short distance away to the right of a large willow tree. "We keep it in the barn, out of the way." She looked thoughtful. "I can't even recall when it was last taken out. The old thing probably won't even start."

"Could we take a look, do you think?" Tom asked. Natasha glanced at him and then her eyes flicked to Danny. She inclined her head.

"I suppose so, yes. I don't see why not," she said, accompanied by a shrug. "Do come this way, it's quicker."

CHAPTER NINE

BOTH TOM and Danny set their mugs down and followed her back out into the conservatory.

"We won't be a moment, Jason dear," Natasha said, turning left once into the conservatory. They had to step over a pair of muddy boots before passing through a door out into the rear garden. The three of them crossed the lawn and made their way to the barn. The entrance was facing away from them. A large wooden door, hanging from a cast-iron rail, that had seen better days was closed.

Tom nodded to Danny and he unhooked the latch and slid the door back on the rail. It moved with ease, despite its poor condition. Inside the old barn, daylight filtered through large cracks in the brickwork. The exterior walls were tied together with age-old clamps, stopping them from parting further. Inside was a ride-on lawnmower, multiple gardening tools hanging from a rack on one wall, but where the Range Rover had once stood, was an empty space.

"What on earth?" Natasha said, gasping, her mouth hanging open. She looked at Tom, then her eyes darted back into the barn and she hurried forwards, looking around as if somehow the two-tonne vehicle was hiding somewhere in the shadows. She turned back to Tom, exasperated. "I–I don't understand. Where is it?"

"When did you last see the car, Natasha?" Tom asked.

She struggled to answer, her forehead furrowing. "I don't know… it's been ages, weeks, maybe months since I've been in here. We don't use the car anymore. We haven't driven the Range Rover in years now. We would have sold it but who would want such an old bucket, especially one that does around fifteen miles to the gallon?"

"What car do you use if you need to?" Tom asked.

"I have a little hatchback." She looked to her left, still shocked by her missing car. "I park it along the side of the house there. I drive… maybe once or twice a month." She laughed but without humour. "The Range Rover isn't even insured anymore!"

Tom gave her a moment to take it all in. "Who else has access to the car?"

She shook her head. "No one. I mean, no one uses our cars."

"What about access to the house?" Danny asked.

She thought hard. "Jason has a carer who comes in three times a week, Tina, just to give me a helping hand. It means I can take myself off for a walk or a cup of coffee in the town. It means I can take a break, you know?"

"Would Tina know about the car out here?"

Natasha shook her head. "I don't know. I doubt it. She has no reason to come out here. No one does. Not even I come out here."

"What about tending the garden?" Tom asked, looking at the array of tools hanging from the racking.

"Oh, yes. There is the gardener, Barry." She looked around,

her eyes finally settling on Tom. "I mean, he's here for a few hours every week, and he knows about the car."

"Where do you keep the keys?" Tom asked.

"In the car," she said. Tom arched his eyebrows and Danny shook his head. "Why wouldn't we?" she asked. "Who would steal a car all the way out here, and who on earth would want to steal that old thing? It's worthless."

"It looks like someone did, Natasha. Could you give us the names and contact details of everyone you know who has been in your house in the past week or two, plus any information regarding visitors, delivery people, cold callers... anyone you can think of?"

Natasha was fiddling with her pendant again, shock evident on her face. She noticed Tom looking at her and nodded. "Yes, of course. Anything you need." She stopped playing with the pendant and shot Tom a searching look. "You said it was involved in a hit-and-run incident?"

"Yes, late last night, in Sandringham."

"Was... anyone hurt?" she asked, fearful.

"A pregnant lady was knocked from the road," Tom said. Natasha gasped. "She had another child in the rear seats, but it would appear they all escaped any serious injury."

"Oh, thank heavens," Natasha said.

"And you're sure no one has been using the car recently, perhaps without your consent?"

Again, Natasha shook her head only this time she was very focussed. "No, certainly not. I don't understand how this has happened."

"There is one more detail, though," Tom said. Natasha looked at him expectantly. "We also found a body in the boot, covered loosely with a sheet of tarpaulin." Natasha stared at him, wide-eyed. "We believe he was killed with a shotgun blast to his abdomen." Natasha's eyes widened further and she teetered on the spot. For a moment, Tom feared she was about to pass out, but she managed to right herself just as Tom moved to prevent her from falling. She raised a hand.

"I'm okay, Mr Janssen. I'm sorry. I felt a little strange then."

"It's understandable, don't worry."

"Who... who is the man?" she asked. "The man you found in the car?"

"We don't know yet," Tom said. "Could it be someone you know?"

She scoffed. "I don't see how. I've never heard of such a thing in these parts," she said, lifting a hand to her mouth. "It's dreadful."

"It is shocking," Tom said. "Rest assured, we'll get to the bottom of it though."

"Who are you people?" They turned to see Jason Law standing at the entrance to the barn, glaring at them. Danny was closest to him and the detective seemed bemused by the question.

"Mr Law," he said, turning towards him. "We're the—"

"Get away from my wife!" Jason screamed, startling Danny with his tone. He hesitated, glancing at Tom but before he could say anything, Jason lunged at him with surprising speed and agility. He shoved Danny who, off balance already and not expecting the move, stumbled backwards, tripping over a box at his feet and falling to the ground.

"Jason!" Natasha shouted but her husband hurried to the racking and lifted a garden rake from its place on the wall. "No, Jason!" Natasha said as he turned around, hefting the rake into the air. Danny, flat on his back, scrambled away from him as best he could. Jason went towards him, swinging the rake in a sweeping motion over Danny who finally managed to put some distance between them. Rolling over onto his front, Danny pushed himself up, trying to stand but failing so flustered was he at the unprovoked assault. As he moved clear, Danny furtively looked behind him as the older man ambled after him, brandishing the rake held tightly in his grip.

"Bloody hell!" Danny exclaimed. By this time, Tom was able to intercept his potential assailant, grasping the shaft of the rake tightly. Jason struggled to pull it away from him, but there was no way he could match Tom's strength. Natasha hurried to her husband's side and slipped an arm around his waist, catching his eye.

"It's okay, love. These are police officers," she said, smiling warmly. Jason's expression softened and he became less agitated, releasing his hold on the rake. Tom backed away, reluctant to turn his back. Danny got to his feet, brushing himself down, his hands shaking.

"Are you all right?" Tom asked. Danny nodded but he was shocked.

"Why are the police here?" Jason said nervously to his wife. "W-What did I do?"

"You haven't done anything, love," she said, putting her other hand gently onto his chest. "They were just here to ask a few questions, that's all." Jason looked at Tom and then to Danny, who was still perturbed and scowling at the older man.

"I-I didn't know. I thought you were..." His expression changed at that moment. The anger he'd shown upon first arriving had switched to fear and anxiousness. Now his expression became vacant, and he looked around them. "I'm cold," he said.

"Let's get you back into the house—"

"No, I have to gather the firewood, otherwise father will be upset with me."

"We'll make sure we get the wood, darling, don't worry. These kind gentlemen will help us." Jason looked between

Tom and Danny, as if seeing them for the first time. His eyes showed fear.

"Who are they?" he asked quietly, leaning towards Natasha but keeping his eye on Tom.

"They're with the police," Natasha said, steering him back towards the entrance. Looking over her shoulder, she smiled apologetically at Tom. He raised a hand to let her know it was okay.

"Bonkers," Danny said, once Natasha and Jason had left the barn and disappeared from view, walking slowly in the direction of the house. "The old sod ought to be locked up."

"You're keen to lock up anyone who takes a dislike to you?"

"Too right."

"I'm not sure there are enough prison places for that."

"Maybe only for the ones who come at me with a weapon then!"

Tom handed him the rake. "If he knew you well, he'd probably have used a scythe."

"Thanks very much, boss," Danny said, returning the rake to its mount on the racking. "Maybe he mistook our dead guy for a burglar and set about him?" Danny said absently, joining Tom outside the barn.

"And blasted him with a shotgun?"

"Why not? The old boy isn't all there, is he?"

"Close up the barn and I'll see you back in the house," Tom said, setting off across the lawn.

Once he reached the house, he found Jason back in his chair, staring out over the garden again. It was as if nothing had happened.

"I'm so sorry about that, Mr Janssen," Natasha said. "It's not at all like him to be violent." She gently rocked her head from side to side. "Sometimes, when he gets very confused, he can become agitated. I've been warned by our GP to expect that, but it doesn't happen very often. I don't know what came over him."

"That's okay, don't worry. We're new people, and I'm sure it's rather daunting if you don't know what's reality any more." Natasha flushed, and Tom realised he could have phrased that better. Now it was his turn to apologise but before he could, she reached out and touched his forearm.

"Don't worry. I know what you meant." Danny appeared behind them, keeping his distance from Jason by remaining on the other side of the conservatory.

"Tell me, Natasha. Do you or your husband own a shot-gun?" Tom asked.

Taken aback, Natasha met his gaze. "No. What use would we have for a gun?"

"So, you've never held a licence?" Tom asked. "It's common in these parts to hold shotgun licences."

"No, we've never had one," she said, glancing at her husband who was staring into space. "And if we did, I don't think we would be allowed to keep it now, would we?"

"No, that's true," Tom said. He glanced sideways at Danny who was still dusting himself off in the places he'd missed. "I think we have everything we need for now, Natasha."

"Do I... need to do anything about the car?"

"For the time being, it will have to stay with us," Tom said. "Once a forensic analysis is complete, then we will see about returning it to you, but that could take some time. After all, it is related to a murder investigation."

Natasha flinched at the mention of it. "I-it's no problem, Mr Janssen. As I say, we haven't used it. If it never came back, I wouldn't mind."

"I'll need to send someone out here to take your finger-prints, yours and your husband's."

"Why?"

"We hope to determine who was driving it and we will need samples of yours to compare against any others we find inside the car. Will that be okay with you?" Tom asked. Natasha looked at her husband, concerned. "It will only take a couple of minutes, and it will be painless."

"Of course, Mr Janssen," she said, turning back to Tom. "We would be happy to do anything we can do to help."

Natasha escorted them to the front door, opening it and standing aside. Danny moved past as quickly as he could, offering her a curt nod farewell and making for the car. Tom paused as he crossed the threshold.

"Tell me, what were you and your husband doing last night? Around ten to ten-thirty?"

"We were here, of course," she said. Tom waited and she realised he was looking for more detail. She began fiddling with her pendant again, concentrating hard. "We had supper around seven o'clock... and then Jason had his bath." She smiled at Tom. "There was no drama around it, which was a blessing. Then... we sat down and watched the television. *The Antiques Roadshow...* yes, there was a Constable painting they'd located, but it was unsigned. Without provenance, it wasn't as valuable as they'd hoped."

"*The Antiques Roadshow*? Last night?"

"On the catch-up thingy," Natasha said, pressing her thumb on an imaginary remote control in her hand. "Honestly, technology is wonderful these days isn't it? To think it was only a handful of years ago that we only had four television channels."

"Yes, it is," Tom said, stepping outside. "Thank you for your time. I'll have one of my officers visit you later today. Will you be home?"

"We will, yes."

Tom thanked her again and walked to his car. Danny was already in the passenger seat, still nursing his pride, and Natasha offered them both a little wave as she closed the door. Tom started the car.

"Do you think someone stole their car, then?" Danny asked.

"If the keys were inside, it wouldn't be difficult."

"Then who knew the car was there?" Danny asked. "You're not going to go stumbling around in the dark looking for it in there are you?"

"No," Tom said, pulling away. "You're not. We'll have to go door to door in the neighbouring houses, see if anyone is missing or saw something last night."

Danny sighed. "More door knocking."

"Do you have a better strategy?" Tom asked. "I'm all ears."

Danny exhaled. "We could…" He frowned. "No, I don't. Although, locking up that silly old buffer wouldn't be a bad start." Tom glanced sideways with a disapproving look. "Sorry, sir. I didn't mean that the way it came out."

"I'm pleased to hear it, Detective Constable."

Danny winced. "Sir?"

"Yes?"

"Is there any chance we can…" he coughed nervously, clearing his throat.

"What?"

"Could we keep that incident, you know, the one in the barn… between us?"

Tom smiled but he didn't reply. Danny fell silent, stewing on his thoughts. The last thing he wanted was for everyone back at the station to hear he'd been bested by an elderly man suffering from Alzheimer's, with a garden rake. Cassie in particular, Tom guessed. He figured Danny could do with a brief lesson in humility, and he left the request unanswered.

CHAPTER TEN

ERIC PRESSED the buzzer at the secure doors. The intercom crackled and he glanced up at the camera in the corner to his right.

"Can I help you?" a disembodied voice said.

"DC Collet, Hunstanton CID," Eric said, showing his warrant card. The latch clicked free and Eric pushed the door open and walked through. Inside the unit, he saw several doors off the corridor to the right and left, used by staff, and made his way along to the nurses' station. The lady behind the desk smiled at him.

"What can we do for you, DC Collet?"

"I'm here to see Lisa Nolan," Eric said. The nurse checked her screen and nodded.

"She's just back from the ultrasound. You'll find her in room seven, just over there," she said, indicating towards the far corner of the ward.

"Thank you." Eric walked over to the door, stepping aside as a porter wheeled another patient out of the ward in a wheelchair. Entering, he looked around. There were six beds in this room, three of them unoccupied or the patients were currently elsewhere.

At the far end, the last bed which happened to be beside the window had a woman sitting up in it. A man was sitting alongside her in a chair, sporting a concerned look, occasionally glancing towards a toddler who was on a play mat at the end of the room, a couple of metres away. This must be where they put patients with young families.

The other two occupied beds were located either side of the entrance and Eric could read their names on the boards at the foot of the bed. Neither was Lisa Nolan, and so he made a beeline for the last bed. The man glanced up warily at Eric as he approached, sitting up from his slouched position. He had close-cropped hair, with a lot of product making it appear wet, gold earrings and a weathered appearance to his complexion. Tattoos were visible protruding from the neckline of his T-shirt and down his forearms.

"Mrs Nolan?" Eric asked.

"Yes," she said, looking up from her conversation with the man beside her bed, who had turned all his attention towards Eric. He presented her with his warrant card.

"DC Eric Collet. How are you feeling?"

"Like she's been hit by a car," the man said before she could answer. Eric inclined his head. Lisa Nolan seemed irritated by the interruption.

"I'm feeling much better, thank you," she said, shooting her companion a dark look. "They expect I'll be able to go home in the next couple of hours. The scan showed no signs of concern about the little one." She put a hand affectionately on her belly. She was heavily pregnant. Eric judged she was possibly only a month away from her due date, maybe less.

"That's good news," he said.

"Yes, we just have to wait for the doctor to sign it off and then we can go home."

"That must be a relief?"

"Very much so, yes."

"What are you doing about catching the lunatic who caused all of this?"

Eric looked at the man. "Are you Mr Nolan?" He gave Eric a curt nod. His demeanour was a lot less friendly than in that of his partner. "Our investigation is ongoing, Mr Nolan."

He scoffed. "In other words you haven't caught them."

"Not yet, no, but we are working on it."

"See?" he said, looking at his wife and shaking his head. "Bloody useless, the lot of them. They'll be there quick enough if you steal a sausage roll from Greggs or something, but when you actually need them to catch a nutter, you've had it."

"Mark!" Lisa said, scolding him. "I'm sure they're doing their best."

Eric smiled. "We are, I promise." He chose to ignore the husband as much as possible, thereby cutting him a bit of slack. There was every chance that he was simply tired, stressed, and certainly rattled by the possibility of what could have happened to their unborn child, his partner and his toddler. If it had been Becca who'd been driven off the road with George in the back, he'd be angry too. "Do you remember much about the accident?"

"She's been through this already!"

Eric smiled. "I'm sure, but the investigation has moved on and it is looking more complicated." He looked back at Lisa. "If you wouldn't mind just going over the details again for me."

"Of course, no problem," Lisa said. "But, like I told the policeman last night, I don't remember much about it. It all happened so fast."

"What do you remember?" Eric asked. Lisa fixed her expression, looking straight ahead, concentrating.

"It was late, and there are no streetlights on the roads through Sandringham." She shook her head. "I didn't see them. They came from nowhere and… just seemed to nudge me. At first, I thought they were just really close to me, like they hadn't seen me or something." She looked at Eric now, on edge. "Then… I felt the car seem to shift, like I was sliding. Thinking about it now, I think they were pushing me. I felt the car going away from me and I tried to correct it, to line myself back with the road but we were on a bend at that point and…" she looked at her husband, apologetic, "I tried, I really did."

"I know you did, love," Mark said, sitting forward and putting a supportive hand on her leg. "A big car like that, weighing in against yours. There was probably nothing you could have done differently."

"What type of car was it?" Eric asked.

"It was an old Range Rover,' she said. "A dark colour, I saw it after… after we crashed."

"After?" Eric asked. She nodded.

"Yes. When they pushed me, and my car started sliding, I completely lost control, and we came off the road. We hit the trees, I remember that because the side windows all shattered and then we rolled over." She was wringing her hands in her lap, reliving the memory had brought back the shock and fear.

"Take your time," Eric said. "There's no rush."

She nodded and her expression took on a distant look. "For a moment – that moment felt like ages, but it could only have been a few seconds – I didn't understand where I was or what had happened. The car was on its side, and not upside down, thankfully, and I didn't know what was going on. It sounds daft…"

"What does?"

"It was like time stood still. It was eerily quiet, and then… Logan started screaming," she said, indicating their son who was playing nearby. Eric smiled at the child who, hearing his name, looked up at them. Logan returned the smile. "He was still safe in his harness, thank God!" Lisa said. "I think he'd been in shock as well."

"What happened then?"

"I knew we had to get out of the car, and I was sort of hanging there, awkwardly, in my seatbelt. It took me a while to get it free and it was while I wrestling with it that I looked out through the windscreen and saw the lights come on."

"The lights?"

"Yes, of the Range Rover. I couldn't believe I hadn't seen it, and then I realised they'd been driving with the headlights turned off."

"So, it stopped? The other driver didn't leave immediately?"

"No, they stopped. The brake lights were on as well. They definitely stopped."

"You have said *they* several times," Eric said, making notes.

"Yes, I saw more than one person inside the car. There was a bit of a commotion."

Eric's curiosity was piqued. "Can you describe it?"

Her brow furrowed. "They were arguing, or fighting," she said, thinking hard. "There was definitely an exchange of views going on. I saw movement in the car. They were very animated."

"How many people do you think were present?"

She exhaled, shaking her head. "I can't be certain. At least two, maybe three, but I can't be sure."

"Did you see anyone get out of the car?" Eric asked.

"Actually, yes," Lisa said. "Someone did get out, and I think they walked to the back of the car…"

"Can you describe them?"

"No, sorry. I'm pretty sure whoever it was got out from the passenger side which was away from me. And, as I said, it was dark and only the rear lights of the car were illuminating them."

"But they didn't come over to you?"

"No, I heard someone yelling and… I saw them hesitate and then got back into the car and it drove away really fast."

"Scum," Mark growled.

Eric nodded, taking it all down in his pocketbook. "You'll get no argument from me, Mr Nolan." He looked up at Lisa again. "What can you tell me about them, the ones in the car?"

Lisa thought hard. "I'm not sure, it might be my mind playing tricks on me… but…"

"Go on," Eric said, "it's best to tell us what you remember. You never know, it might be useful, even if you don't think it's relevant at the moment."

"Well, when I thought I was losing control of the car, I looked in my mirror and seeing the car behind me, so close, shocked me and I looked round. I remember… seeing the driver. Our eyes sort of met, and he looked just as surprised as I did. He was staring at me, open-mouthed." She shrugged. "Like I say, I'm not sure it was like that but it's what I keep seeing when I think about it. It's really surreal."

"During high-stress traumatic events, your brain can almost slow things down as it processes everything going on around you. It's what people refer to as seeing things happening in slow motion."

"That makes sense. So, maybe I did see that?"

"I wouldn't be surprised," Eric said. "What do you remember about the driver?"

"Young," she said, then chuckled. "Not that I'm old, but he was younger than me."

"How old, would you say?"

She pursed her lips, considering it. "Twenty-something. Early twenties, I'd say. He had short hair, shaved at the sides not cut, and he was white. Sorry, I know that's rubbish."

"Not at all it's great, very detailed under the circumstances, thank you. You're doing very well," Eric said, and Lisa smiled.

"Are you going to catch the little sod then?" Mark said through gritted teeth.

"We'll do our best, Mr Nolan."

"Don't patronise me," he said, scowling at Eric. He seemed to look him up and down. "How old are you anyway? I'll bet you're about the same age as the guy who put Lisa in here."

Eric was used to being treated this way. Despite the onset of lines caused by parenthood, he still managed to keep his boyish looks. At least for now. "I can assure you, Mr Nolan, we are taking this very seriously, and we are making progress."

"You've found them already?"

"No," Eric said, and Mark bristled, "but we do have the car." Mark settled at the mention of that, but he remained unhappy. "We are processing the car at the moment and hopefully we'll get some fingerprints from the interior."

"You're going all out then?" Lisa said. "We watch the crime shows on the telly, and I wouldn't expect you to look for fingerprints in a car accident. Especially one where nobody died."

Eric winced momentarily, and Mark picked up on it. "What aren't you telling us?" he asked.

Eric contemplated brushing the question away, but she was involved and it was only fair to keep them advised. He glanced towards their son, who seemed focussed on the toys he was playing with. Even so, Eric lowered his voice. "When we found the Range Rover this morning, we also found… the body of a deceased male in the back of the car." Lisa gasped and Mark blinked in surprise.

"A body?" Mark whispered. Eric nodded.

"I can't say anything else at this time, but I'm sure you can understand that we are treating this with the utmost importance."

"Ah… so if there was no body there, you'd be washing your hands of it," Mark said. Lisa glared at him and he lowered his gaze from Eric, putting his hands together in his lap.

"What happened to him?" Lisa asked.

"We are still investigating," Eric said. "But we are treating it as suspicious."

"Right, okay," Lisa said quietly.

"Try not to think too much about it," Eric said, attempting to reassure her with his confidence. "I think the accident was an unfortunate occurrence—"

"Unfortunate?" Mark said.

"What I mean is, I think the accident was unrelated to whatever led the man to be in that situation." He smiled at Lisa. "I know it's difficult, but please try to put it out of your mind as best you can. You have a lovely family, and another on the way. Focus on getting yourself home."

"Thank you, I will."

Eric took out one of his contact cards, placing it on top of the bedside cabinet. "Here are my contact details. If you think of anything else that you think might be relevant, please give me a call. Once we have more information, I'll be sure to update you."

Lisa nodded, smiling appreciatively, but she was clearly rattled. Eric regretted telling her now. It wasn't information she needed to be burdened with at this time. It could have waited. He thanked her and then turned to leave. He was halfway towards the corridor when he heard footsteps behind him.

Mark Nolan fell into step alongside him, and Eric slowed.

"Listen, I'm sorry about before," he said. Eric inclined his head, signalling that he understood. "It's just that this whole situation has been quite a shock, you know?"

"It's okay. It is a lot to take in," Eric said, pulling up. Mark was hesitant, looking around and running a hand through his hair and waiting for a passing nurse to go by.

"You know, this…" he grimaced, "the man you found. Do I have anything to worry about?"

"What do you mean?"

"Well, people don't usually drive around with dead bodies in the boot, do they?"

"No."

"Well then," Mark said, shifting his weight between his feet. "Lisa saw the driver."

"Yes."

"So, she's a witness. She could *identify* him."

"Ah, right," Eric said. "I see your point. I don't think you have to worry."

"Do you know who the guy is, the one who died?"

"No, not yet."

"Well then…"

Eric met his eye. "Look, I can understand why you're asking, but they wouldn't know that Lisa can identify them. Everything happened very quickly—"

"But she could be in danger. What are you going to do about it?"

"Sorry," Eric said. "I don't understand. Are you asking for protection? I don't believe that's necessary."

"I pay my taxes," Mark said. "And you need to do your

job." Mark jabbed a finger into Eric's chest. The anger had returned.

"I can assure you, we are doing our job, Mr Nolan," Eric said, looking down at the finger still pushed against his chest. Mark took his hand away. "Now, you have my number, and if you feel threatened then give me a call and I'll send some officers around to your house. But there's no reason to believe that your family are in danger, Mr Nolan. No reason at all."

"Right," Mark said, taking a step away from him. "I hope you're right, for my family's sake." He stopped, glaring at Eric. "If anything happens, I'll be holding you accountable, DC Collet."

Eric nodded and remained where he was as Mark Nolan turned and stalked away, back to his wife's bedside. Eric couldn't help but think there was more behind Mark's animosity than simply fear for his family's safety.

Mark Nolan appeared to have an instant dislike for him, if not for the police in general. Eric couldn't help but wonder if the man had had involvement with the police in the past. It was something he planned to look into when he got the chance, back at the station.

CHAPTER ELEVEN

THE TEAM GATHERED in the ops room. Cassie passed Eric a cup of coffee she'd brought for him from the canteen. Danny frowned at her.

"Where's mine, sarge?"

"Oh," Cassie said, patting her pockets theatrically with her free hand. She stopped, pouted, and then smiled at him. "Sorry, I think I spilled yours on the way back up here."

"Cheers," Danny said, but any further conversation ended as Tom clapped his hands, drawing eyes to him at the front of the room. The CID team was joined in the briefing by a handful of uniformed constables who Tom had managed to round up for canvassing duties. His staff were experienced investigators, but they were a small team and having two murder inquiries underway at the same time stretched them.

"Can I have your attention please?" Tom said. Everyone took their seats or remained standing but focussed on Tom. "We are going to have a round-up of where we are with your individual assignments. Cassie, what have we had back from All Saints Church?"

Cassie cocked her head. "Not much, sir. The belfry has been processed and other than signs of more than one person being present, there isn't a lot of detail." She consulted her notes. "There isn't a great deal of traffic at the middle-floor level, and we have a lot of dust gathered on the timbers. This was disturbed by two different sets of footwear. The good news is we do have several footprints where tread style and depths are quantifiable, and the chewing gum wrapper you found, but that's about it."

"The wrapper?" Tom asked.

Cassie winced. "Still trying to determine the brand and origin. The language used in the ingredients, which is the piece you found, is Polish and, as far as we can deduce, it isn't sold here in the UK, but there are several Polish delis and suppliers in operation in these parts and hundreds more elsewhere in the country. Any of them could be importing the product for sale."

"Okay, keep at it. What about Martin Odiham?"

"Personal life or forensic analysis?"

"Analysis first, please. I've already spoken to Doctor Paxton, but if you could fill everyone else in."

"There was evidence of him taking a beating, but we knew that already. Toxicology has no sign of alcohol or drugs in his system, and no trace evidence was found under the fingernails. He took a beating, but he didn't fight back or at least, there are no defensive wounds visible."

"What about Odiham's personal life?"

"Widowed," Cassie said. "Lives alone in his cottage in Castle Acre. He retired from his work nineteen years ago and came to West Acre about ten years ago, becoming church warden soon afterwards."

"What work did he do?" Tom asked.

"He worked for an insurance company," Cassie said. "I've

looked into his work record, and he wasn't involved in anything controversial or particularly groundbreaking. I spoke with the HR department, and he was well regarded, diligent and popular, as far as I can tell."

Tom was thoughtful. "There is a great deal of time passing between retirement and his death. I find it difficult to see how the two could be connected. What was found at his home?"

"Still processing it, sir," Cassie said. "Although it is a small property, he had a lifetime's worth of clutter in there. It's hard to know what's important and what can be disregarded with no context to work with. It'll take time."

"The car?" Tom asked.

Cassie nodded. "The fire investigator called it a basic incendiary device, which I think is professional speak for a petrol bomb or similar. Simple, crude but effective."

"He came up with something in a hurry once he knew we were at the property."

"That would be my assumption, sir. It's likely he drove Odiham's car back to his house, to get what he wanted from inside perhaps, and then when he realised the police were there already – maybe sooner than he expected – he got rid of any trace of his presence in the car." She shrugged. "I wonder if he had planned to do similar to the house."

Tom took a deep breath. "I'm pleased he didn't do so with us inside."

"A murderer with a conscience," Cassie said, drily.

"Or one who thinks we'll pull out all the stops if he kills a couple of police officers," Danny said, "but we'll be less inclined to do so with one old boy and a burglary."

"You could be right, Danny," Tom said. "There's always the possibility he didn't find what he was looking for in the house and doesn't want to risk destroying whatever it is."

"Have we any idea what that might be?" Eric asked. Tom shook his head.

"Not until we can figure out a motive, no." Tom looked at the information board, focussing on the photograph of Martin Odiham. "Cassie, keep digging. The burglary at the cottage tells us Odiham was targeted. It wasn't a random attack." Cassie nodded, and Tom turned to Eric. "Eric, the Range Rover, please."

"The scene has been processed and the body has been removed and taken to Doctor Paxton for the postmortem. The deceased was wearing a thick jacket and aside from the obvious gunshot wound, we didn't see any other obvious signs of damage to the body. Paxton says he'll be through," Eric checked his watch, "in about an hour or so, from now. The victim wasn't carrying any identification, no driving licence, wallet or keys. Nothing like that."

"Any indication as to who else was in the car with him?"

"I spoke to the driver of the other car involved in the collision, Lisa Nolan." Eric looked up. "She's expected to be released from hospital later today, and both she and her child are okay. She is pretty sure there were multiple people in the car, a minimum of two anyway. The Range Rover stopped at the scene and a passenger got out, momentarily looking over at her before being encouraged back into the vehicle. Then, it took off, leaving her in the car."

"Tossers," Cassie said. "Although, murderers don't have a particularly strong moral compass, so she was probably better off being left alone."

"What about the driver?" Tom asked Eric. "Did she see them?"

Eric nodded. "Briefly, but it all happened at speed. She gave me a description of him but how reliable it is seeing as it was during the accident itself, remains to be seen. She said he was young though, in his twenties." Eric riffled through the folder in front of him on his desk. "However, the scenes-of-crime technicians have done a good job and managed to lift some prints from inside the car." Eric produced a document and scanned it. "Now, whoever was in the car wasn't completely daft. They tried to erase any sign of their presence on the interior, wiping the steering wheel clean, door handles, internal and external, including the exterior boot release button... but they did miss the rear-view mirror. Here, the techs were able to lift two partial fingerprints."

"That's good news," Tom said. "Is it anyone we know?"

Eric consulted his notes. "It's not a complete match," he said, grimacing, "but it's close enough to give us a name. Finn Harper. He's a resident of Hunstanton, lives at an address in Crescent Road. He has been on our radar before, but as a teenager. He has a handful of shoplifting charges under his belt, two arrests for aggravated assault, but no convictions, and a caution for possession of Class C drugs."

"Sounds like a real charmer," Danny said.

Eric agreed. "Murder though?"

"It would be a significant step up for him," Tom said. "Anything related to guns?"

Eric shook his head. "No, he's pretty much just a petty thief, but someone decent people would want to steer clear of."

"Known associates?" Tom asked.

"Nothing in the database," Eric said. "I was waiting to see what you wanted to do before I went round to his house."

"I think we'll do that," Tom said, "as soon as we're through with the briefing. You can take Danny with you. If – Lisa Nolan, was it? – is right and Finn wasn't alone in the car, then the only way we'll learn who else was there is to ask him."

"Maybe he's stepping up his game," Cassie said. "Or he

has already done so but been a bit more clever about it in recent years. How old is he? Twenties, you said?"

"That's what Lisa said," Eric told her. "His file says he's twenty-one."

"He's been a busy boy for twenty-one," Tom said. "Where is the Range Rover now?"

"In the yard, sir," Eric said. "We had a low loader drop it off half an hour ago."

"Right," Tom said, looking at Danny Wilson. "What have you got for us on the owner of the Range Rover, Jason Law?"

Danny cleared his throat, picking up his notebook. "He's a retired secondary school teacher. He taught Humanities subjects at various schools, primarily in the Black Country, but he originates from Hampshire on the south coast." Danny arched his eyebrows. "He's also a licensed lay reader, or he was, before he lost his marbles."

"Yes, Natasha said so. Where did he do it?" he asked absently.

Danny consulted his notes, searching for the answer, smiling with apparent relief that he'd noted that down. "Several churches in the Walsall and Dudley area, but I can't find any reference of him here in Norfolk."

"Has he ever held a shotgun licence?" Tom asked. Danny shook his head.

"And he has never had so much as a parking ticket either. He's as clean as freshly laid snow."

"You sound disappointed," Cassie said.

Danny shrugged. "Not at all… I just—"

"Don't like him," Cassie said, smirking knowingly. "I can't imagine why that might be the case."

Danny's eyes narrowed and when Eric also grinned, he rolled his eyes. No one else commented, but it was clear to him that Tom hadn't kept the incident with the rake to himself.

"Eric, how did you get on with the holiday homes around the sailing club at Snettisham?"

Eric looked glum. "Ninety percent of them aren't currently occupied, sir. The wind hasn't been there for the sailing in the last few days and that's the driving factor for people to be staying on the lake."

"What about the caravan park?"

"Reduced occupancy," Eric said. "It's been a poor summer, and numbers are down across the board. The caravans lining the access road to the sailing club are the least occupied because they're the furthest from the water. Anyone coming or going in a vehicle wouldn't be seen beyond that last line of caravans." He sighed. "And the path along the shore north towards Heacham and south towards Lynn isn't well lit. At the time the car was dumped, no one was about to see them."

"I suspect they knew that," Tom said absently. "Finn Harper would know that." Eric nodded. "Okay," Tom said, looking around the room. "I want to continue with the canvassing of the neighbours," moving to a map of the local area, pinned to another board, "around Martin Odiham's cottage in Castle Acre and also the properties near to the Laws' house. We're working pretty much blind here, and we need something to get things moving. With a bit of luck, that break will come once we've been able to chat to Harper. Until then, stay diligent and make a note of anything that strikes you as interesting, however small or insignificant it may seem."

There was a murmur of agreement from all of those assembled and Tom ended the briefing. As bodies filtered out of the room, Tom saw Tamara waiting at the rear. He hadn't seen her come in, and she'd likely caught the end of the meeting. Tom caught Eric's attention.

"You can head round to Harper's as soon as I've spoken to the DCI," Tom said.

"You're the DCI now, sir," Eric replied, and Tom smiled.

"You know what I mean."

He walked towards Tamara and she met him halfway. They were alone as the others returned to work at their desks. "Do you have a minute?" she asked.

"It's about all I do have, yes," he replied. Tamara smiled, looking past him at the information boards.

"I miss this, you know."

"What, the briefings?"

She laughed. "Okay, not the briefings, but being involved."

"You were promoted barely—"

"And I'm already regretting it," she said, lowering her voice. "If I'd wanted to work in administration, I'd…" she shook her head, "have done something else."

"That bad?"

Tamara ran a hand through her hair, smiling in greeting to Cassie who waved to her. "You know, with two murder cases underway, Major Crimes would usually be crawling all over us to take one or both off our hands."

"They've got their own problems," Tom said.

"They do," Tamara agreed, wrinkling her nose, "and they're trying the age-old distraction technique of whaboutery when it comes to getting themselves out of a sticky situation."

"Trying to cast shade over us?"

"Exactly," Tamara said, heaving a sigh.

"It won't work."

"No, it won't," she agreed. "But it will cause a smell and some of that is going to come our way. I know we did everything by the book but… they are itching to turn us over." She fixed Tom with a stern look. "Do you know what I mean?"

He nodded. "I won't let you down," Tom said. He looked around the room at Eric, Cassie and Danny. "None of us will."

She reached out and touched his forearm. "I know."

CHAPTER TWELVE

CRESCENT ROAD WAS LOCATED at the southern end of the town, slightly elevated with a view out across The Wash over to Lincolnshire which was easily visible on a clear day. The housing stock was a mix of traditional Victorian terraces and newer single-storey houses built in the 60s when the old town expanded.

"That one," Eric said, pointing to an end of terrace brick and sandstone property. Unusually for the town, this house had access to the side which they had partially extended the house into, but also left enough space for cars, whereas many of the traditional houses in the seaside town were constructed before such space was needed. Danny parked the car in the street outside.

The calm weather of the previous few days had been replaced now, a northerly breeze rattling in off the water bringing with it a sudden drop in temperature. Danny drew his coat about him, as they walked up the short path to the front door, signalling for Eric to stand off to the right. He kept a watchful eye on the side of the house just in case their quarry decided to run.

Danny rang the doorbell. They didn't have to wait long before a woman opened the door, peering out at them. Not recognising Danny, she glanced at Eric just as Danny took out his identification.

"Mrs Harper?" he asked, and she nodded. "We're hoping to have a word with your son, Finn. Is he at home?"

"Finn?" she asked, frowning. She clicked her tongue against the roof of her mouth, rolled her eyes, and pulled the door wider. "I knew he'd been up to something."

"Why would you say that, Mrs Harper?"

"If you knew my son, you wouldn't have to ask. Do come in," she said, stepping back and turning to lead the way into the house. "Finn!"

"What is it, mum?"

"The police are here to see you—"

Footsteps thundered down the stairs and a figure rounded the newel post, presumably Finn, almost colliding with his mother and he was gone in a flash.

"Finn!" his mother shouted.

"Eric! Around the back!" Danny bellowed, but he didn't wait to see the detective constable take off down the side of the house. He tried to get past Mrs Harper who remained standing in the middle of the hallway, inadvertently blocking Danny's path, and she put a hand to her chest in surprise. "Excuse me, Mrs Harper," Danny said, manhandling her aside as best he could. The woman gasped as Danny ran past her, through the house and into the rear. The building had also been extended into the garden, creating a very narrow but spacious property.

Danny had lost sight of Finn once he disappeared into the depths of the back of the house and fearful of passing him, he had to slow down as he entered a kitchen at the back of the property. A large chimney stack separated what

Danny figured was the original room from the extension at the rear.

There was no sign of Finn. Danny continued on. Hearing animated voices coming from outside, he found a set of sliding patio doors open. Stepping out, a hooded figure sprinted back from the side of the house, Eric giving chase and Danny fell into step alongside him.

"Stop!" Eric yelled but Finn Harper had no intention of doing so, if anything he found another burst of speed.

"Get after him, Eric!" Danny said, confident they had him cornered. At the end of the garden was a stone wall, six feet tall with large vegetation beyond it offering another barrier. Finn zig-zagged across the lawn, only just managing to keep out of both Danny and Eric's grasp. At one point, Danny took hold of his hoodie and tugged at it, but it was unzipped at the front and Finn managed to spin, pulling his arms free and leaving Danny holding only the fleece, off balance. He tripped over his own feet and fell over. "Bloody Nora!"

With incredible agility, Finn feinted to move to his left only to shift to his right, catching Eric off guard, and used the waste bin beside the wall for leverage to clamber up it. Without regard for his safety, Finn vaulted the wall, pitching headfirst over the lip and falling through the undergrowth. Eric attempted the same manoeuvre but got his angles all wrong, the bin shifting under his weight and flipping over onto its side. Eric pitched backwards, hitting the ground on his back with a thud, exhaling heavily upon impact.

"That hurt," Eric said, seeing Danny towering over him. Danny cast the hoodie aside and made to climb the wall himself, but by the time he was sitting astride it he could see Finn had successfully disappeared. Beyond the mix of bushes and trees was an alleyway running between the properties whose gardens backed onto one another. If you weren't already aware of it, you would never know it was there.

"Damn," Danny said. Eric was back on his feet, nursing his back. He squinted up at Danny.

"The boss is going to be furious," Eric said, rubbing the base of his back. Finn Harper's mother had come to the patio doors and was watching them, a look of deep concern on her face.

"That's twice today," Danny said, keeping his voice low and still searching for any sign of Finn Harper… but to no avail.

"Twice what?" Eric asked.

"Twice I've been made to look a complete idiot."

"Don't worry about it," Eric said as Danny swung a leg back over the wall and dropped down into the garden beside him.

"You think it'll be okay?"

"Nah, it's just everyone expects it from you now."

"What?" Danny asked as Eric set off back to where Mrs Harper was waiting, arms folded across her chest. She didn't seem too alarmed at what she'd just witnessed. Danny hurried after Eric. "Does everyone think I'm useless or something?" he hissed, gently tugging on Eric's arm but his colleague ignored the question.

"Mrs Harper," Eric said, brushing some grass clippings from the arm of his jacket, "do you know your son's where-abouts yesterday?"

"Are you going to tell me what this is all about?" she asked defiantly. She had a look on her face. This woman wasn't going to take any nonsense.

"We need to speak to Finn about an incident that we believe he was involved in, Mrs Harper. A car accident that took place late last night."

"That can't be," she said. "My Finn doesn't own a car."

Eric and Danny exchanged a glance and Danny pursed his lips, then nodded. "It wasn't his car, Mrs Harper."

"Oh, for heaven's sake!" she said, throwing her arms in the air despairingly. "Are you telling me he stole a car?"

"That's what we need to speak to him about," Danny said.

"And then he crashed it?"

Danny winced. "Again—"

"That's what you need to speak to him about?"

Danny nodded.

"Do you know where your son might be headed?" Eric asked.

"You could speak to that wastrel he spends all of his time with."

"And which particular wastrel would that be, Mrs Harper?" Danny took out his pocketbook and clicked the end of his pen.

"Ollie," she said, folding her arms again. "Oliver Chalk. If he's got himself wrapped up in something illegal, then I'd wager Ollie has something to do with it."

"Is Ollie a bad influence?" Eric asked.

She snorted with derision. "A bad influence, you ask?" She tutted. "That boy was born to be locked up. Mark my words, that's where he'll end up. I just pray to God he doesn't take my son there with him."

"Do you know where we can find Ollie?" Danny asked.

"Officially, he's what you would deem *of no fixed abode*."

"And unofficially?"

"There's a squat just off the seafront, but I don't know where exactly," she said. "Finn knows full well he's not supposed to be hanging out with that boy, but if there's trouble then he'll not be far away."

"And if he didn't go there," Eric said, "where would he go?"

"Your guess is as good as mine, young man," she said. "Although, you could always ask Alexa."

Danny cocked his head. "I'm assuming you don't mean the online device?"

"No, Alexa… the girl that he and Ollie have been knocking around with."

"Finn's girlfriend?" Danny asked. She shrugged. It was clear she didn't approve of the girl. "And what can you tell us about her?"

"Not much. She's orphaned. Lives across town with her grandparents, but I don't know where. They raised her, Finn told me – decent people by all accounts – but she's a bit of a tearaway."

"Please don't take this the wrong way, Mrs Harper," Danny said, "but you don't seem all that surprised by any of this."

"I gave up trying to police that boy some time ago. Whatever I did with him, for him… or to him, never worked. It's probably my fault." Danny made to assuage her self-deprecation but she cut him off. "I raised him, shaped him. If the parent isn't to blame when they turn out as a wrong-un, then who is? I told him this was his last chance," she said, a cloud darkening her expression, "and this is how he repays me."

"We don't know the full story yet, Mrs Harper," Eric said. "It may not be as bad as you think."

"Two plain clothes detectives knocking on my door, and he makes a run for it." She shook her head. "I may not be the brightest, but it doesn't look like innocence to me." She raised a finger towards Danny. "Well, let me tell you this, when you find him you just let him know that I'll have his things packed for him and I'll leave them out here in the garden. He'd better collect them before it starts raining again because he'll not be coming back into my house."

Eric coughed awkwardly but Danny smiled. "I'll be sure to let him know, Mrs Harper."

They left via the passage along the side of the house. Once in the car, Danny took out a mobile phone and started scrolling through the screens.

"Hadn't we better check in back at the nick?" Eric asked.

"What's that?"

"Shouldn't we let the DI know we... um... lost Finn."

"DCI," Danny said quietly, still concentrating on the mobile in his hand.

"Whatever," Eric said. "We ought to though, right?"

"And have everyone think I'm an idiot?" Danny glanced sideways at Eric. "I don't know about you, but I don't fancy being ridiculed twice in a day."

"But—"

"Shh," Danny said, frowning. "I'm busy."

"Sorry to interrupt your social life—"

"There we are," Danny said, turning the screen towards Eric.

"What's—"

"Alexa Willis," Danny said, grinning. "Pretty girl, if you can get past the tattoos, I suppose."

"What's wrong with tattoos?"

Danny shrugged. "Nothing at all, if ink is your thing. Not mine though."

"Hey, how did you find her?"

Danny held the mobile aloft. "Finn dropped this when he scaled the wall."

"You didn't!"

Danny nodded. "I sure did. Who's the idiot now?" Eric

snapped his head around, scanning the area as if someone might be watching.

"I can't believe you did that—"

"Did what? I found a lost device, and it happened to be unlocked." He smiled at Eric. "I'm trying to find the owner."

Eric shook his head. "The boss will not be happy about—"

"Not if you tell him, he won't, no. Keep schtum, Eric, and you and I can redeem this regrettable episode. Right?"

Eric sighed. "Any idea where we can find them?"

Danny was already scrolling through some photographs stored in the phone's memory. He opened up one particular shot, angling the screen so Eric could see. It was taken down by the seafront, but it looked more like the area between Heacham and the caravan parks on the south side of Hunstanton than in the town itself. The image was a selfie, two males and one female. Finn Harper was one of them and the blonde girl between the two males looked very much like Alexa Willis.

"I guess the other one is Chalkie himself," Danny said, "don't you think?"

"Likely."

"Come on then, let's go and find this beachfront squat of theirs."

Eric took a deep breath. "All right, but if they're not there—"

"We'll fess up," Danny said, holding his left hand in the air, folding his fingers. "Scout's honour."

"You were never a boy scout."

"Says who?"

"You're using the wrong hand for starters!" Eric shook his head. Danny started the car and putting it in gear, looked behind them and reversed to turn the car around.

"So… who thinks I'm an idiot?" he asked, hearing the fear in his own voice.

"Everyone, Danny," Eric whispered. "Everyone."

CHAPTER THIRTEEN

"I KNOW I said to bring me more interesting subjects, Tom," Doctor Paxton said, leaning forward and peering over the rim of his glasses as Tom entered the room, Cassie a half step behind him, "but I wasn't expecting you to be so swift." Paxton was greeting Tom but he looked past him to Cassie, smiling warmly. "Cassandra, delighted to see you again."

Cassie sighed, glancing around the morgue. "I would like to say the same, but I can't, so I won't."

Paxton's smile broadened. "Your tongue is as razor sharp as ever, DS Knight."

"I sharpened it just for you." Cassie returned his smile.

"Delighted," Paxton repeated. "Come, come." He beckoned them over as he stood up and led them to the mortuary slab. The body was covered by a simple sheet, the pathologist having already completed his examination. They joined him and Paxton lifted the sheet back to reveal the face and upper body of the man found dead in the boot of the Range Rover.

Tom gave the body a cursory look. The man had been curled up inside the car, as well as covered by a tarpaulin, and this was the first time Tom had been able to get a good look at him. He was a heavy-set man, muscular and imposing. His body was tattooed, the left arm with what Tom judged was a Celtic pattern whereas the right was more of a sleeve: different images and patterns merged together.

He looked to be in his forties, early to mid. His hair was close cut, and recently too, based on the length and the tidiness of the shaping. He had more ink across his chest in the form of a bird of prey's wing tips, the wings wrapping around his body from the rear and coming across his shoulders, sweeping down towards his pectorals. If you imagined a bird landing on his back and enveloping him with a large wingspan, you wouldn't be far off. Tom had never seen such a dramatic design.

Paxton saw him studying it. "He will have had a high threshold for pain, this one," the doctor said. Tom glanced sideways at him. "Just think how long he will have spent lying on his front while all of that was sketched out, inked, and then factor in the scabbing and the recovery time." He wrinkled his nose. "Maybe he enjoyed the sensation of pain."

Tom exhaled, looking the man up and down again. "We'll never know."

"It's a real work of art," Cassie said.

Paxton nodded glumly. "Someone made a right mess of it at the rear though," he said, crossing to his little side desk and returning with a folder in hand. He passed a set of photographs to Tom and although he'd seen many of such images before, he was still taken aback. He handed them on to Cassie. "Shotgun wound to the back," Paxton said. "Close quarters, too." He took up a stance as if he was holding an imaginary shotgun, mimicking the recoil with a slight movement of his arms. "Look at the spread pattern," he said, stopping Tom on one particular image. "I'd estimate the shooter was standing four feet behind him, perhaps less. The barrel will obviously have been almost two feet closer than that."

"Unless it was sawn off," Cassie said.

"No," Paxton said, staring at the deceased. "Again, the spread pattern is quite telling. If the barrel was reduced in length, or sawn off, as you say, then the spread pattern of the shot would be much wider. Had the shooter been within a foot, then perhaps we would see the same but I'd expect to see powder burns and a greater impact from the wad column."

"The what?" Cassie asked. It was Tom who answered.

"The wad column is what holds the shot pellets in place inside the hull of the cartridge and separate from the powder charge. Essentially, it's like a bucket, and it keeps the pellets together as they pass along the barrel. They used to be made of paper or cardboard, but these days they are usually plastic."

"Very environmentally friendly," Cassie said.

"Biodegradable," Paxton added, "and it's often designed to disintegrate and drop away from the barrel upon exit allowing the pellets to continue on their trajectory. In this case," he said, cocking his head, "I found elements of the wad inside the wound itself. The concentration of the pellets, their spread pattern, and a bit of know-how," he said, tapping the end of his nose, "helps me calculate the distance from the body along with the shape of the weapon's barrel."

"Did he see it coming?" Tom asked.

"I have no way of knowing to be sure," Paxton said, arching his eyebrows, "but I think it unlikely. The wound was square on where the shooter was standing. If he was aware of the shooter or their approach, he may well have turned, or tried to turn, and thereby offered a very different profile."

"Executed?" Tom asked.

Paxton was thoughtful. "He was standing upright when he was shot. He's a tall man, a smidgen over six foot three inches.

He pitched forward, face first onto the ground. There is soil in his left ear and some of it caught in the eyelids of his left eye. I imagine he made a sound when he hit the ground." Paxton looked to the ceiling.

"What is it?" Tom asked.

"I was just wondering… if a giant of a man falls in the forest, and he is alone, does he make a sound?"

Tom inclined his head, ignoring the pathologist's eccentricity. Cassie arched her eyebrows at Tom and he stifled a smile.

"Not that he was in a forest, mind you," Paxton said, focussing on the body again. "The soil has a high concentrate of silica — that's sand, DS Knight – which is common in these parts."

Cassie rolled her eyes. "Can we place the body at a scene, presuming we can find it?"

Paxton nodded. "With a high percentage of probability, yes. I would think so. Do you have such a location for comparison?"

"No, not yet," she said.

"Oh, shame."

"Can we rule out the area around the sailing club?" Tom asked.

"I would say so, yes. There isn't enough sand present. I think you'll be looking for a site more inland, and also…" he checked his notes, "there are other contaminants present in the samples."

"What type of contaminants?"

"Chemicals," Paxton said. "I can't tell you which ones exactly, but samples have been sent off to the lab for analysis. They were only trace amounts, but it might help narrow your search as to where this chap met his end."

"Is there any evidence of a struggle, defensive wounds or the like?"

"No, nothing to indicate he was on the defensive. I did manage to find strong samples of skin beneath the fingernails though. The lack of any indication of defensive injuries or indeed offensive ones, makes me believe the deposits were added without duress."

"Meaning?" Cassie asked.

"*Meaning* there are no cuts or abrasions on his knuckles, or any sign of bruising to his body. His clothing is intact and in good condition, albeit with a gaping hole in the back of his jacket and undergarment," Paxton said. "These factors tell us he wasn't fighting for his life nor was he fighting with anyone per se. However, he took hold – a firm hold – of someone quite recently which is where the trace evidence was caught beneath the fingernails." He pursed his lips, nodding slowly. "Interesting."

"That's one word for it," Cassie said. Paxton glanced quizzically at her. "Confusing, is another."

"I wouldn't disagree," Paxton said, and then turned to Tom. "Anyway, I've sent samples away for you."

"We didn't find anything we could use to identify him within the car or upon his person," Tom said. "Do you have anything for us?"

"Besides the obvious," Paxton said, "I've taken fingerprints for you, naturally, and you might think that with all of the body art that he'd give us the name of a loved one or perhaps the mention of a significant place close to his heart to help narrow it down for you, but there isn't." Paxton frowned. "Or, at least, nothing clear. I have photographed and documented all the visible tattoos. There are one or two which may prove related to somewhere. There's a church, just here," he said, indicating one of the tattoos on the sleeve arm. "The spire is rather notable, and I dare say it actually exists rather than being the figment of the artist's imagination. Tattooists tend to use visual original pieces to copy from rather than making it up as they go along, so to speak."

"There are no steeples like that in Norfolk," Tom said.

"No," Paxton agreed, "but I strongly suspect this gentleman isn't from hereabouts. I don't think he grew up in this country."

"You sound confident on that presumption."

"Oh, I am." Paxton donned a set of gloves and picked up a metal implement, stooping beside the deceased's head before using it to gently prise the jaw open. "You see here," he said, both Tom and Cassie peered into the man's mouth.

"What are we looking at, Doc?"

"Fillings," he said, "good old-fashioned dentistry from the days of drill and fill, before we became more focussed on a lighter touch and therefore less intervention."

"And that's significant because?" Cassie asked.

"The composition of the amalgam, Cassandra," Paxton said. "That used in continental Europe is very different to ours, or was at the time this work was done, and when you move further east and cross the line of the former Iron Curtain, it changes again."

"Where was the work done?" Tom asked.

Paxton pursed his lips. "I'm still working on that, for certainty, you understand? But if you put a gun to my head – or my back – I'd say Eastern Europe. Poor quality work, I would say too. The amalgam wears over time, and that is to be expected, but there are several minor cracks in the occlusal fillings on the lower left and that shouldn't be happening based on when I think the work was done." He shook his head. "I suppose we get what we pay for."

"Can we track his dental records?" Cassie asked.

"With work done abroad?" Paxton asked, then shook his head. "Doubtful, unless he's on file somewhere and you know where to look. The best we can probably hope for is to narrow it down to a region," his eyebrows flicked optimistically, "maybe a country, if we are extremely fortunate, but I wouldn't expect that to be the break you might be hoping for."

"Anything else you've found that might be of interest?" Tom asked.

"There is something that might help you narrow down the search, Tom. He's certainly been an active boy," Paxton said. "Medically speaking, he's kept my colleagues busy over the years. He has a stainless steel pin in his ankle. It must have been a nasty break at the time, several years ago, mind you. I suspect he still feels it when it's cold outside." Paxton flicked through his notes, found what he was looking for and tapped the entry with his forefinger. "The pin has a serial number. They are marked at manufacture, making it easier to keep track of batches in light of failures and so forth."

"If we can trace the serial number to the manufacturer…"

"Then you'll know the country it was supplied to, and possibly even the hospital it was shipped onto," Paxton said. "Depending on the country, they might even be able to tell you when the surgery was performed and who on. I wouldn't hold your breath though."

"It's something," Tom said.

"There's more, although it just speaks to the lifestyle of the man," Paxton said, consulting his notes, "rather than offering help to identify him. He has other historic injuries which have all healed. Two scars, one on the upper left thigh and another in the lower abdomen. Knife entry wounds, I would say, based on the size, pattern formation and the shape of the scar tissue. Slightly more exotic, however, is the bullet wound to his shoulder."

"Bullet wound?" Tom asked.

"Yes, again, all healed, and I must say, he was rather lucky.

It was likely a small-ish calibre round, and it passed primarily through flesh, chipping the clavicle upon entry and merely lending the shoulder blade a glancing blow before exiting his body. A good old through-and-through as we used to call it in the military."

"Do you think he could be ex-military then?" Tom asked.

"I think it would be a good place to start, Tom. Bearing in mind his physical condition – aside from being dead – his age profile and medical history," Paxton said before shrugging. "However, I'm not a detective. That's your job."

"Can you keep us posted on the lab results?" Tom asked.

"Of course."

Tom thanked him and he made to leave with Cassie. Doctor Paxton waved to them or, as Tom suspected, to Cassie as they walked out into the corridor.

"What is it with that guy?" she asked under her breath. "He belittles me at every opportunity but fusses around me like... like..."

"Like what?" Tom asked, amused.

Cassie shook her head. "He does know that he isn't my type? For him to be my type would require his undergoing of *a lot of surgery* that he would find invasive."

Tom laughed. "He's old enough to be your father."

"Exactly, it's creepy."

"You stand up to him," Tom said, holding the door open for her as they walked out into the car park. "I think he respects that."

"Hmm... even so, it's weird. People ask why I call him Doctor Death..." she shrugged. "I don't know what to tell them."

"Maybe he sees you as the daughter he never had."

"Eww..." Cassie said, wrinkling her nose. "Although, I suppose that's preferable to the alternative." She shuddered theatrically. "Can we talk about the dead guy? I'd much rather talk about murder."

"Sure," Tom said, unlocking the car. "We need to put a name to the dead man's face. Let's follow up on all local missing person reports, just in case. However, I suspect he's from further afield. Get onto the Border Force and start running through names recently entered the country at Norwich Airport. If he's come into Norfolk direct, recently, then he'll likely have come via Schiphol."

"And if he came in through London months ago?" Cassie asked, buckling her seatbelt.

"Then we are going to have to do some more work, aren't we?" Tom said with a smile. "The military angle interests me. At his age he would represent an experienced front-line soldier if he was still serving unless—"

"Unless he's now off doing other things," Cassie said. "There's been a massive take up in private contracting in the last ten to twenty years, and that hasn't been confined to ex-service personnel in the West."

"All the more reason to put a name to the face. Start circulating his picture around the local hotels. Maybe someone will be missing a recently checked-in guest."

"As if we haven't got enough criminals of our own, we're importing them now too."

"He's a victim, Cassie. We'll treat him as such until we know otherwise."

"Understood, sir. I never doubted it, but... there's something odd going on in all of this."

Tom couldn't disagree.

CHAPTER FOURTEEN

ERIC SIGHED. They'd been sitting in the car at a neighbouring property for over an hour. Cassie had phoned him twice now and followed it up with a text message after he didn't answer the calls. Having read the message, he exhaled heavily, slipping his mobile back into his pocket.

"Do you want to make any more noise?" Danny asked, "Because you already have my attention."

Eric pursed his lips. "We don't even know if he's in there," he said, hunkering down in his seat and folding his arms across his chest. Danny didn't reply but he must be thinking the same thing. "How long are we going to sit here?"

"You need to be somewhere?"

"I'd like to see my wife and child at some point, yes," Eric said. "I don't want to stay here watching that dump all day and all night."

The building two doors down from them was little more than a cabin. A cabin might be stretching it because it was a ramshackle affair, particularly when compared with others along the seafront. Timber clad, most likely back in the 1970s, it clearly wasn't cared for. The neighbouring properties were of mixed construction, some being timber framed, whereas others were built from brick, raised on pillars to see above the established sea defences and also to protect the majority of the building from tidal flooding which was common in these parts.

Whoever owned this cabin didn't come here much. It was dilapidated, the timber cladding rotten, with single-glazed windows held in place by crumbling frames. The gardens to the sea-facing front of the property were full of old junk, and that would be an eyesore on the promenade if it weren't for the thick weeds and brambles encapsulating it. The rear wasn't much better, being something of a jungle much like the front.

It was prime real estate for a squat. Eric wondered if someone had inherited the property years ago and either they never came here or lived so far away as not to want to travel here, perhaps living abroad. The properties to either side were holiday homes as well, and therefore the owners may not even be aware of the squatters next door. They may even hope that a resident, illegal or otherwise, might make more of an effort to improve it, benefiting all parties.

That hadn't happened yet.

"Do you think he's in there?" Eric asked.

"Yes!" Danny hissed, impatient. "If I didn't, I wouldn't be sitting here, would I?"

"It's just…"

"Just what, Eric?"

"We've been here for a while, that's all."

"And?"

"And I need the toilet," Eric said quietly, holding the take-away coffee cup loosely in his hand, silently regretting going for a large one earlier.

"Go behind the secondary defence," Danny said, thumbing

towards the earthwork barrier on the other side of the road. They'd parked their car in the rear access to a property two doors down from the squat. It offered them a decent vantage point to see anyone approaching the cabin. There was also the access from the front by way of the promenade but it was a hefty walk in either direction to Hunstanton or Heacham, depending on whether you went north or south. Eric looked across the road, assessing the option.

"There's a caravan park on that side."

"It's not close. You can go in the dunes—"

"What if a kid walks past with her bucket and spade? It'll be a nightmare."

"Ah… kids go pee-pee in the dunes all the time."

"I'm not a kid, though, am I?"

Danny cocked his head. "True. Come on then," he said, cracking his door open.

"Come on then… what?"

"Let's go and see if we can borrow a toilet," Danny said, getting out. Eric did likewise.

"Where?" Eric asked, closing his door and feeling the wind pass across him now he was out of the sheltered interior of the car. Danny nodded towards the squat.

"They probably have the water connected. These sorts usually do." He set off towards the cabin and Eric hurried after him, his need to wee disappearing.

"What if he's not there?" Eric asked.

"There's only one way to find out, Eric."

"Shouldn't we get a few more bodies, just in case he makes a run for it again?"

Danny stopped abruptly, Eric bumping into him. Danny turned to Eric, raised his hands before him, and fixed him with a stern look. "I have no intention of going back to the station and trying to explain how we lost our only suspect while we were chatting with his mum. Okay?" Danny set off again.

"How will you explain it if we lose him twice?" Eric asked but Danny continued on, shaking his head and wagging a finger in the air.

"That's not going to happen," Danny said. "It can't. I won't allow it. I'll go through the front—"

"What?" Eric asked. "We can't just pile in there."

"Why not?"

"Because we don't know he's there, for starters. We have no warrant—"

"Eric, just back me up, okay."

"We should get more people then."

Danny shook his head, advancing on the property and waving his hand to Eric, signalling him to make his way around to the front. Each property was fenced off, some with wooden stock fencing but others, like this one, by chicken wire. They should have done something similar to this approach earlier, rather than gifting Finn Harper an opportunity to escape from his mother's house.

Eric slipped down the side of the neighbouring property and clambered up the slope to the wall atop the concrete promenade running along the sea front. He hopped over the fence and stooped low when entering the front garden, making his way along the wall. It wasn't easy with so much clutter and vegetation to navigate. At one time, whoever used this place must have taken a boat directly out onto the water from here, because there were old nets clumped together in a pile and an upturned topper beneath the brambles. They hadn't moved in years though.

Eric hunkered down beside the closed door, listening intently to any sounds from inside. There were none. The windows were all covered by thick net curtains, stained brown by years of neglect. They were very effective at keeping prying eyes from seeing inside the cabin though. Silently inspecting the door frame, Eric could see that one swift kick would probably be all he needed to take the door off its hinges.

This was madness, though. It would be one thing to face the DI having lost their only suspect but this… this was something else. Danny had better be right. He took a deep breath, steadying himself. Harper would run, just as he had done earlier. The thing is, they had no idea how many people were inside the cabin. It was a high-risk strategy, particularly when you considered it a face-saving exercise.

He didn't have time to think on it, hearing a thud come from the front. There was a second and then a third accompanied by splintering wood.

"Police!" Danny yelled, and Eric prepared himself. Even though he was ready, he was still almost caught by surprise by the speed with which the door flew open and a figure made to sprint past him. Eric was ready enough though, pushing off and rugby tackling the body as soon as it came through the door. Eric heard him exhale heavily as they collided and both came down onto the ground, hard.

Eric expected a battle, but his opponent gave up without a fight, clearly winded. Eric handcuffed him before rolling him onto his side. Finn Harper gasped for air, but it wasn't serious.

"Ah… you've bloody hurt me, mate!"

"Deep breaths," Eric said. "It'll pass soon enough." He looked to his right, Danny running out of the door and pulling up when he saw Eric had things under control.

"See," Danny said, breathing heavily, "I told you he was here. Just call me Sherlock."

"Jammy is what I'll call you," Eric said, standing up.

Danny shrugged. "Yeah, that too."

"Anyone else inside?" Eric asked. Danny shook his head.

"The place is a mess though."

"How many squats have you been in?" Eric asked. "You sound surprised."

"No, not like that. It's been turned over, and I mean given a proper trashing."

"Like Martin Odiham's cottage?"

"Yeah, I'd say so," Danny said. "Mind you, I suppose it depends on how bad it was before." He gently kicked the sole of Finn Harper's shoe. "What do you say, Finn, your mates' messy pups or what?"

Finn Harper looked up at them, his breathing was more composed now. "No comment."

"Oh God," Danny muttered. "He's going to be one of those, isn't he?" Eric dropped to his haunches beside Finn.

"Listen, it'd be in your best interests to speak to us, Finn. We can place you in the car."

"No, you're mistaken!" Finn retorted, although fear edged his tone. Eric inclined his head.

"Well, you're going to have to do a lot better than that, Finn."

"Sod off," Finn replied.

Danny smiled grimly. "Well, that's better than no comment, I suppose."

Eric nodded and something caught his eye in the long grass to the left of Finn's shoulder. He rose and walked over, picking up a mobile phone. He looked back at Finn, dusting off the sand that'd found its way onto the screen. Eric exchanged a glance with Danny, who seemed equally curious. Eric held it aloft.

"Yours, I presume, Finn?" Harper looked away and then closed his eyes. "You must be a popular chap, to be needing two mobile phones, Finn."

"Very popular," Danny said, nodding. Eric put the mobile

in his pocket and then took a firm hold on his captive's arm, first helping him onto his knees and then awkwardly up onto his feet.

"Are you going to tell us who was in the stolen car with you, Finn?" Eric asked as he walked him back into the cabin.

"No comment."

Eric sighed. "One step forward, two steps back," he said, arching his eyebrows as he passed Danny.

CHAPTER FIFTEEN

Finn Harper's clothing rustled as he shifted his weight in his seat. After booking him in, he was given a white paper coverall to wear and his clothing taken from him to be sent away to the lab for analysis. Now, sitting in an interview room, he sipped at a cup of tea Eric had brought in for him. Tom sat opposite him, and Eric pulled out the chair beside his boss.

Tom studied the young man. He was calm, and very collected bearing in mind what he was linked to. Was he someone who thrived in a stressful situation or did he not understand the position he found himself in? Tom started the recording device, introducing all those present for the benefit of the recording.

"Do you still waive your right to legal representation?" Tom asked. Finn nodded, and Tom pointed to the digital recorder.

"Yes, I waive my right to legal representation," Finn said in as monotone a voice as was possible, setting his vending machine plastic cup down on the table, sitting back and folding his arms across his chest. He was no stranger to a police interview room and was clearly accustomed to the environment and everything that came with it. This fact was what piqued Tom's curiosity even more with him dispensing with the need of a solicitor.

Perversely, it made Tom warier rather than thinking he had the advantage.

"Where did you steal the car from?" Tom asked. Finn lifted his eyes from the cup he was nursing, slowly rotating it on the table before him.

"What car?"

"The Range Rover you dumped at Snettisham Sailing Club."

Finn shook his head. "I don't do sailing."

"Is that so?"

"Yeah. I don't like water." He wrinkled his nose. "It scares me, being out of my depth."

Tom nodded solemnly. "I think you're right. You are out of your depth." Finn smirked. His confidence was bordering on arrogance. "I don't want to waste each other's time," Tom said. "We know you were in that car."

"What car?" Finn repeated, his smirk changing to a broad smile.

"The Range Rover we found your fingerprints inside," Tom said.

The smile faded slightly but Finn seemed unfazed. He shrugged. "Nah, you're fitting me up."

"You did a good job of wiping down the car's interior," Tom said, opening the folder on the table in front of him, and beginning to sift through the papers. He looked up at Finn, sliding a crime-scene photograph, taken of the car's interior cabin, towards him. Finn didn't flinch but he did break eye contact with Tom and momentarily glance at the photo. A stickered arrow pointed to the rearview mirror and the location of the fingerprint. "You were not quite as thorough as you thought though. In fact, it was all very half-arse. There were still many prints left from the owners as well. It looks like you did it in a hurry. Keen to be somewhere, were you?"

Tom waited patiently. Finn was processing the information, likely playing out possible explanations and scenarios in his head. It was all part of the game. Finn was an experienced player, as was Tom. Finn was pensive, but Tom continued to wait. Eventually, Finn merely shrugged.

"So what? You have a fingerprint. Big deal."

"It proves you were in the car." Tom raised a quizzical eyebrow. "Would you care to offer us an explanation for why that would be?"

Finn sniffed. "I probably got a lift."

"Usually hitchhike, do you?"

"On occasion," Finn said. "If needs be."

"When?"

"No idea," Finn said. "I don't have a car, so I tend to grab a lift whenever I can, you know?" He held his hands up. "Could have been anytime in the last few months."

"Tell us about the driver," Tom said.

"Can't," Finn replied, stretching out his arms before folding them again. "Sorry, but my memory isn't that good these days. I'm – what do they call it? – absent-minded."

"Convenient," Eric said. Finn turned the corners of his mouth down, exaggerating the expression.

"The location of the fingerprints suggest you were in the driving seat," Tom said.

"And?"

"Did the owner let you drive them as well?" Tom asked. "You know, when you were hitching a lift."

"I can't remember," Finn said. "I'm—"

"Absent-minded," Tom said. Finn grinned at him and

nodded. Tom sat forward, resting his elbows on the table and making a tent with his hands. "I tell you what, seeing as you're struggling with details, how about I fill you in on the details we have and see if that jogs your memory."

"Sounds good to me," Finn said, taking a sip from his tea. He grimaced. "Is this the best you can do? It's a bit watery."

"Sorry," Eric said. "Budgets are tight these days."

Tom scanned the paperwork in front of him as he laid it out. Taking a deep breath, he lifted his gaze to Finn.

"So, we have a stolen Range Rover that was involved in a hit-and-run accident on the Sandringham Estate... which left a pregnant woman and her two-year-old son in hospital—"

"Now that is a shame," Finn said. "To think that someone would be involved in such a thing, and," he narrowed his eyes, craning his neck towards Tom, *"leave the scene*, is an awful thing to do."

"Isn't it?" Tom said, feeling his emotions prickle at Finn's intransigence. "What sort of person would do such a thing?"

"A selfish person," Finn said. He arched his eyebrows. "Is she all right?"

"The driver?" Tom asked and Finn nodded. "She's been discharged from hospital."

"Baby and – toddler, was it – okay, too?"

"Yes, no thanks to you."

Finn smiled. "I wasn't there."

"Well," Tom said, "the lady driving the Astra was able to give us a description of the person driving the Range Rover and we are confident she will be able to identify them."

"Ah... but she hasn't done so far?" Finn asked. Tom ignored the question.

"The car was later dumped outside the Snettisham sailing club where it was discovered and reported to us the following morning." He lifted his eyes to meet Finn's. "How am I doing so far?"

"It's a fascinating story," Finn said. "I mean, it starts slowly, tails off in the middle and I do hope you have a far more entertaining climax to it, otherwise the audience will probably give a thumbs down in the reviews."

"Let's see what we can do to accommodate you," Tom said, smiling and looking down at his notes. "Now, upon inspection by my colleagues, it became apparent there was something – I think you'll like this, Finn – of interest, under cover, in the boot of the abandoned car."

"Was there?" Finn asked, sitting forward. "What was it?"

"A dead body," Tom said flatly. Finn stared at him, expressionless. His lips parted slightly and there was an involuntary twitch in his left eyelid. "Is that entertaining enough for you?"

"I-I don't know nothing about a dead body."

"Oh… but you know something about… something?" Tom asked. For the first time, Finn seemed rattled, if only a little. He shook his head firmly. "Okay, let me continue. The body found in the boot of the car was deceased, and do you know how they died?"

Finn shook his head. "No, I don't know how he died."

"He?" Tom asked, glancing sideways at Eric. "Did I say it was a man?"

"No, sir," Eric said, staring hard at Finn. "You didn't mention it."

Finn coughed. "W-What else would it be?"

"A woman," Eric said, "if it wasn't a man. That's still how it works, even these days where the gender lines are blurred. Isn't that right, sir?"

"Yes, you're right, Eric." Tom took a deep breath, fixing Finn with a stern look. "Tell us again, Mr Harper, how you know nothing about anything. And while you're doing that,

making your pitiful denials, my colleagues are busy scrutin-
ising the clothing you were wearing today, picking apart your
mum's house for everything you own, going through your
social media posts, bank account… we've obtained a warrant
for your mobile phone records…" he took a deep breath, "and
we're pretty much turning your sad little life upside down."

Finn closed his eyes and Tom thought he saw his hands
shake but he quickly hid them in his lap below the level of the
table. "I didn't kill anyone."

"Now we're starting to get somewhere," Tom said. "Forget
about telling me what you didn't do. Perhaps you could start
with what you did do, yes?" Finn nodded, sitting upright. He
was agitated, to the point Tom began to wonder just what he
did know about the body in the car.

"Look," Finn said, using his hands animatedly, "I took the
car, all right. I did. I'll hold my hands up to that but… I
swear," he leaned towards Tom, "*I swear* I don't know
anything about no body."

"Come on, Finn!" Tom said.

"I don't! I mean," he said, the pitch of his tone rising, "we did
see the guy in the back… and then… and then… I panicked."

"You panicked?" Tom asked. Finn nodded furiously.
"When you saw the body?"

"Exactly, yeah. Wouldn't you? You're driving along and
then realise there's a dead guy in the boot!"

"So who was in the car with you?" Eric asked. Finn's head
snapped to his left, looking at Eric.

"I didn't say—"

"You said *we*," Eric told him, "and unless you expect us to
believe you were driving along and happened to lift the
tarpaulin in the boot, then it stands to reason someone else did
that. Someone sitting in the rear passenger seats. So…" Eric

looked thoughtfully towards the ceiling, "by my count that's a driver – you – a passenger in the front seat and at least one person in the rear seats."

Tom nodded. "That's… forgive my maths, Finn, but at least three people in the car—"

"Plus, a dead guy," Eric added.

"Plus one," Tom said. "Care to give us those names, Finn, seeing as you're being honest now?"

"I didn't kill anyone," Finn said, sitting back, defiant.

"Not good enough, Finn," Tom said. "I need names, otherwise this is a great story but we only have your word as to the validity of any of it."

"It's the truth!" Finn pleaded.

"You don't have much credibility in the bank, though," Tom said, glancing at Eric. "What do you think DC Collet?"

"I think he's not being truthful, sir. I mean, he hasn't even told us where he stole the car from. Has he?"

"No, he has not," Tom said, turning back to Finn who was growing more uncomfortable as the seconds ticked past. "Where did you get the car?"

"I found it—"

Tom laughed. "You'll have to do better than that. You'll be telling us you bought it off a bloke in the pub next!"

"We were hanging out down at West Acre Ford and it was just there… keys in the ignition, unlocked."

"Just… there?" Tom asked, struggling to accept the plausibility of such a half-baked suggestion.

"It was!" Finn said, sitting forward. "It was parked strangely, like it had been left where it stopped. The key was in the ignition… and…" he sighed, "we just took it for a bit of a laugh, that's all."

"A bit of a laugh?" Eric asked.

"Yeah! It's not like we were going to sell it or anything. I mean, it's well old, and drives like it too."

"The accident. Tell us about that," Tom said. Finn took a deep breath, steadying himself. Tom felt they were getting more of the truth from him now.

"I was driving," he said, "I accept that's what was going on… then," he hesitated. "Then we realised there was a body in the boot and," he shook his head, "I must have taken my eyes off the road, just for a second, that's all, and then I hit that other car."

"And you decided to drive away rather than check everyone was all right?" Tom asked.

"Look! I just realised there was a dead fella in the back of the car," he said, raising his voice. "It's not like that was a normal turn of events, you know what I mean?"

"She is heavily pregnant, and had her other child with her—"

"I'm sorry! Yes, I should have got out and… done something. Called someone."

"But you didn't."

"I am sorry, you have to believe me!"

"What about the body," Tom said. "Did you touch it?"

"Hell no! I don't want to touch a dead guy, no way. I wanted to get as far away from it as I could, as soon as I could."

"So you dumped the car beside the sailing club?"

"We did, yes," Finn said. "Then I walked back along the seafront to Hunstanton, and I went home."

"Did you take anything from the body—"

"No! I told you, I wanted to get rid. Fast as I could."

"So we won't find any of your DNA on the body?"

"No!" Finn said, seemingly assured of his position. "You won't."

"How about your friends. Did they interfere with the body?"

"No, why would they?"

"I don't know," Eric said drily, "just for a laugh, maybe?"

Finn glared at him. "I swear. We just dumped the car and legged it. I know we did wrong, especially by the woman in the other car, but I made a mistake… in the heat of the moment, that's all." He looked between Tom and Eric. "I guess you two are boy scouts and never make mistakes, huh?"

Tom shook his head. "I've never run a woman and her child off the road late at night and left her there, no. But that's me."

"But she's going to be okay, right? I mean, her and the baby…"

"And the other child," Eric said, clearly angry, bearing in mind he had a son of a similar age.

"Yeah," Finn said. "I've said I'm sorry, but what else can I do?"

"First off, you can give us the names of everyone else in the car with you, and don't give me any of this nonsense about not wanting to grass on your friends. This is a murder investigation, and you are front and centre of it." Tom sat forward, tapping the table's surface for dramatic effect. "Names. Now."

CHAPTER SIXTEEN

"So, Finn Harper has admitted to stealing the Range Rover," Tom said to the group, "and to being in the driving seat when the collision with Lisa Nolan occurred."

"Where did he take the car from?" Tamara asked. She was sitting in on the briefing, keen to see how the case was developing. Tom pointed to a pinned location on a map, mounted on the information board.

"From West Acre Ford," Tom said. "He claims to have found the car with the keys in the ignition. Finn, and his friends, took the car for a bit of fun and then realised there was an additional person in the boot of the car. He claims this is when the accident happened, the shock of realising they were driving a car with a dead body in the boot."

"Do you believe him?" Tamara asked.

"He was tight-lipped until we gave him the evidence that proved he was in the car. Then, he was more agreeable. He's given us the names of the other two, Oliver Chalk and Alexa Willis, who were with him that night." Tom took a breath. "We may not have the full story but he's being helpful. As soon as we can speak to his friends, then we'll be able to see just how honest he's become."

"West Acre… where was the car taken from?" Tamara asked.

"Great Bircham," Tom said. "That's where the car is registered to, and the owners are unsure of when it went missing from the barn they store it in."

"What do we know about Chalk and Willis?" Tamara asked. Tom pointed to Eric, signalling him to pick up the narrative.

"Ollie Chalk has a colourful background," Eric said. "He's twenty-eight, so a few years older than both Finn Harper and Alexa Willis, both of whom are in their early twenties. He is originally from Hastings, down on the south coast, and how or why he moved to Norfolk is unknown, but he did so after leaving the army."

"Who did he serve with, Eric?" Danny asked. Eric consulted his notes.

"The Light Dragoons," he said. "A light cavalry unit used primarily as an advance unit. I've been onto his former regiment and Chalk served deployments in Bosnia – his first deployment role – Poland and combat operations in Afghanistan." Eric inclined his head. "Apparently, Trooper Chalk's record wasn't spotless. I spoke to a senior officer who described him as a competent gunner, and a popular member of the team but he had disciplinary problems. He didn't particularly care for the chain of command which got him into all sorts of trouble."

"Did he leave of his own accord?" Tom asked.

Eric nodded. "Yes. He was injured in a car accident and his recovery wasn't considered strong enough to enable him to return to active service."

"What about since he moved to Norfolk? Do we have any experience with him?" Tamara asked.

"No, he hasn't come up on our radar until now. Finn Harper told us he's been squatting at the cabin on the seafront for over a year now. Where he was before that is anyone's guess but, by my calculations, there's a six-month window between his getting out of the army and him coming across Finn, here in Hunstanton."

"And the other one?" Tamara asked. "Alex…"

"Willis," Eric said. "She lives with her maternal grandparents here in Hunstanton. Her parents divorced when she was two years old, and her mother passed away when she was seven. She's been with her grandparents ever since." Eric shook his head. "There is no father listed on the birth certificate and, as far as I know, he's not involved in her life."

"Is she known to us?" Cassie asked.

"Oh yes!" Eric said, blowing out his cheeks. "She's been picked up by uniform on no fewer than fourteen occasions for various shoplifting offences. Multiple cautions on that front. She has been arrested and cautioned for drug possession, and one count of solicitation," Eric said, arching his eyebrows. "But that was three years ago and, from what I can understand, she had had a falling out with the grandparents and left home. She wound up in King's Lynn which is where the offence was recorded. Seemingly, she was turning tricks – pretending to offer services – taking the money without providing what she offered. After that, she returned back to the family home."

"Any recent offences?" Tom asked.

Eric shook his head. "On the face of it, she's cleaned herself up—"

"Or got better at getting away with things," Cassie said,

smiling. "Was there any sign of these two when you picked up Harper at the squat?"

"No," Danny said. "Only Finn was present, although the place had been given a proper going over. I know some squatters take care of the properties they live in, but even those who don't tend not to utterly trash the place. They do still have to live there, after all."

"What are you thinking?" Tom asked. "That it was burgled?"

Danny shrugged. "Why anyone would burgle a squat is beyond me. Unless someone was owed something. Perhaps a drug debt or something similar? I guess that's possible."

"Did you ask Finn about it?" Cassie asked. "When you picked him up, I mean?"

"He was none the wiser," Eric said. "At least, that's what he said at the time."

"Do we know the whereabouts of these other two, Chalk and Willis?" Tamara asked.

"No, we don't," Tom said. "Finn was spooked by Danny and Eric showing up at his mum's house. After he gave them the slip," Danny and Eric both averted their eyes from Tom's gaze, "he went to the squat, expecting to find them there. When we are done here, Cassie and Eric can go over to Alexa's grandparents' house and see if she's there."

"Right," Tamara said, her eyes drifting across the information boards. "If Oliver Chalk has no ties then there is every possibility, he'll not be hanging around these parts, especially if he's been linked to a dead body. Have his description put out to neighbouring forces, just in case."

"Already done," Tom said. Tamara smiled.

"Of course it is," she said. "Are you done?" Tom nodded, bringing the briefing to an end. Everyone moved away to carry on with their allocated tasks. Tamara beckoned Tom over and the two of them went into his office, Tamara closing the door after them.

"What's up?" he asked.

"Martin Odiham," she said. "Where are we with his murder?"

Tom absently rubbed his chin. "No further forward. We're struggling to find a motive, let alone a suspect. The forensic examination turned up no sign of anyone other than him. Whoever was looking for something in his house left barely a trace of themselves that they were there. If they had been a bit more methodical about their search, rather than ransacking the entire cottage, then we might not have known they were there."

Tamara took a seat and Tom did the same, behind his desk. "What about the car?"

"Burnt out," Tom said. "I can only presume that the person who took it – probably the man who killed him – was concerned that they'd left a trace of them inside it or was unwilling to take the risk, firing the car's interior to cover themselves."

"That was risky," Tamara said, "with you inside the cottage."

"It was," Tom agreed. "They are a cool character, that's for sure."

"What about Odiham himself, are there any leads there?"

"Not that we've found," Tom said. His brow furrowed. "He is a widower. He has no children, and no living next of kin that we've been able to trace. He retired a few years ago, from a middle-management job. His financial history is solid. He owned the cottage outright, has no debts, no credit cards or outstanding loans. His current account has over twenty thousand pounds available to it." He scratched the side of his head. "There's no indication of substance abuse, he wasn't an alcoholic. Everyone we've spoken to describes him as a very decent man, a kind man, and no one has a bad word to say about him." He sat back in his chair. Tamara was listening, thinking hard.

"It sounds to me like he wouldn't be a target," Tamara said.

"I agree, and if his house hadn't been turned over, I would argue he wasn't the target. That said, nothing appears to have been removed from the house. Nothing that one would expect in a burglary, at any rate. There was a substantial amount of cash in the writing bureau in the sitting room. That was turned out onto the floor along with everything else, but not taken. There were several vintage watches that would fetch a tidy sum at a pawnbroker, too. They were left, along with a few electrical items; a tablet and a laptop. Again, not particularly high value, but they'd be taken by any competent burglar."

"Even an incompetent one would take one or two of those," Tamara said.

"It doesn't make any sense," Tom said. "It looks targeted, but there's no reason for it."

"Unless…"

"Unless?" Tom asked.

"Unless he wasn't the target at all," Tamara said. "Maybe… he was in the wrong place at the wrong time."

"Mistaken identity?"

Tamara shrugged. "Yes, maybe."

"That will make things more complicated," Tom said, frowning. There was a knock on the door. "Come in!" Tom called. The door cracked open, and PC Marshall peered around the door at them.

"I'm sorry to interrupt, sir."

"That's okay, David. What can I do for you?"

"We've had a phone call, sir," the constable said. "From a hotelier in the town. He thinks he recognised the sketch of the deceased man as one of his guests. He says he's not seen him for a couple of days, and when he saw the sketch we distributed, he swears it's him."

"A hotel here in town?" Tom asked. The constable nodded. Tom glanced through the window. Cassie had already left and presumably taken Eric with her. Danny had a telephone clamped to his ear.

"Should I give it to one of the—"

"No, I'll take it," Tom said, checking his watch. He had time before he was due at home. Despite running two separate murder investigations, he'd promised Saffy he'd be home to eat with them this evening. Bearing in mind what she was going through at the moment, he had no intention of letting her down.

PC Marshall entered the office, crossing to Tom's desk and passing him the details of the hotel. He smiled at both senior officers and departed.

"What are you doing with Finn Harper?" Tamara asked.

"I don't know, yet," Tom said, slipping the piece of paper into his pocket. "We'll hold him for now, at least until the forensic tests from his clothing come back. The clothes he was wearing and also those we took from his mum's house. There are no signs of him having been in a fight, scratches, cuts or abrasions. We also ran a gunshot residue test on his hands, but that came back negative."

"The residue only lasts for a few hours, so that's inconclusive," Tamara said.

"Yes but, if nothing else, it will get him thinking. Even if he wasn't the shooter, he may have been present and helped lift the body into the car, regardless of his denials. I'm not quite ready to give him the benefit of the doubt." He was reflective. "So, we'll hold him for now, apply for a custody extension if we need to."

"If you don't find anything else linking him to the murder then you may not get the extension," Tamara said.

"No, that's true. With a bit of luck we'll find his friends and that'll shed a little more light on the situation, clearing or incriminating him."

"And the dead man?"

"I'll let you know once I've had a look in his hotel room," Tom said. "As of this moment, we suspect he's from Eastern Europe and has a military background. Aside from that, he's quite a mystery."

"Keep me posted?"

"You can count on it."

"On other matters," Tamara said, sitting forward. "How is Cassie?"

Tom was pensive. "Playing things close to her chest."

"That's Cassie."

"I thought you'd know better than me," Tom said. "She's still staying at yours, isn't she?"

Tamara nodded. "Yes, but she slips away to her room as soon as she can. She says she doesn't want to cramp my style with David."

"Oh, is he living at yours now?" Tom asked. He knew David and Tamara were growing closer, but he'd been so busy lately, as had the team that, socially, he was behind the curve.

"He may as well be," Tamara said, smiling coyly. "But it's not official."

"That would put too much pressure on you, wouldn't it?" Tom said playfully.

"Something like that, yes. Anyway," Tamara said, seeking to move the conversation back to Cassie, "I'm worried Cassie is bottling it up. She has to address what happened before she can move past it."

Tom sighed. "I don't disagree, but it's Cassie. She's… not one to share."

Tamara nodded. "Just keep an eye on her, would you?"

CHAPTER SEVENTEEN

THE DOOR CREAKED OPEN, and Tom's guide flicked on the light switch beside the entrance. The hallway of the basement flat was gloomy and there was a telltale odour of damp.

"This flat has its own access," the owner said, stepping aside and allowing Tom to enter. "We let it out more like a self-catering apartment rather than incorporating it into the hotel. It's popular with people who are travelling on a budget, those who are planning to be out and about. The views aren't great, but you are literally within a stone's throw of the beach and the pier arcade."

"Do you let it often?" Tom asked.

"It's popular because it's cheap." Cook noticed a flicker in Tom's expression, and he seemed irritated by it. "I know it's not a palace but men like Mr Farkas don't seem to mind."

Tom looked around the entrance. The decor was dated and probably hadn't been updated since the 70s. The carpet had a swirling pattern to it, multiple shades of red and burgundy which did little to lift the space. The walls were papered with a contrasting floral design, but the original Victorian cornicing was still in place. It was heavily painted in gloss white, or had been, but was now suffering from the same effect of ageing as the rest of the flat.

"When did Mr Farkas check in?" Tom asked. The man, Simon Cook, an overweight, balding man in his early sixties, thought hard, scratching his temple as he did so.

"Three days ago, if I remember right. I'll check for you," he said.

"Did you check him in or someone else?"

"No, no, it was me. We run the place," he said, looking around them, "me and the wife. It's only us. We used to have more staff, but we are winding down these days. We are semi-retired now, and don't stress about occupancy rates anymore. It keeps us ticking over until the day we cash in and sell the lot."

"Sounds like a good plan," Tom said. "I could do with something similar myself. Things never seem to let up in my job."

"No sign of crime coming down then?" Cook asked casually. "You hear all the time about crime rates dropping but it's because people don't bother reporting the crimes these days."

Tom smiled. "Don't believe everything you read in the papers." Cook shifted awkwardly.

"I didn't mean… you know, any offence."

"None taken." They walked on into the flat. The only natural light came from a bay window to the front but that was positioned below street level and with the sun having already set, it didn't offer anywhere near enough light into the interior.

"We have another flat that backs onto this one, but that has a small courtyard terrace at the back. I added that myself, just to give the occupants something a little more to combat the lack of a sea view." The hotel, now being run more as a guest house, was on Cliff Parade in Hunstanton.

The terraced Victorian properties, all multi-storey build-ings, were once either grand hotels or the coastal homes of wealthy merchants who came to the coast to escape the smog of coal-fired London back when the English seaside towns were in their heyday. Once the advent of travel to foreign climes took hold, the appeal of coming up to the north Norfolk coast waned and when the railway lines were shut down, places like Hunstanton declined.

Now, though, towns like this were enjoying a rebirth of sorts, people rediscovering what was available on their doorstep. Businesses were starting up, property developers cashing in and what threatened to become ghost towns of once popular haunts were growing again.

Tom peered into the galley-style kitchen. It was messy with aluminium takeaway food trays piled up on the surface. The incumbent didn't seem too fussed about using the facilities. There were a handful of empty beer bottles which added to the stale smell in the air. Nothing excessive, by way of alcohol consumption, but whoever was staying here hadn't made much of an effort to keep on top of things.

"What did you make of him?" Tom asked, moving on to the main reception room of the property, the forward-facing living room. Cook shrugged.

"He didn't say much. He was polite enough, but I figured he couldn't speak much English."

"He was foreign, then?"

"Oh yes." Cook frowned. "I don't know where he was from though."

"You mean you didn't take a look at his passport or anything?"

"No, why would I do that?" Cook countered. "He'd paid in advance through the portal advertising the booking. To be honest, I'm not bothered who he is or where he's from, as long as I get paid."

"Fair enough," Tom said, entering the room. The bay window was covered by a thick curtain which was three-quarters drawn, and Tom pulled them back allowing what little light of the day remained to flood in. There was a small two-seater sofa against one wall and a shallow table before it. A television was mounted on the wall opposite, the cables hanging down beneath it. A round table was set off to one side of the bay window, in the corner, and there were two dining chairs. It didn't appear to have been used but a bowl of half-eaten cereal was on the table, the milk having formed an odd-looking layer upon the surface.

Simon Cook heaved a sigh. "Not very house proud, these Eastern Europeans, are they?"

"He was staying here alone?"

"As far as I know, yes. But like I said—"

"As long as they pay the bill, who cares?"

"Yes, that's right," Cook said defensively. "This isn't a police state."

"Do you recall him saying why he was here in town?" Tom asked. "Visiting friends, here on business?"

"He said he was sightseeing," Cook said, looking around. He seemed doubtful. "He didn't say what he was here to see… the inside of this flat, by the look of it."

"The bedroom?" Tom asked, seeing an ashtray that was practically overflowing. He stooped to examine the filters. They were branded but he couldn't read it, the language being alien to him. It certainly looked Eastern European, Slavic in style.

They left the living room and Simon Cook led them along the corridor deeper into the gloomy interior. There was a second pendant in this part of the hall, but the bulb had blown. Reaching the door, Tom touched the man's arm, gesturing him aside so Tom could enter first. He pushed the door open and switched on the light. This room had no window to the exterior. It was once painted white but the brightness on the walls had long since faded.

An unmade bed was in the centre of the room. Another door off to their right led to a small en suite shower room. Tom found minimal toiletries present. A free-standing wardrobe was on the opposite side of the room and inside Tom found a holdall and a couple of changes of clothing, but nothing else.

"He travels light, doesn't he?" Cook said. Tom silently agreed. There were no personal effects of note that Tom could see. He donned a set of forensic gloves and picked up the holdall from the foot of the wardrobe, setting it down on the bed. It was a brand he wasn't familiar with. He unzipped it, scanning the inside. The clothes in the room were laid out neatly in contrast to everything else in the flat.

The bag itself appeared to be more or less empty but Tom found the base of the holdall to be rigid. Rapping his knuckles on it, there was a distinct hollow sound. Usually, these types of bags had a layer of rigid board at the bottom to help maintain the shape and form of the material. This one seemed different though. Tom ran his fingers around the outside of the holdall, finding the base to be firmer and more pronounced than he might expect. Returning to the inside, he felt the edges of the base board, finding a drop at each end and along the side. There must be a compartment or something inside.

Teasing up the edge, he lifted the board clear to find a hidden pocket. It was perhaps a quarter of an inch deep. Inside Tom found a box, fashioned from a material he'd never come across before. Something was loose inside and the box opened at one end. Tom gently opened it, allowing the contents to slide out onto the bed. The first thing he saw was a passport. He picked it up, the crest on the front indicated it was a Slovenian passport. He opened it to the identification page, recognising the face of the deceased currently lying in the morgue.

"Oskar Kolar," Tom said to himself. It was unmistakably him. The only issue was that this wasn't the only passport he could see on the bed. The second he picked up was apparently issued in Bulgaria under the name of Darian Hristov. There were three more passports, issued in Hungary, Poland and, lastly, France. The French passport listed the man's birthplace as Dakar, the capital city of the former French colony, Senegal.

Besides the multiple forms of identification there were several envelopes, each containing substantial volumes of cash. Tom was aware of Simon Cook, standing in the doorway, watching what he was doing.

"That… er… looks like a lot of money." Tom didn't say anything but closed the envelopes and put them back on the bed. He would need to have this room secured and properly processed. Tom took out his mobile and snapped a picture of each passport. The same photo had been used for each one, and giving the inner pages a cursory check, he found there were stamps in all of them. They'd been used fairly frequently. Either that or they were stamped to give that impression, adding to their credibility.

Tom turned and gestured for Simon Cook to leave with him. Cook was very interested in what Tom had found, but fortunately he'd only really seen the money. Tom regretted allowing him to accompany him, but he didn't officially have a warrant to search, so it was done with Cook's leave.

"Is it him then?"

"I believe so, yes," Tom said. There was no point in denying it. They walked back to the front door. "I'm afraid we'll need to examine the flat in greater detail. It will be off limits until such time as I can have that arranged."

"I see," Cook said, looking over Tom's shoulder. "What do you think happened to him? The dead man, I mean."

"That's what I'm trying to find out. When did you last see him?"

"Oh…" Cook exhaled. "The morning after he checked in. He came around to the main reception looking for information."

"What sort of information?"

"Local attractions, historic sites… that sort of thing."

"And where did you direct him?"

Cook's brow furrowed. "I had my hands full with a delivery for the bar. We have a bar in the guest house, it's not open every day but we offer service three nights a week and then there's the restaurant."

"Did Mr Farkas eat with you?"

"No, not that I remember."

"And the historic sites, which of those was he interested in?"

"Nothing specific," Cook said, thinking hard. "I gave him a selection of flyers that we keep at reception. It wasn't much, but like I said, I don't think his English was very good and… I was very busy."

"Can you show me?"

"Yes, of course."

They stepped out of the basement flat. Cook closed the door and the lock clicked into place. Tom barred his way and arched his eyebrows as the man hesitated before reluctantly handing him the key.

"You have a spare, I presume?" Tom asked.

"I do, yes."

"Can I ask you not to enter the property until we give you the green light? It's now a crime scene."

"Y-Yes, of course." Tom wondered if all that cash would still be present once he managed to get a team down here. He didn't want to think badly of him, but he'd spent enough time around people to know what temptation could do to the best of them.

They made their way around to the main entrance to the building on Cliff Parade, mounting the steps and walking into reception. A woman was sitting behind the desk, scrolling on a mobile phone.

"It's the police, love. They needed to search Mr Farkas's flat. He's dead." She seemed shocked, her eyes flitting between her husband and Tom. "And, you should see it, he's got a lot of cash downstairs as well." Tom felt that same pang of regret at allowing Cook to join him as he walked around the flat. It was a schoolboy error, but no one was perfect.

"Perhaps you could do me a favour, Mr Cook – and Mrs Cook – and keep what you know about Mr Farkas to yourselves for the time being. We need to keep a lid on information getting around until we know what the situation is. Could you do that for me?"

"Absolutely!" Simon Cook said, nodding firmly. "We'll do our bit, won't we, love?"

"Yes, certainly." Tom felt Mrs Cook wasn't quite as eager with her response as her husband had been, and Tom doubted they'd stick to it anyway. The mobile in her hand, which she was already glancing at, suggested news would travel swiftly. He was grateful for the fact Cook hadn't been standing at his shoulder when he was looking at the passports. He'd need to get some uniformed officers down here as soon as possible to seal the flat.

Then they'd have to work out which identity – if any of

them – truly belonged to their dead body. Simon Cook busied himself in front of a small stand on a sideboard to the left of the reception desk. He gathered together a number of leaflets and flyers, before returning to Tom and proudly handing them to him.

"I'm pretty sure these are the ones I gave him." Tom flicked through the clutch of glossy leaflets. They were all architectural or historic buildings, in locations in and around Hunstanton, as far along the coast as Holkham, Holt and Sheringham, Tom's hometown and further afield, inland. None of them were family-oriented places, reflecting that Farkas was a lone traveller.

"And you're sure you gave him all of these?" Tom said. One of the flyers stood out to him. Cook nodded.

"Yes, he was keen to see that one in particular," he said, pointing to the flyer on top of the pile in Tom's hand. Tom raised it in the air towards him.

"This one? Are you sure?"

"Yes, absolutely. I told him they would appreciate the visit because they are still fundraising for the restoration project. It's a real community affair."

Tom turned the flyer in his hand, studying it. It was an information leaflet centring on historic parish churches in Norfolk. The main photo depicted a unique clock on a bell tower where the numerals on the face had been replaced with the words *Watch and Pray*, written in gold leaf.

It was the clock face of All Saints Church at West Acre.

CHAPTER EIGHTEEN

"Mrs Willis?" Cassie asked as she was greeted by a wary look from the lady peering around the door at her. She nodded but didn't speak, looking past Cassie at Eric. "Detective Sergeant Knight, from Norfolk Police."

"What is it you want?"

"We are looking for Alexa, is she home?"

"No, she isn't." The woman made to close the door, but Cassie put her hand on it, gently holding it open. Alexa's grandmother was a slight figure offering little resistance.

"Mrs Willis," Cassie said firmly, but with an accompanying smile. "Could we have a word with you, please?" She hesitated, but nodded curtly, stepping back and opening the door wider.

"You'd better come in."

"Thank you, you're very kind," Cassie said. She glanced back at Eric who followed her into the house. It was a well-kept home, everything seemed to have its place and was stored accordingly. The kitchen was immaculately presented at the rear of the house overlooking the garden and a small arch opened up into the living-dining room.

A man was sitting in an armchair, presumably Alexa's grandfather, reading a newspaper, and he seemed startled to see his wife lead two people into the room.

"This is my husband, Dean," she said. Looking at him with a glum expression, she indicated Cassie and Eric. "These are police officers, Dean."

"The police?"

"They're looking for Alexa."

"Whatever for?"

Cassie smiled a greeting at the man and looked at his wife. "Mrs Willis—"

"Beryl," she said, "please… sorry, I've already forgotten your name."

"Knight, Cassandra Knight," she said, glancing sideways at Eric. "And this is DC Eric Collet. We're sorry to spring a visit on you unexpectedly, but we believe Alexa… your grand-daughter?"

"Yes, she is," Dean said.

"We believe Alexa may have witnessed an incident, and we want the chance to speak to her about it."

"An incident? What kind of incident?" Dean asked.

"A traffic accident," Eric said. "There was a hit-and-run, and we think she will know what happened."

Dean's eyes narrowed, and Beryl was nervously toying with her necklace. "Do you usually send two plain clothes detectives to interview a witness to a car crash?"

Cassie smiled politely. "It can happen, yes. It is dependent on the circumstances of each case."

"So… someone died?"

"No, there were no serious injuries to anyone in the vehicle." The answer only made him more suspicious.

"And what does our Alexa have to do with any of this? She doesn't even have a driving licence. She wanted lessons for her birthday but," he glanced at his wife, "we're not exactly rolling in money these days. And we spent more than enough on that girl over the years as it is."

"Oh, Dean. She's been no trouble—"

"She's been nought but trouble for years," Dean retorted, folding his paper and almost throwing it to the carpet at his feet. "It's you, mollycoddling the girl all her life that's the issue."

Beryl seemed embarrassed, shooting Cassie an apologetic look. "I'm so sorry," she said. "Alexa does manage to get herself caught up in things from time to time."

Dean snorted derisorily. "Caught up," he muttered.

"She's a good girl, really," Beryl said. "She just makes poor choices—"

"Like the poor choice of taking up with that druggie layabout," Dean countered. "She used to be a good girl, but all that changed from the age of nine."

"Can you put a name to this particular druggie layabout?" Cassie asked with a straight face.

"Wally something or other," Dean said, shaking his head.

"Ollie," Beryl corrected him. Dean shrugged. He'd chosen the name purposely. She turned back to Cassie. "Oliver. But I'm afraid I don't know his last name."

"That's okay, don't worry."

"What is it you think Alexa can help you with?" Beryl asked. "Helping identify the driver?"

"Confirming who stole the car is more like it," Dean said. His wife glared at him but he turned to Cassie. "Well, tell me I'm wrong."

"We would rather speak to your granddaughter directly, Mr Willis."

"She nicked it then?" he asked. "She might not have had lessons, but that girl can drive, I know she can."

"We have someone in custody who has admitted to driving the car and to leaving the scene, Mr Willis."

"But not Ollie?" Dean asked. Cassie shook her head.

"So, you've picked up the other Musketeer then, have you? Finbar the Terrible?" Cassie didn't confirm anything but he searched both of their expressions, and took their silence as confirmation. "He's another waster, if you ask me."

"Well, they didn't ask you, did they, Dean?" His wife bristled at his attitude, but he was unfazed, merely shrugging and reaching for his newspaper. "What is it you think they did?" she asked, nervously.

"When did you last see Alexa?" Cassie asked, ignoring the question. Beryl thought about it, lifting a hand to her mouth. Cassie saw it shake slightly until she steadied it on her face. It could be nerves or a condition she had; Cassie wasn't sure.

"I-I think it was the day before yesterday," she said, her eyes darting to Dean for confirmation. He stared straight ahead, but he hadn't opened his newspaper again, it remained folded in his lap. "We… had words with her."

"Words? Regarding what?" Cassie asked.

"Regarding the company she is associating with, that's what," he said, his tone turning aggressive. "Bloody ungrateful little mare she's becoming—"

"Dean!"

"Well, it's true. After everything we've done for her, she comes and goes as she pleases, makes no contribution to the running of the home, let alone what she steals from us. It's a liberty, that's what it is."

"She's just a girl—"

"She was. Now she's a grown woman, who takes from the hands that feed her… and… and gives it to that scum she hangs around with."

"You don't approve of Alexa's choice of friends then, Mr Willis?" Cassie asked, stating the obvious.

He bristled. "No, I do not. She was a lovely little girl up until she approached double figures... and then she went the same way as her mother."

"What happened to Alexa's mother, if you don't mind me asking?" Cassie said.

"Fell in with the wrong crowd," Beryl said quietly.

"Fell in!" Dean said, shaking his head, shifting in his seat. "You always made excuses for the girl, that's what got her in trouble in the first place."

"It wasn't like that. She... was a sensitive sort."

"She was a wastrel, that's what she was," Dean said, raising his voice. His wife became more agitated, and Cassie figured they'd had these conversations before, probably on many occasions. She doubted they ever found common ground either. "She went looking for trouble and found it with ease."

Beryl became upset, quickly excusing herself so she wouldn't cry in front of them. Dean looked guilty as he watched her hurry away, his face flushing with embarrassment.

"It must be difficult," Cassie said. He looked at her. "When your child sets the boundaries of their own life and makes poor choices."

"Yes... do you have children, DS Knight?"

"No, I don't."

"Well, when you do, you'll learn. You can give them every opportunity, sweat blood and tears to do right by them, but don't expect them to offer you respect. That's not how it works."

"Is it transactional then?" Cassie asked. Dean shot her a quizzical look. "Do you give them what you think is valuable and expect their devotion in return? Or do they not get to make their own choices?"

"I… I don't know what you mean."

"Just a thought," Cassie said, with a slight smile. "What did happen to Alexa's mum?"

"She got in with the likes of that Ollie character. She kept pumping that God awful stuff into her veins and one day…" he looked away and Cassie saw his eyes gleam as they teared up. "Anyway, the coroner says it was accidental, that she didn't mean to take as much as she did, but I know different."

"What do you think happened?" Cassie asked him. He met her eye.

"She knew how much she could and couldn't take in one go. It wasn't an accident, she knew what she was doing."

"You think she took her own life?"

"I do, yes. The social services had taken little Alexa away from her," he said sourly. "You can't blame them, what with the conditions she was living in and the state of her life, of herself."

"And after she passed away, you took on Alexa?"

"We did. I couldn't see her grow up in the care system." He shook his head forcefully. "I'm sure it's full of compassionate and well-meaning people, but not for my granddaughter. We messed up with her mother, but I swore we'd do a better job this time around."

"And how's that going, do you think?" Cassie asked, straight-faced.

"We do our best, DS Knight," he growled. "But that girl has too much of her mother in her. She's a free spirit, and I doubt anyone will tame her."

Cassie arched her eyebrows. There were a lot of thoughts in her head, but it wasn't really any of her business. "Do you know where we might find her?" Dean shrugged. "It is important, Mr Willis. I wouldn't ask if it wasn't. I genuinely believe she is a witness—"

"Who also took part in stealing a vehicle, right?"

Cassie sighed. "Likely, yes, but believe me, that's the last thing we're interested in at this time."

"What else is going on here?" Dean asked. "You're not telling me everything, are you?"

"We really need to speak with Alexa. Do you have any idea where we can find her? Please."

Dean stared at Cassie, his expression darkening but he relented. "There's an old cabin, pretty much a dilapidated shack, down on the seafront. That's where they hang out... doing whatever it is they do."

"Thank you," Cassie said, glancing sideways at Eric. "Is there anywhere else she might go, if she didn't feel she could go there?"

Dean thought about it for a moment. "I suppose there's her cousin. She always got on well with him, and I guess she may turn to him if she was in trouble."

"Can you give us his address?" Eric asked, taking out his pocketbook. Dean shook his head.

"No, I don't know that side of the family. They are on the layabout's side."

"Alexa's father?" Cassie asked. Dean nodded. "Where can we find him?"

"In prison, I suspect," he said, snorting.

"What's his name, the cousin?"

"Mark... something, I don't know."

Cassie thanked him. She took out one of her contact cards and gave it to Dean. He glanced at it and set it down on the table beside his chair.

"If you think of anything else, or if Alexa comes home, please could you let me know?"

Dean locked eyes with her. "Just how much trouble is my granddaughter in?"

"It will be much better for her to speak to us sooner rather than later, I'll say that."

He inhaled deeply. "When she shows up, I'll call," he said. "You have my word."

They didn't see Beryl before they left so they showed themselves out. Dean was deep in thought when Cassie peeked in through the front-facing window as they walked back to the car.

"He's a bitter man," Eric said.

"I think he's done his best," Cassie unlocked the car.

"What was all that about?" Eric asked, opening his door. Cassie shot him an inquiring look. "Before, when you were baiting him about his parenting technique."

"Oh, that was nothing," Cassie said, getting in. Eric did the same.

"Yes, it was," Eric pressed her. "You strongly disagreed with his stance; I could tell."

"Well, it's none of my concern but..."

"But?"

Cassie heaved a sigh. "It's very easy to lay down the law, to tell others they have to conform and respect you in the process."

"Respect your elders, that's what my mum raised me to believe," Eric said.

Cassie inclined her head. "Yes, people often say that, but... if you rule like a dictator, sooner or later, there's going to be a rebellion." She started the car, glancing sideways at him and putting the car in gear. "Whether you like it, or feel you deserve it, is utterly irrelevant."

CHAPTER NINETEEN

SAFFY MET Tom at the door, jumping into his arms before he managed to close it behind him. He lifted her up, mock groaning under her weight, and spinning her around in the air. Russell, ever in tune with the mood of his favourite member of the Janssen pack, ran circles around them, barking excitedly.

"I wish I got this reception every day when I came home," Tom said, smiling at Saffy. Her arms were draped around his neck, and she was grinning at him. "What's that you have there?" he asked, studying her smile.

"I have a wobbly tooth," Saffy said, wiggling the incisor with her tongue.

"Argh, don't do that," Tom said, smiling. "That creeps me out."

"What?" Alice said, standing at the door to the kitchen. "A big bad policeman like you, scared of a wobbly tooth."

"Give me criminals every time," Tom said, making to put Saffy down but she tightened her grip, wrapping her legs around his waist and interlocking her ankles. "I've got a barnacle," he said, lumbering towards the kitchen with an exaggerated gait. "Call the boat yard, I need to have my hull stripped!"

Saffy was laughing heartily. The smell of cooking was in the air.

"We have Saffy's current favourite for dinner tonight," Alice said.

"Current favourite, is it?" Tom asked. "Which would be?"

"Lasagne," Saffy said, "with garlic bread – slices, not sticks – and a salad."

"You… a salad?" Tom asked.

"I can eat a salad," Saffy said. "It's healthy, especially on top of the carbs that come with the pasta and the cheese."

"I'm surprised, I thought you wanted to eat less meat," Tom said.

"It's vegetable lasagne, of course," Saffy said.

"Ah… you've been spending too much time with your Aunt Tamara," he said, jovially, "filling your head with all this vegan nonsense."

"It's not nonsense," Saffy said, pouting as he carried her into the kitchen, and she allowed him to set her down. "Being vegan is good."

"Are you… wanting to become a vegan?" Tom asked. Saffy wrinkled her nose. "The sausages aren't as nice."

"Apart from sausages," she said thoughtfully. "And pepperoni pizza. Life isn't living without that."

"Good point," Tom said, recalling an image of Saffy picking the pepperoni slices off the pizza and setting them aside before eating it. He thought it best not to mention that point, pepperoni being her preferred choice of topping each and every time.

"Can the two of you set the table while I plate up?" Alice said and both Tom and Saffy set about the task side by side. Russell hopped onto his bed in the corner of the dining room, ears pricked, expecting the odd morsel to fall from the table soon enough. He would be ready.

Alice opened the oven door, and a cloud of steam escaped, which she ducked away from. Tom and Saffy were exchanging cutlery and place mats when Tom's mobile rang.

"Don't answer it!" Saffy said, grinning. "You're on your dinner break."

"I am on my dinner break," he said, silencing the call but noting it was from Cassie. She was likely going to update him on the search for Alexa Willis. They finished the table off, and Saffy stepped back, proud of their accomplishments. Tom high-fived her.

"Saffy, darling, can you get us all a glass of water?" Alice looked at Tom, frowning. "The side veggies need another couple of minutes."

"Double vegetables?" Tom said, smiling. "Lucky us!" Saffy rolled her eyes at his sarcasm. His smile widening. Alice nodded towards his mobile which he'd set aside on the counter.

"You have time to take that call, if you like."

"It can wait," Tom said. Alice inclined her head. She knew him well.

"You'll only be thinking about it all through dinner if you don't."

"I'll just be a minute," Tom said, scooping up the mobile and walking quickly through to the living room. He dialled Cassie's number, and she answered straightaway.

"Sorry to trouble you, sir."

"No trouble. How did you get on with Alexa?"

"The grandparents haven't seen her in a couple of days, they're a bit vague about it to be honest."

"Intentionally so?"

"No, I don't think so. They're good people and will help if they can… but we have a more pressing concern."

"What is it?"

"We've got another incident, a body has been found out at West Acre Ford, not far from where Finn Harper claims to have stolen the Range Rover from."

"What? You're kidding."

"A family out for an evening dog walk came across it in the water and called us. Sheriff is out there now." Cassie paused, allowing him time to process the news. "Do you want me to handle it? I know you have responsibilities—"

"You go over," Tom said, "and send me a pin of the location and I'll be there as soon as I can," he said, turning and looking into the dining area. Saffy was sitting in her chair, watching him intently. He smiled but she didn't return it, her feet swinging anxiously beneath the table.

"If you're sure?" Cassie asked.

"I'll be there," he said, hanging up. Putting the mobile in his pocket, he went back into the dining room, Alice bringing the first of the dishes over to the table. "I'm starving," he said, taking the first plate from Alice and putting it down in front of Saffy. She looked up at him questioningly.

"Do you have to leave again?"

He gave her a serious look. "I'm allowed a meal break," he said. "It's in my contract." Saffy smiled and Tom pulled out his chair, sitting down. Alice set his plate down in front of him and he thanked her.

"When do criminals take time off?" Saffy asked. Tom exhaled heavily, smiling at Alice who took a seat beside her daughter, opposite Tom.

"It seems like they never do," Tom said.

"And crime is their business?" Saffy asked.

"Yes, I suppose it is."

"Then… how do you have a life away from work, if they are always at work?"

Tom didn't have a satisfactory answer but both Tom and Alice had agreed that they'd always choose to answer questions truthfully wherever possible when it came to how they would raise Saffy. He couldn't ignore it. Alice was watching him closely, waiting to see how he'd manage this one.

"I guess," he said, biting his bottom lip momentarily, "bad people will always try to get away with doing bad things. And we, I mean, all of us," Tom said creating an imaginary circle in the air with his hands.

"Who don't do bad things?" Saffy asked, and Tom nodded.

"We have to find a way to counteract what those people do, and sometimes that means we have to work when we don't want to." Tom sucked air through his teeth. "Does that make sense?"

Saffy nodded. "So… you'll be going back to work after dinner then?"

"I'm afraid so," Tom said. "Tonight is one of those times."

Saffy cocked her head, cutting forcefully into her lasagne. She was still sticking a fork in her food at a ninety-degree angle and then practically sawing through the meal with the knife, and using the wrong hands in the process, but she seemed comfortable with his explanation.

"Is that okay, love?" Alice asked.

"Yes," Saffy said. "We can't let them win, can we? The bad people I mean."

"That's right," Tom said. "We can't."

"It must really suck being an adult," Saffy said. "Having to work when you don't want to."

Alice laughed. "There's plenty of that to go around," she said drily. Tom smiled.

"Isn't there just!"

CHAPTER TWENTY

TOM APPROACHED the turn-off for West Acre Ford. Located some distance to the east of the village of West Acre, winding its way through the valley that bears its name, the River Nar could be forded close to Low Road. The approach road to the ford itself was no longer in use with vehicles prohibited.

Tom pulled his car into the small car park at the high point above the shallow incline leading to the ford. Locals travelled from some distance on a summer's day to bathe in the chalk stream, a popular location with families as it was safe for children to play in the water. From here, open paths through grass meadows stretched to both the east and west.

The old access road down to the ford was blocked by a liveried police car and Tom greeted the constable standing beside it.

"Good evening, sir," he said rotating at the shoulder and gesturing down the road. "DS Knight is already at the scene along with PC Marshall." Tom scanned the vehicles in the car park, spotting a familiar car. The constable noticed as well. "The FME is here as well, sir. She arrived about twenty minutes ago, shortly before the scenes-of-crime team."

Tom thanked him and set off down the road for the short walk to the river. Most of the time the water passing over the ford was barely above knee height with a gentle flow. During wetter periods the river would rise much higher and would broaden to encompass the walking paths running alongside it. In these times, the water could become dangerous, especially for children. Recently though, there was no reason why someone should get into trouble here. The water was clear, slow moving and shallow.

Cassie noted Tom's approach from her vantage point at the water's edge. Doctor Williams was beside her. Tom looked past them and saw a two-man police diver team bringing a body across the water to their side. A forensic photographer, standing in the knee-deep water, took several close-up shots prior to them lifting the body out of the water.

As Fiona Williams knelt down, inspecting the deceased, both Tom and Cassie gave her room to carry out her examination, standing back and making their own observations.

The body was male, in his late twenties or early thirties, Tom guessed. He didn't have a stitch of clothing on him and his upper body and arms were decorated with tattoos of varying shapes and sizes. He was white, his skin very pale but this could have been more pronounced due to the length of time he had spent in the water.

Tom saw Fiona point to several places on the upper body and the sound of the photographer's camera shutter clicked in the silence. Tom turned his attention to the river. The water looked so serene, clear and unblemished, slowly passing them by with the underwater vegetation gracefully swaying with the flow. An owl hooted from within the nearby trees, probably wondering why so many people were here this late at night.

It was a fairly common route for locals to walk their dogs,

in all weathers. Russell enjoyed leaping into this water from time to time as well, and he figured the body couldn't have lain in the water for long without being spotted by a passer-by.

"Who found the body?" he asked.

"That couple," Cassie said, indicating with a slight nod towards a man and a woman, standing off to their right with PC Marshall. They had a black Labrador at their feet. The dog was lying down, settling in for the wait. "They were on an evening stroll, pretty much the same walk they do each night, sometimes alone, sometimes together and at varying times, but," she shrugged, "they saw it, caught in the reeds on the far side of the bank."

"Do we think this is where he went into the water?" Tom asked.

"Unclear," Cassie said. "I have a dog handler walking the bank trying to find evidence of where he may have been thrown in."

"Thrown in?" Tom asked. "You're confident."

"I am," she said grimly. "I know there's a time for skinny-dipping but not in this weather." She shook her head. "Someone stripped him butt naked and threw him into the water. Whether he was alive or not at the time remains to be seen."

"I think Cassandra is quite right, Tom," Dr Williams said, standing up, brandishing a thermometer in her hands.

"Which bit?"

"You have the clearest murder victim I've seen without a telltale shotgun wound or something similar," she said, checking the temperature gauge. "To pre-empt your expected question, I'd estimate time of death was anywhere between twelve to fifteen hours ago."

"He can't have been in the water for that long, surely?" Tom asked. She agreed.

"My time window is caveated by the need to take the water temperature, because that can skew body cooling times and affect the liver temperature test. However, I'm confident enough in that window."

"So, the body was brought here and dumped?" Tom asked.

"That's my guess, yes. Either that or he was killed somewhere nearby, perhaps on the river's edge, and then somehow managed to find his way into the water after death."

"Dubious," Cassie said.

"I agree," Fiona replied. "At any rate, I expect Dr Paxton won't find water in his lungs which will confirm it, but I am certain he was dead before going into the water and for quite some time." Cassie looked around the area. Tom knew what she was thinking.

"There are better places to dump a body than this," Tom said. "You can't drive down here for a start. The chance of being seen on the way in or out is high. Risky."

Cassie frowned. "Maybe he went in further up the river and it carried him down here?"

Tom was doubtful. "This stretch of the water picks up some speed but there are various points upstream where it is virtually standing still. I doubt the current would bring a body very far, not unless the river was much higher." He looked around again, thinking hard. "Perhaps there's another reason."

"Such as?" Cassie asked. Tom had no answer. He looked to Fiona Williams.

"Any idea of the cause of death, assuming you're correct and it isn't drowning?"

"He's been severely beaten," she said, her forehead creased. "The bruising hasn't had a chance to come out prior to his death, but the early signs are present. I've noted multiple cuts and lacerations to the upper body, as well as the arms and legs." She looked at Tom, then glanced down at the body, dropping to her haunches. Tom did the same beside her. "You'll see here, for example," she said, pointing to the left side of his chest, "two-inch cuts, precision ones as well."

Tom looked. The wound was more of an oval than a slice or cut, which he would expect. With a gloved finger, Fiona gently pinched the external edges above and below the wound, gently moving the skin together. The wound closed up, forming a slit. Even Tom could see how smooth the lines of the wound were.

"That would need a sharp blade," he said.

"A scalpel, I would say," Fiona said. "Wielded with control… needing a steady hand, not a random slash."

"How many injuries?" Tom asked.

Fiona's eyebrows flicked up momentarily. "I've counted over a dozen, but it's beyond my scope. The postmortem will tell you more. Very few of them would be life-threatening by themselves."

"Death by a thousand cuts," Tom said.

"He was tortured," Cassie said. Tom nodded. "Is there a killing wound?"

"This one," Fiona said, pointing to a wound at the heart. "It looks much deeper, a little over an inch wide. I suspect that was the killing blow." She took a deep breath, looking away. "But he suffered… he suffered a lot before he passed away."

"Is there anything else you can tell us, Fiona?"

"He had a drug problem," she said, pointing to the creases of his arms at the elbow. "Heroin, I would guess based on the repeated needle punctures and his general physical health. He's thin for a man of his age, and you can see the receding gums from around his teeth. A lack of nutrients, suppression of appetite and generally not taking care of oneself… it is very obvious if you're used to dealing with addicts."

Tom caught sight of the man's shoulder, piquing his curiosity. He leaned closer, angling his head to see better.

"What is it?" Cassie asked.

"A regimental crest, tattooed on his arm." Tom read the motto written inside the four pointed cross. "*Viret in aeternum. Merebimur.*"

"What does that mean in the language of the living?" Cassie asked.

"*It flourishes forever,*" Tom said quietly.

"Catchy," Cassie said.

"And *we deserve it,*" Tom added. He cast an eye over the body. Did anyone deserve this?

"It would be handy if someone had left him with some ID to help us out," Cassie bemoaned. Tom inclined his head.

"He's ex-military." He looked at Fiona. "Late twenties or early thirties?" She nodded. "We're looking for someone who fits this description and I doubt it's a coincidence."

Cassie heaved a sigh. "Ollie Chalk, by any chance?"

"That'd be my guess," Tom said. He looked down at the dead man. "I think that's one less person we have to be out looking for."

"Sir!" Tom looked across to the other side of the riverbank where a uniformed constable was trying to get his attention, a German Shepherd sitting by his side. "There's something I think you need to see."

Tom and Cassie had to walk some distance along the riverbank before they could find a suitable crossing place. The far side of the river was much less travelled for that reason, and it was a good ten minutes before the officer managed to guide them to where they could see what he'd found.

They were upstream of where the body was found

snagged in the reeds, perhaps a hundred metres or so away. The constable led them through a clutch of trees and undergrowth, emerging a few moments later in a small clearing. To the north lay open fields, whereas to either side the trees and almost shoulder-high vegetation enclosed the space.

At the centre of the clearing, in a patch of well-trodden grass they found the unmistakable discolouration on the ground that could only be blood. Around the clearing were discarded pieces of clothing. The dog handler stood at the outer edge, the dog excitedly pacing on the spot.

The volume of blood on display, still visible despite the length of time it had to soak away, was telling. This wasn't only the murder site, but the torture location as well.

"Geez…" Cassie whispered. She looked around the clearing. "What do you think, a drug deal gone wrong?"

"Does Oliver Chalk look like the kind of guy who has the money for a business deal worthy of this?"

Cassie arched her eyebrows. "Non-payment of a debt?"

Tom exhaled heavily. "Dead men can't pay."

"True. A warning then?"

Tom thought about that. The body was left in a spot where it would be discovered fairly soon, with the added bonus of washing clean any potential trace evidence of the perpetrator from the body. "A warning to who though?"

"We have to find Alexa Willis," Cassie said. "Until we know what's going on, anyone in this guy's orbit could be at risk."

Tom nodded silently. Cassie was right. Something wasn't adding up, and Finn Harper was their only link to any of this. The only living one, at any rate. He just hoped they weren't too late in finding Alexa.

"You never did give me the details of what happened at

Alexa's home." Cassie looked at Tom with a resigned expression.

"Her grandparents thought she was most likely with Ollie Chalk," she said. "And I sure as hell hope they are wrong."

"Could she be anywhere else?"

"Maybe she'd go to a cousin for help. Some guy by the name of Mark, but that's all they know."

"Then we'd better find Mark," Tom said flatly. "As soon as possible."

"Agreed."

"And get someone back to Chalk's squat," Tom said. "Pick it clean. I want to know everything we can about Oliver Chalk and what he's been up to."

CHAPTER TWENTY-ONE

Eric pressed the doorbell again, stepping back and glancing over at the front window. The curtains were drawn but the lights were definitely on. The upstairs windows were also covered by curtains, but he thought he heard movement inside. He rapped his knuckles on the door as well just for good measure.

A figure came to the door and Eric took a half step backwards just as the exterior porch light came on. Lisa Nolan opened the door, peering through the crack at him. When she recognised Eric, she closed the door, freeing the security chain and opened the door fully.

"DC Collet," she said, tightening the large fleece dressing gown she was in. "This is a surprise."

"I apologise for the late visit, Mrs Nolan. Do you think I could come in for a moment?"

"Yes, of course," she said, beckoning him inside. The entrance hall was cramped. It was narrow as it was but there was a pushchair folded up behind the door with a variety of shoes scattered around it. There was a shoe rack but that had overflowed. Eric stepped around the clutter. "I'm so sorry about the mess," Lisa said. "What with everything happening in the last few days things have been a bit crazy."

"That's okay, don't worry," Eric said. "I have a little one at home too, so I know how it is. How is your son?"

"He's asleep at the moment," Lisa said, leading him into the living room. Her husband Mark was sitting on a bean bag on the floor, playing a video game. "He struggled a bit to get to sleep the first night we were home. I think seeing me in the hospital and the shock of the accident unsettled him. I'm sure he's okay now though."

Mark Nolan glanced up and seeing Eric he dropped his controller and removed the headphones he'd had on. He stood up. "Sorry, I didn't hear the door."

"It's a good job I didn't fall asleep with Logan, isn't it?" Lisa said, pointedly looking at her husband.

"Yeah… well, I was just catching up with the lads, you know," he said, glancing at the television. Red lettering flashed up, informing Mark he'd been killed.

"It looks like you've met your match," Eric said.

"You game?" Mark asked.

"No, not at all," Eric said. "I wouldn't have the time even if I wanted to."

"Neither would my husband," Lisa said, "if he got off his backside and found work."

"Oh, not this again," Mark said, with a sigh. He looked at Eric, picked up the remote control and turned off the television. "What can we do for you, DC Collet?"

"I have some pictures I'd like you to take a look at, Lisa," Eric said, tapping the outside of the folder he was carrying. "We're hoping you can confirm who was in the car that hit you."

Mark's eyes narrowed. "I thought you'd already arrested the driver. That's what we heard, right Lisa?" She nodded.

"That is correct, Mr Nolan," Eric said, "but there is another angle, a wider investigation, that we are following up." Eric opened the folder, taking out a clutch of photographs. He looked around, spying a dining table pushed against the wall in the corner. "Do you think we could lay them out there for you?"

"Of course," Lisa said, crossing to the table and starting to clear things away from the surface. She looked at her husband, watching on forlornly. "You could help, Mark."

"Yes, sorry," he said, hurrying over and being more of a nuisance than a help, pushing things around rather than picking them up and moving them out of the way. After a few minutes, they had a clear area for Eric to lay out the pictures. It was a line up, only using photos rather than people. Eric pulled out a chair and Lisa sat down. "I can try, but everything happened so quickly."

"No pressure, Lisa," Eric said, "just do your best."

She nodded and Eric laid out the first six photographs. In this set was one of Finn Harper and having scanned the pictures a couple of times, she pointed to him. "That one," she said firmly.

"Are you sure?" Eric asked.

"Yes, he was driving. I recognise him. It all seemed to be happening in slow motion, like he was pushing my car rather than hitting it with force. There was no great bang or anything."

"That's great," Eric said. "Well done." He gathered up the photos and then took the next batch. He laid them out much as before, and when he was ready, he indicated for her to look at them. Mark hovered at her shoulder, also looking at the pictures. Lisa went back and forth, her forehead furrowing as she studied them. Looking up at Eric after a few moments, she shook her head.

"I'm sorry," she said. "I don't recognise any of them."

Eric smiled. "That's okay, don't worry." This second line up had a photograph of Ollie Chalk amongst them, taken during his army days, supplied by his former regiment. They'd managed to crop the image, removing any sign of a uniform. The man had changed since then, and Eric wasn't surprised that she hadn't picked him out. Eric took those pictures away, laying out the third set. These were all women.

Mark blew out his cheeks, glancing towards the kitchen, Lisa was paying attention to the images as Eric set them out before her.

"Anyone fancy a cup of tea or something?" he asked.

"No, I'm fine, thank you," Eric said, absently.

"I will, love," Lisa said, glancing at the clock on the wall. "Decaf though please, at this time."

"Yeah, of course," Mark said, walking through into the kitchen. Eric finished and stepped back to allow her to see all the photos clearly. She scanned them, stopping abruptly. Eric thought there was a flicker of recognition, and her finger traced one particular image.

"What is it, Lisa?" he asked.

"This one," she said. Eric looked down, seeing her finger pointing to Alexa Willis. Lisa looked up at Eric. "It's her. She was there."

"Are you sure?" Eric asked. "It was dark, and you said it all happened quickly.

"Yes, I saw her... not during the accident, but after."

"When you were stationary?"

"Yes," Lisa said, nodding furiously. "She got out, I'm sure she did. I saw her face in the red glow of the brake lights... but... I think I know her, sort of."

"You know her?" Eric asked, his curiosity piqued. "Where from?"

"I-I… didn't realise before," she said, looking towards the door into the kitchen. "Mark!" she called but her husband didn't answer. "Mark!" she said again, only this time, louder. "Come and see this." He didn't reappear, and Eric heard the switch on the kettle click, the telltale rattle of the appliance ceasing as it switched off. "Tch… where's he got to?"

Eric crossed the short distance to the doorway and looked into the kitchen. Steam was rising from the kettle but there were no mugs set aside. A draught of cool air drifted across the kitchen from the back door, open to the night air. There was no sign of Mark Nolan. Eric went through into the kitchen and poked his head out of the back door, scanning their small garden. He still couldn't see Mark, but the side gate was swinging gently on its hinges.

Eric made his way back inside to where Lisa waited.

"I think he's gone," Eric said.

"Gone? Where could he have gone?"

"I don't know," Eric said. Lisa was bewildered, looking round at Eric, open-mouthed. Her gaze drifted back to the photograph, and she frowned. "What is it?"

"I remember where I've seen her before," she said, shaking her head. "It was a long time ago… but I think it's her." Eric waited. Lisa focussed on him again. "I think she's Mark's cousin… Alexis or something, her name is. I mean, they're not close at all, but we bumped into her in town once. Mark spoke to her. I had the little one running around and I'm… yes, I'm sure he said she was his cousin or something."

"Are you sure?"

Eric heard a screech of wheels outside, and he walked across to the front window and parted them, peering out. A dark-coloured van rounded the bend down the road, but whether it was this vehicle that had made the noise, he couldn't be sure. Other than that, there was no one else around. Everything was still. A dog barked from somewhere. Even though the orange glow of the streetlights lit the area pretty well, Eric didn't expect to see Mark Nolan cowering behind a bush somewhere. Did Mark see the photo of his cousin and make himself scarce so as not to be put on the spot?

"Yes, I'm certain," Lisa said confidently. "It's her. She's a bit older, and her hair is different from how she had it back then, but it's definitely her."

They heard movement upstairs, and a moment later a child called out. Lisa looked up at the ceiling and then apologetically to Eric. "That's my Logan."

"Sounds like he needs his mum," Eric said.

"Would you mind?" she asked.

Eric shook his head. "No, of course not."

Lisa got up from the table, stealing a last look at the photograph of Alexa Willis. She glanced at Eric. "I don't know what Mark is playing at." She went out into the hall and Eric heard the squeak of the treads as she made her way up the stairs, reassuring her son she was on the way to see him.

Eric took out his mobile phone, peeking out through the curtains once again, and still seeing nothing of note. He called Cassie. She answered.

"Eric, how did you get on?"

"She was able to confirm Finn Harper as the driver, but didn't recognise Ollie Chalk…"

"I sense there's more?"

"Yes… it's really odd, but the husband appears to have done a moonlight flit while she was going through the galleries."

"Why would he do that?" Cassie asked.

"Lisa, Mrs Nolan, picked out Alexa's photograph," Eric said. "And she thinks she is Mark's cousin."

"Mark?" Cassie asked. Eric heard the change in pitch.

"Yes, Mark Nolan, Lisa's husband. It's one hell of a coincidence," Eric said, looking towards the hallway and the stairs, checking Lisa wasn't about to walk in on the conversation. "I guess she could be mistaken—"

"No, she's probably bang on," Cassie said. "Alexa's grandparents said that her cousin was called Mark, remember?"

Eric sighed. "Damn. I didn't…"

"None of us did, Eric, don't worry. None of us did."

"What should I do?"

"Ask the wife where her husband has been since she came out of hospital. See if he's been acting odd, making strange phone calls or disappearing for hours at a time."

Eric scanned the room, seeing empty crisp packets, cans of beer and the games console. "I get the impression he doesn't venture far from home," he said, noticing the butts of hand-rolled cigarettes stubbed out in the ashtray. Upon closer inspection, they weren't cigarettes but joints, the torn covers of cigarette papers, lying on a nearby table, giving it away. "I thought he was being more polite this time around. He gave me a load of backchat in the hospital, but tonight he was as nice as pie."

"See if his wife knows where he likes to hang out. Maybe he'll lead us to Alexa."

Lisa walked back into the living room, starting as she saw Eric was on the phone.

"Will do," Eric said, hanging up and smiling at her. "Lisa, do you know where Mark might have gone to?" She seemed unsure. "A place he hangs out, someone he might call upon if he or someone he knew was in trouble?"

"I-I… I don't know," she said.

"He's not in trouble, Lisa," Eric said, trying to reassure her.

"At least not yet. He might be soon, though, if I can't speak to him."

"What has he done?"

"Nothing," Eric said, "but… I'll be honest with you, Lisa. His cousin, Alexa, is linked to a murder investigation and we need to speak to her." Lisa gasped, putting a hand to her mouth. "One of her acquaintances has already been hurt," Eric said, not wishing to alarm her unnecessarily. "And Alexa, as well as anyone around her, could find themselves in danger. Do you know where Mark would go?"

Lisa seemed to think things through, looking pensive. "But he's not in trouble?"

"No, but he could be in danger. If you know where he might go, then you have to tell me. It's for his own good."

"There's only one person he'd turn to," Lisa says.

"Who?"

"The guy he… scores his gear from," Lisa said, averting her eyes from Eric's gaze. "If Mark was in trouble or needed help, he'd turn to him."

"What's his name?" Eric asked. She shook her head, but Eric didn't believe she didn't know. "Lisa, I need a name."

"I don't know him. I haven't smoked weed or taken anything else since I fell pregnant with our first child. I wish Mark would stop as well, he's just wasting his life." She looked at Eric earnestly. "I swear, I don't know him. He's a new guy. He's only around a year or two."

"Do you know where I can find him?"

"He's not nearby. Mark has… run up debts with the local dealers, so much so that he's even spending the child benefit on keeping people away from the house, and so he's had to go further afield to find someone willing to… you know?"

"Supply him on tick," Eric said, nodding. "Where does this dealer live?"

Lisa's brow creased and he could see the moral torment she was going through, loyalty to her husband versus keeping him from harm. "He has a place, a cabin, on the seafront just outside Hunstanton." She glanced at Eric with a pleading look. "Don't let anything happen to him, DC Collet. He's not a bad man."

Eric walked out through the kitchen and into the garden, dialling Cassie's number again.

"It's me. Is Danny still down at the squat?"

"Yes, why?"

"Ollie Chalk is Mark Nolan's dealer, and Mark might be on his way there now."

Cassie thought about it for a moment. "I'll have Danny, and the forensic team pull back and watch, see if we can pick him up."

Eric ended the call and went back inside. Lisa was clearly upset, and Eric felt for her. "You did the right thing," he told her. "For everyone concerned." She nodded but she seemed unconvinced. Eric's eyes drifted to a pile of paperwork on the table next to him. On the top was a formal letter and it caught his eye. He gestured towards it. "Is that from your insurance company?"

"Yes," she said wiping tears from her eye. "It's about the accident. We aren't fully comprehensive on the insurance and so without the other driver to claim from, because the car was stolen… apparently, we don't have a leg to stand on." Her voice quavered at that point. "As if I don't have enough to worry about already."

"Try to focus on yourself," Eric said, although the words sounded hollow. "You and the baby, and the one upstairs." She nodded but didn't reply. Eric looked again at the letter. "Your car, is this description right?" Eric asked, inclining his head towards the letter.

"Yes, why?"

"You drive a black Astra?"

She nodded. "I did, yes. They've written it off though. Without an insurance payout I can't afford to repair it anyway or buy another car."

"I wish I had something positive to say," Eric told her. "But I hope things improve for you."

"Thank you. You're very kind."

"When Mark comes home, please have him call me," Eric said, passing her one of his contact cards. Lisa took it. Eric saw himself out. Walking back to his car, he thought about the accident that had put Lisa's car off the road. The Range Rover had traces of white paint down the side, not black.

CHAPTER TWENTY-TWO

Tom entered the room, the constable who had been present along with Eric departed and Tom pulled up a chair opposite Finn Harper. Finn was sitting casually in his seat, arms folded across his chest. Tom took a deep breath before running through the formalities to begin the interview.

Finn had no longer waived his right to legal representation and the duty solicitor was sitting alongside him. It wasn't a representative Tom knew. He was young, possibly fresh in the role which could work one of two ways. He might be more agreeable as a result or he was the latest graduate who was looking to make a name for himself.

"DCI Janssen," the solicitor said before Tom could ask any questions. "My client has been in custody for approaching thirty-six hours which, correct me if I'm wrong, is the length of the extension granted to you by the court. I trust you will soon be bringing charges against my client in the matter of the hit-and-run accident? He has admitted to this," the solicitor said, glancing disapprovingly at Finn, "and I want it on record that he has fully cooperated with your investigation at every stage."

"Duly noted, Mr Johnson," Tom said. He then turned to Finn. "Mr Harper, let me be candid, seeing as your time with us will soon be at an end." A trace of a smile was visible on the solicitor's face. "I don't believe you have been entirely truthful with us."

"My client admitted to taking the car without permission, his involvement in the road traffic accident, and he also gave you the names of the other occupants. What else would you expect from him, DCI Janssen?" Tom saw Finn smirk. Clearly, his legal advisor had been in his ear and exuded a lot of confidence. Tom opened the folder in front of him, taking out photographs of the Range Rover. He laid them out, and Johnson looked at them but Finn remained as he was.

"These are images taken of the Range Rover you admittedly stole, and the damage sustained in the accident."

"We know this DCI Janssen—"

"You'll note," Tom said, ignoring the solicitor, "the traces of paint in the photos, paint that transferred from the vehicle you collided with and stuck into the scrapes and gouges of the car you were driving." Tom stared at Finn, their eyes locked. "Look at them."

Finn sighed and sat forward, studying the images. Then he sat back. "So what?"

"You see the white paint?" Both Finn and his representative nodded once they'd exchanged looks. "The curious thing is the car Lisa Nolan was driving was a black Vauxhall Astra." Johnson glanced at his client, but Finn kept his eye on Tom. "And so, I put it to you, Mr Harper, that not only were you involved in the accident which left Lisa Nolan and her child in the hospital, but there was another incident prior to that."

Finn turned the corners of his mouth down. "I don't know anything about that."

"Really?" Tom asked and Finn nodded. "Well, our witness

stated that your car appeared out of nowhere that night and then collided with her. She was surprised not to have seen you. That got me thinking…"

"Thinking what?" Johnson asked.

"On a road through Sandringham, where there are no lights, a few houses but none close to the scene of the accident… how did you manage not to be seen?"

Finn pursed his lips, feeling the eyes of Tom, Eric and his solicitor on him. He shrugged. "Don't know. Maybe she wasn't paying attention."

"You would have been lit up like a Christmas tree at that time of night on that stretch of road. My guess is that you were driving without headlights on. Now, I wonder why you would be doing that?"

Finn shrugged once again. "You said it, it's a guess."

"I'll have to ask the other occupants," Tom said, opening the folder again.

"Why don't you do just that, Detective Chief Inspector," Johnson said, although Tom detected a chink in his absolute confidence.

Tom laid out a photograph in front of Finn. When Finn looked down at it, his eyes widened. Tom put another on top, followed quickly by one more. All of them were crime scene photographs of Ollie Chalk's tortured and mutilated body. Johnson gasped. Tom fixed Finn with a stern look.

"I would love to, but your friend isn't talking anymore."

"What do you mean by this, Mr Jans—"

"What I mean, *Mr Johnson*," Tom said firmly, "is that your client's friends are being picked off, one by one. We have been unable to locate Alexa Willis. No one has seen her for a couple of days, and we have had no joy in tracking her down. We have a working hypothesis that everyone inside that car has become a target. As far as we know, the next body we find will be hers."

"I-I… I don't know what to say…" Finn stammered.

"You can start with the truth, Finn," Tom said, folding his arms across his chest. "Because, if you don't," he glanced at the door, "I'll do exactly as your legal representative says and charge you with what you've admitted to. I'll bail you, and then you can go out on the street and fend for yourself." He tapped the photos of Ollie Chalk with his forefinger. "But, right now, I think you're in the safest place possible. All that can change, obviously." Tom looked at Eric. "Have the custody sergeant prepare the paperwork. Finn can go home in about half an hour."

"Wait!" Finn said, sitting forward. Johnson tried to intervene.

"Perhaps I should speak to my client in private—"

"You can't let me out…" Finn said, his eyes darting to the topmost photo of his friend. "I-I don't want to die."

"Finn," Johnson said, "the DCI is trying to scare you—"

"No!" Tom said, pointing at the images. "Whoever it was who tortured your friend to death is trying to scare you. And it should be working, and if it isn't then, quite frankly, you're an idiot."

"DCI Janssen!" Johnson said, but Tom dismissed his interruption with a flick of his hand.

"Right now, I'm scared to death on your behalf, and I am also the only reason they can't get to you." He stared at Finn whose demeanour shifted. He was nervous. Tom could feel it.

"Look," Finn said, holding up his hands and adopting a conciliatory tone, "I told you what happened…"

Tom grimaced. "No, you didn't, Finn. You told me the bare minimum you thought you could get away with and no more." He looked at Eric. "We're getting nowhere with this. I say we bail him and let him fend for himself—"

"No, wait!" Finn said. Tom looked at him. Finn forced a smile. "Let's just wait a moment… and talk about this."

"Okay, what would you like to tell us?"

Finn steadied himself, ignoring the protestations of his legal counsel. "What I said before – about not knowing there was a body in the back – was true. On my mother's life, I swear—"

"Let's not go there, Finn," Eric said. "Your word isn't credible, and I think we'd rather not put anything on your mother. I think she's suffered enough."

Finn shook his head. "We found the car, just like I said," he explained, gesticulating with his hands for emphasis, "parked up near West Acre Ford."

"What were you doing there?" Tom asked.

"Smoking a bit of puff, you know? Just hanging out, the three of us. We heard the car approach, it's an old diesel Range Rover… you can hear them a mile away, real throaty."

"Did you see it?"

"Only the headlights… through the trees." Finn was thinking hard, his lips pursed, his eyebrows knitted. "We heard the engine go off and someone got out, slamming the door shut."

"Then?"

He shrugged. "Then… nothing. For a minute we all thought some local jobsworth might have called you lot on us. Some guy had walked his dog nearby earlier, tutting at us for sitting around and having a laugh."

"Go on," Tom said.

"We didn't think any more of it. We had a few cans… a bit of a smoke and when we were ready, we set off home. That's when we came across the car." He was clearly concentrating, trying to recall as many details as he could. "Anyway… it was parked up on the verge at the foot of the access road, you know the one I mean, just along from the ford?"

"I know it," Tom said.

"Yeah, well it was unusual. No one is supposed to take their cars down there any more." He shrugged. "It was unlocked, the driver's door was only closed on the first catch."

"So you decided to take it?"

"No!" Finn said, then relented. "Not at first." He looked at Tom, sheepishly. "At first we had a look inside to see what was in there."

"To see what you could steal," Eric said.

"Yeah," Finn said, nodding. "There wasn't anything of value. It was a piece of crap. I'm amazed it was still running." His expression changed, turning regretful. "The keys were still in the ignition. Whoever brought the car there had been gone for a good half hour, maybe more. We wondered if they'd just dumped it there. It was half on the verge at a weird angle, like they'd abandoned it where it stopped." He laughed a dry chuckle. "Ollie said we should take it for a spin. Alexa told him not to be so daft, but I went along with it." He frowned. "And… we did. It was a spur of the moment thing and that's when everything changed."

"What happened?" Tom asked, confident they were getting to the truth now. Finn took a deep breath, lifting his eyes to the ceiling.

"We'd barely been out on the main road, Low Road, heading towards West Acre and this guy," he frowned, exhaling, "came up on us really fast. He was all over my arse, weaving left and right. I thought he wanted to get past but there was no safe space to overtake. He angered me, I'm not going to lie, and I flicked him off, you know?"

"And then?"

"I eased off," Finn said, "when we got onto a straight but instead of them passing, they came alongside, looking in at us." He scoffed. "I mean… we know some sketchy types and all, but these guys… they were something else."

"Guys? How many?" Tom asked.

Finn shook his head. "At least two, but I was too busy driving, and they freaked me out. They were alongside, revving their engine and the guy in the passenger seat was waving at us to pull over." He laughed without humour. "There was no chance of me doing that."

"What car was it?"

"A BMW, three or five series, I'm not sure," he said. "White, definitely white."

"And then?"

"The tosser slammed into me, and I instinctively swerved away from him, almost losing control of the car." His expression had taken on a faraway look now. "He hit me once, and I thought maybe it was accidental, but then a second and a third time. We were bouncing off each other at one point, me steering into him to stop myself from being shoved off the road."

"But you kept it under control," Tom said.

"I did, no idea how, mind you. We were heading through Sandringham by that point, and there was a fork in the road coming up. I could see sparks coming up from between the cars, and they were screaming at me to stop – from the other car – and Alexa was screaming. Hell, everyone was screaming! At the last moment, I broke away and swerved left. I only just made the turning, well, I didn't but it's a Range Rover so I mounted the verge and bounced over onto the other road."

"Did you lose them?" Tom asked.

"I saw their lights flickering through the trees as they came about to come after us, but I've done a bit of," he rocked his head from side to side, "illegal four-by-four driving through the woods of the Sandringham Estate. Only on the periphery, you know? I wouldn't want to get shot by your lot on protection duties," Finn said.

"You're playing with fire there," Eric said.

Finn smiled. "It adds to the excitement, the prospect of getting caught doing that there."

"You left the main roads behind then?" Tom asked. Finn nodded.

"Yeah, that's right. I switched off the headlights and went into the trees. We had to go slow, obviously, but I kinda knew where I was. We picked our way through, coming out on a different road a quarter of a mile away from where we went in." He grinned at Tom. "Lost them, good and proper! Once we were back on the road, that was when Ollie saw the body in the back." He sighed, shaking his head in resignation. "Alexa flipped! And… I was still giving it beans just to try and get away from the area, just in case. I mean, we had no idea what was going on, you know?"

"You still had the headlights off at this point?" Tom asked.

"I did, yeah." He sat back, sinking low in his seat. "I didn't see her. I should have…"

"That's when you collided with the car driven by Lisa Nolan?"

"Yes. At first, I thought it was them… that they'd found us again, somehow. I managed to stall the engine; I don't know how. It's so old I'd probably run it too hard, and it was on the verge of giving up."

"Did you not think to offer help?" Eric asked, evidently annoyed.

"I wasn't thinking at all!" Finn said. "Alexa got out… Ollie shouted at her to get back into the car. She was going to help, see if they were all right but… with the body in the back, those fellas in the Beamer… I just wanted to get gone, as fast as possible."

"You should have helped her," Eric said. "Regardless of what else was happening around you. She's pregnant."

"*I know!*" Finn exclaimed. "I'm not a perfect human being, sue me!" Eric exhaled stiffly, and Tom placed a calming hand on the DC's forearm.

"You got the car started again," Tom said. Finn nodded. "And what of Alexa?"

"She got back in," Finn said, "reluctantly. She… er… thought she recognised the car."

"It was driven by her cousin's wife," Tom said. Finn drew a hand down his face, rubbing at his mouth and chin. "Did she say that?" Finn shrugged but didn't answer. Tom guessed she did, but he still wasn't willing to share everything, especially if it made him look bad. "What did you do then?"

"We wanted to dump the car as soon as possible, somewhere out of the way where we were less likely to be seen."

"The sailing club?" Tom asked.

Finn nodded. "I couldn't believe they had a function on that night. I thought I'd screwed up, but actually it worked in our favour. Who would notice *another* Range Rover parked outside the club? Then, we walked back along the seafront before splitting and going our separate ways. Ollie walked towards his place with Alexa, while I cut across town back to my mum's."

Tom was satisfied this was a fair representation of what occurred. However, he didn't believe it was complete. He conveyed that to Finn Harper with a look.

"The body," Tom said.

"What about it?" Finn asked nervously.

"You said you didn't look, and you didn't touch it. That's not true, is it, Finn?"

CHAPTER TWENTY-THREE

Tom placed the sealed bags down on the desk. They all gathered around them. Both of the mobiles were switched off, and Tom opened one bag, allowing Cassie to open the other. Tom held his up, then switched it on.

"This one is Finn's," he said, turning the screen to face him as it lit up with the brand's logo during the initial start-up phase.

"And this one," Cassie said, turning hers on as well, "Finn took from the pocket of the man with many names, lying dead in the back of the car they nicked."

Tom tapped in the PIN code Finn Harper reluctantly provided to them earlier. Cassie's screen flashed up requesting either a fingerprint or an access code.

"I expected as much," she said. "I don't suppose we can get Doctor Death to work his voodoo on the body in the morgue, reinflate his fingers with water or something to unlock this screen?"

"That's an option for tomorrow, certainly," Tom said. "Assuming, of course, it was his mobile."

"You think he might have stolen it as well?" Danny asked.

Tom had no idea. It was likely it was the man's mobile, a burner probably, seeing as everything else in his possession turned out to be false. Via Interpol, they'd been able to determine that every passport discovered in the rented flat was false, or at least, he wasn't any of those individuals. They all existed, but he wasn't one of them. His true identity was still very much unknown.

"He was wearing a watch, too," Eric said. "Apparently, Finn cashed that in at a pawnbroker down in King's Lynn the following day. We'll send some uniforms round there tomorrow to pick it up."

Tom put Finn's mobile down, turning his attention to the other one. They'd need to get into that somehow, but it was an iPhone, and the encryption on those was notoriously difficult to break without help from the manufacturer. They'd likely need a court order to obtain that assistance and, although it would be forthcoming under the circumstances, it would take time. That was a resource he was aware they had little of.

"Have someone—"

Tom was cut off by Finn's mobile ringing. All eyes turned to the phone, caller ID was withheld. The call rang off moments later. Tom picked it up, seeing a number of notifications dropping down from the top of the screen, recent texts, missed calls and emails. Tom opened up the missed calls log, seeing multiple calls from withheld numbers. There were also several from the previous twenty-four hours from Alexa Willis.

"Have Harper brought back into an interview room please," Tom said to no one in particular. Eric hurried to his desk, picking up the phone. Meanwhile Danny's desk phone rang and he answered it, immediately waving to Tom, drawing his attention. Tom walked over to stand beside him at his desk.

Danny put the phone against his chest for a moment. "Forensics have come back with the results of the DNA taken from beneath our mystery man's fingernails, sir," he said, returning to the call. Danny listened, nodding from time to time and then he leaned forward, unlocking his desktop and clicking through into his emails. "Yeah, I see it. Thanks." He hung up, put the receiver down and opened the email attachment. "They got a hit on the database, sir," Danny said, glancing Tom's way, before focussing on his email.

"Do we have a suspect?" Tom asked.

"Yes," Danny said quietly, "and no." He sighed, bowing his head. "It's a DNA match to a cold case, back in…" he studied the screen again, "1990. Down in some small village in Surrey."

Tom perched himself on the edge of a desk. "What was the case?"

"A double homicide, sir." Danny looked up at him. "A man was beaten to death in his home by an intruder, while his wife was abducted." Danny sucked air through his teeth, righting himself and shooting Tom a grim look. "They found traces of an unknown individual's DNA at the crime scene, as well as the wife's blood stains but her body was never found. It's officially still an ongoing murder investigation, but no one's been actively working on it for… yeah, thirteen years, following a cold case review in late 2012. That was when the DNA analysis took place."

"At that time," Tom said, "DNA would still have been a relatively new part of an investigation. They caught Pitchfork – the murderer of those teenage girls – in… 88, I think. The technology probably wasn't as advanced then as it was when they carried out the review. Whose DNA did we find under the fingernails?"

"That of the same unidentified individual who left theirs at the scene." Danny looked again at the information that had been emailed through to him.

"Presumably left by the perpetrator?"

"Yes, that's what it says here. The victim found at the scene was beaten about the head with a baseball bat which was still present. It says here, the body was beaten so badly that the blows chipped the end of the bat, and the splintering of the wood may have been what captured the killer's DNA." Danny shrugged. "I guess he got careless handling it. Lucky break for us there."

Tom sat quietly, considering the implications for their case. "This was in 1990?"

"Yes."

"And there have been no other hits on that sample related to any other crimes?"

Danny shook his head. "How is that even possible?"

"It is unlikely, I agree," Tom said. "It's probable he went away somewhere, prison for instance. In this case, abroad, I expect."

"Why abroad, sir?"

"From memory, 2001, it became a thing for us to gather a suspect's DNA for any offence when they were arrested. Not so, in 1990. Anyone who carries out such a murder is unlikely to have that as their first or one and only crime. It takes a strong stomach to bludgeon someone to death." Tom shook his head. "If he'd stayed in the country, he'd have committed more crimes and that sample would have flashed up some-where. I'd wager he left the country."

"Or kept his nose clean between kills for... over thirty years," Danny said. He laughed then. "And I doubt that. Gaps between kills get shorter, not longer, as time goes by."

"Exactly," Tom said. "Something has made him active again, brought him back to the UK." He cupped his chin in one hand, thinking. "Have all the files related to the Surrey case sent up to us. Let's see if we can pull the two cases together. Maybe we can help one another out."

Danny scoffed. "If they haven't been able to find him in over thirty years, what chance do we have in a few days?"

"But we have what that inquiry team didn't." Danny looked at Tom with an optimistic look. "We have the finest detective constable in the whole of East Anglia working on our case, don't we, Danny?"

Danny smiled. "I'll get right on it, sir."

Tom got up from the desk, walking across to the information boards. He looked at the photos of the three who stole the car. One was in custody, another missing and the third had been tortured to death. If they were to believe Finn Harper's account then these three unfortunate souls stumbled across someone attempting to dispose of a body, and not just any body, but that of a man who Tom suspected to be responsible for the murder of Martin Odiham inside All Saints Church. Having learned from the hotelier of the man's intense interest in All Saints Church, could it be a coincidence that a murder happened there soon after and then he suffers the same fate within the subsequent twenty-four hours? No, this man was involved.

By taking the car they'd exposed the killer, or killers, and it would appear as if these men decided that potential witnesses – obstacles – needed to be erased. Alexa was probably next, and his own thinly disguised threat to Finn Harper was actually pretty accurate. The safest place for him to be at this time was inside a police cell. Something still wasn't adding up though.

Why did they kill the man who killed Odiham? What motive did either party have for the initial murder, of Odiham and then killing his killer? Ollie Chalk, as well as

Finn and Alexa, could simply be collateral damage, caught up in events they were not involved in. The classic *wrong place and wrong time* situation, that could easily shape, or take, a life. He had to presume that the reason they'd been unable to locate Alexa likely meant she was already in danger and, in the worst-case scenario, she was already dead.

He hoped that wasn't so. After all, the bodies of Martin Odiham and Ollie Chalk had been left with little regard for concealment or stealth. If Alexa was dead, then her body would be found fairly soon. The fact they hadn't discovered her body told him they still had a chance. Although that window was probably closing.

"Sir!" Tom was snapped away from his thoughts, seeing Eric hurrying over to join him. "Harper is in an interview room downstairs. The custody sergeant wants to know if we should call his solicitor back in?"

"We'll see. He might not need him."

"Sir?" Eric asked, then lowered his voice, "With the investigation team due any minute, wouldn't it be wise to play it straight down the line?"

Eric was right, of course. Tamara had made that point herself, but Tom had a feeling that if he played this completely straight then there was every possibility that the next body they came upon would almost certainly be that of Alexa Willis.

"Come downstairs with me, Eric," Tom said, pointing towards the two mobile phones now back in their respective evidence bags, "and bring those with you."

Five minutes later, Tom entered the interview with Eric a half step behind. He nodded to the uniformed constable, who had been keeping an eye on Finn Harper until they arrived, indicating for him to leave. Finn eyed them warily, Tom setting the two bags containing the mobiles down in front of him.

"Right, Finn," Tom said, leaning his balled fists on the table, towering over the other man, "you are proving to be a popular boy in your imposed absence from society."

"What's that?" Finn asked. He looked past Tom and Eric at the closed door. "Where's my brief?" He sat back, folding his arms defiantly. "I'm not saying a word until he gets here."

"This isn't an interview, Finn," Tom said. Finn looked at him and then at Eric, who stared at him, impassive. "This is an opportunity for you to help your friend, and yourself come to think of it."

"What?" Finn asked, but Tom had his attention. Tom opened the bag, removing Finn's mobile and putting it back down in front of him.

"You've been receiving phone calls the whole time you've been staying with us."

"So what?" Finn said. "People like me. What's it to you?"

"Your friends usually withhold their numbers from you?" Eric asked.

"No."

"Good, because I don't think the caller is a friend of yours." Tom glanced sideways at Eric. "How often are they calling?"

"Ten calls since nine o'clock," Eric said. "Someone has a massive love-in for you, Finn."

"You're not a dealer, are you, Finn?" Tom asked. "People miss their dealer when they drop off the radar."

He scoffed, sneering his answer. "No. That's… that's what Ollie did." His demeanour changed at the mention of his friend.

"That's what we thought," Tom said. He pulled out a chair and sat down. Eric remained where he was, standing nearby, but he leaned against the wall. Finn's eyes flitted between both of them, unsure.

"What's going on?" he asked. Tom arched his eyebrows quizzically. "If you're not going to ask me any questions… what's going on?"

"We're waiting, Finn," Tom said softly. "We're waiting."

"For… what?"

As if on cue, the screen of Finn's mobile lit up as a call came through. They all looked at it, *Private Number* showed on the screen. Tom sat forward.

"Are you going to answer that?" Finn lifted his eyes to Tom, uncertainty clear in his expression. "Go on, you wouldn't want to miss it." Tentatively, Finn picked up the mobile, treating it as if it was a trap and the mobile might explode. "On speaker, if you don't mind," Tom said, "and we," he gestured to Eric, "are not here."

Finn tapped the screen, putting the call on the loudspeaker setting. "Hello," he said quietly.

"Finn Harper?" a heavily accented voice said.

"Y-Yes, who is this?" he asked, glancing at Tom.

"You have something of mine, Finn. I want it back."

Finn's eyes darted to Tom and then Eric, flustered. "I-I don't know what you're talking—"

"You have something of mine, and I have something of yours."

"What—"

An anguished scream came over the line, startling everyone in the room. It was a woman. By Finn's reaction, Tom realised he knew her.

"Finn!" she said, through tears. "Finn, you have to help—"

"Alexa!" Finn said. She didn't speak again, but she did shriek as she was struck across the face, the telltale slapping sound of a firm hand meeting skin.

"*You have what I want*," the voice said. "Give it to me and I will give you your friend."

"What is it you want?" Finn asked, all sense of bravado having long since evaporated.

"You took it from the car. Do you have it?" Finn's eyes darted to the second mobile phone, just as Tom suspected.

"I have it!" Finn replied.

"Good. Return it to me."

"I'm… not sure if I can," Finn said nervously, looking at Tom.

"Return it to me or I will return your friend to you in the mail, one piece at a time—"

"No, don't do that!" Finn said, raising his voice. His eyes were on Tom, who nodded slowly. "I-I can get it to you," he said. "I'm sure I can."

"Good. It is the right decision, I think. Alexa will appreciate your cooperation. Sadly, for your friend, Oliver, he was less cooperative."

"How… how will I get it to you?"

"I will send you instructions, Finn. You will follow them."

"I will, yes."

"If you deviate from the instructions, then I will hurt your friend. I will cause her very much pain, you understand?"

"I do. I understand."

"Good, then you will do as I instruct you. If you do not follow my instructions to the last detail, I will hurt your friend more than I have already."

"I understand," Finn all but whispered, the magnitude of the conversation weighing heavily on him.

"You will be alone, Finn Harper. If you are not alone, then the next time you see Alexa, she will look like the meat counter of your local supermarket."

Finn gasped. He looked like a little boy now, a far cry from the appearance he'd crafted for himself in the last couple of days. "I... I'll do it. I will."

"Good," the man said, ending the call. Finn stared at Tom, his eyes glazed.

"What am I going to do?" he asked.

"It looks like you're going on a little tour of Norfolk," Tom said. Finn frowned, looking at Eric who inclined his head.

"You'd do anything to help Alexa, wouldn't you, Finn?"

Finn nodded, but he looked ready to cry.

CHAPTER TWENTY-FOUR

THE FOLLOWING MORNING, Tom had assembled as large a team as he dared. During his time in the Metropolitan Police, in London, he had been part of large surveillance operations where they'd tracked multiple targets in both moving vehicles and on foot. For every individual they wanted to keep a twenty-four-hour watch upon, they would need sixteen personnel, along with multiple unmarked vehicles. All of these resources would allow for frequent rotation of surveillance teams, leaving the target unaware of their presence.

On this occasion, however, they knew who they would be following and, more importantly, the target would also know they were being watched. The trickiest element to the operation was that they had to assume that the person or persons they were hoping to reveal would also be aware of this.

Finn Harper had not only dropped out of sight, but he'd been off the grid on his socials and uncontactable on his mobile phone. The police, as well as his mother, knew this was because he was in a police station cell. Regarding those who were trying to find him though, it was unclear what they knew. They hadn't made any reference to the fact he was in the police station when he answered the phone call under Tom's supervision. Nor did they seem too bothered when he answered.

Perhaps both Ollie Chalk and Alexa Willis had been unaware of Finn's detention. If so, then Tom could be certain his team had the advantage, for it is hard to spot someone following you if you're not expecting them. There was an alternative though. And it was a scary scenario.

Whoever murdered Ollie and the unknown foreigner Finn discovered in the stolen car and probably having kidnapped Alexa, were operating with scant regard for the rules of law or morality. They could well know exactly where Finn was when they contacted him. If this was the case, then there was no doubt they would have a plan to deal with the police scrutiny. It was this notion that concerned Tom.

"Okay, listen up," Tom said, clapping his hands together indicating for a bit of quiet. Everyone settled. All of those present knew how important it was for this operation to go smoothly. "You've all been assigned your pairings, vehicles and communication designations. Keep the chatter to a minimum so as no one runs the risk of missing notifications." Tom looked around the assembled faces. "I'm the lead on this one. I'll ask all of you to follow instructions to the letter. We're dealing with a ruthless individual, and there may be more than one of them. Assume they will be looking for signs of us just as much as we are for them. Cars, keep your distance. We're not likely to be in built-up areas, and we'll stick out like a sore thumb if we stay too close."

"Any chance of more unmarked cars, sir?" Cassie asked.

"No, I'm afraid not," he said. "We have as many bodies as we can gather on short notice and we'll have to make do." Cassie nodded. "Now, I want us to keep eyes on our target at all times. He is wired for sound, and we will track the GPS signal from his phone, but we're in Norfolk and it's likely we will lose signal from time to time. That's why it is imperative we keep a direct line of sight. Does anyone else have any questions?"

Danny raised his hand. "How can we be sure our target doesn't screw this up?" There was a murmur of general laughter, but it quietened quickly enough.

"He won't," Tom said. "I'm sure of it." He checked the time. All they were waiting for was the phone call to tell them where Finn Harper had to be. "Okay, stay sharp out there. I want everyone going home safely tonight, and I want these sick individuals in custody."

Tom ended the briefing. Now they simply had to be patient. They didn't have long to wait though. Within the hour, the call came through. Finn Harper was sitting in an interview room along with Tom and Eric. He took a deep breath and tapped answer. They didn't have the call on speaker this time. Doing so changes the sound of the voice and they didn't want to risk tipping them off that Finn had company, police company at that.

"Hello," Finn said nervously.

"You will go to the pier amusements in Hunstanton. You have twenty minutes to arrive."

Finn glanced pensively at Tom. "And what do I do when I get there?"

"You will go to the rear, underneath the pier, and you will wait."

The call ended just as Finn made to ask another question, one of several written down on a piece of paper in front of him. He never got the chance. He looked at Tom, apologetically. "He didn't give me—"

"It's okay," Tom said.

"Hunstanton pier it is then," Eric said.

"To begin with," Tom said. Eric shot him a questioning look. "That will be the first port of call, but they won't be there." He took a deep breath. "We're not dealing with idiots or Monday morning centre-forwards, Eric. Whoever is behind this has it well planned. They'll give us the runaround, try to flush out anyone else who's following or paying attention. Only when they're happy are they going to reveal themselves."

"Cheery," Finn said glumly. Tom picked up the mobile phone.

"Time to go," he said.

Fifteen minutes later, Finn Harper made his way across the green and past the old bandstand on his left. He descended onto the end of the promenade which ran beneath what was left of the old pier which was not that old, having been replaced following a second fire, leaving only the entrance to the pier in place. No longer did it stretch out over the water as it had done in its heyday.

The modern building stood on huge concrete pillars, and it was here that Finn Harper was to wait. The tide was in, and the wind, as strong as it was, drove the waves hard against the sea wall throwing spray high into the air, seawater landing all along the promenade. The barriers were all closed today to prevent any possible flooding of the town's seafront. The roar of the waves was such that he was concerned he wouldn't hear the mobile in his pocket ring.

Taking out the phone, he stared at the screen, waiting. It had passed the twenty-minute mark, and a fleeting thought occurred that maybe this was a merry dance that the killers didn't intend to play. A distraction perhaps to allow them to focus police resources on a futile enterprise whilst they got on with what they really wanted to do.

The thought also occurred to him that maybe this whole escapade was an attempt to get him out into the open, allowing them to terminate another witness. Looking around, he couldn't see any signs of the police, just as was supposed to be the case. However, it did leave him with a sense of vulnerability.

To his left was the promenade, effectively closed off from public footfall due to the waves breaching the sea wall. It would be easy to be caught in a wave and dragged back into the sea at this point. It had happened before, and the chances of survival would be slim. Not necessarily by way of drowning. The body would be driven repeatedly against the sea defences and smashed to bits long before you had the chance to drown.

To his right was the remaining stretch of promenade leading up to the famous Hunstanton Cliffs, given over to the sailing club and some permanent beach cabins, a semicircular concrete facade with the most basic of storage for its owners. There were very few vantage points of where he stood, beneath the pier. He wondered if the line-of-sight rule had already been compromised.

But still, he waited.

A lone dog walker passed by him, and the man cast a sideways glance at him but didn't return the polite half smile he was offered. He was in his sixties, and it was unlikely the killer would be walking a small poodle. He checked the time, and then looked at the mobile phone again, wondering how long it would be.

The mobile rang. He answered.

"Hello?"

"You are alone, as instructed?"

"I am."

"You are to go to your right. In front of the sailing club,

you will see a white BMW. You will find the key fob in the glove box."

"And then?"

"You will find instructions in the car."

"Right…"

"One more thing."

"Yes?"

"You are to throw this mobile phone into the sea."

"Did… you say—"

"Into the sea. Do it now."

The call ended. He looked around, knowing that this was one of the ways the surveillance team could follow him. Reluctantly, he stepped forward just after a wave hit the wall and the swell retreated, launching the mobile into the air. He sighed, seeing it disappear beneath the surface. With a nervous glance back along the promenade, he walked towards the sailing club.

The white BMW was parked exactly where described. The doors were unlocked, and he scanned the accident damage along the side as he got in. This was the car used to repeatedly ram the Range Rover the other night. He opened the driver's door, stooping low to examine the interior, half expecting to see someone lying in the rear seat, hidden from view by the privacy glass. But the car was empty.

He got in, closing the door. The interior was just as one would expect, although he did a cursory check for a microphone or a dashcam that might be pointed at him rather than the outside. There was nothing of the sort. He thought this might be a hire car, based on it being completely sanitised with no litter, debris or personalisation in place.

He reached across, popping open the glove box. There was a user manual and service book, along with the key fob. Around it, secured with an elastic band, was a piece of paper.

He took off the band and unfurled the paper. Reading aloud, he said, "Drive the car to Drove Orchards. Park in front of Eric's. You have ten minutes."

He did a quick calculation. Drove Orchards was a small business park along the coast, consisting of takeaway shops, a farm shop and a children's clothing store. For the north Norfolk coast, it was a busy place, but at this time of the day there would be very few people around. It was about ten minutes journey time from where he was. He'd better not pick up a tractor or something on the way or he would be late.

"I guess I'm going to Eric's. Hope they want me to pick up some fish and chips while I'm there," he said for the benefit of those listening, just in case they'd missed it the first time he read the note aloud. He heaved a sigh, his fears easing, and started the car.

The road swept up the hill beside the green, and he turned left onto Cliff Parade, driving along the elevated seafront towards Old Hunstanton. He was fortunate with the traffic. Now that the number of tourists present in the area had eased, the traffic on the narrow coastal route had lessened as well.

The route took him from Old Hunstanton, past Holme-next-the-Sea and on towards the picturesque coastal village of Thornham. Drove Orchards was located just before reaching Thornham itself, a turning on the left off the main road. Pulling into the gravelled car park, he slowed the car down, coming to a stop as he examined the area.

As expected, there was no one else present. The restaurants and takeaways wouldn't get busy until later in the day. For now, his was the only car in the car park. Another vehicle passed by on the main road and he wondered if that was one of the tracker cars following on. They couldn't turn in behind him, because it would give them away.

Whoever had chosen this location had comprehensively

done their homework. There were no cameras in Drove Orchards, likely inside some of the premises, yes, but not overlooking the car park itself. There was also only one route in and out, and one road passing by. The surveillance team were going to have to be very focussed to keep him in sight.

First the pier, and now this place. They knew what they were doing and that concerned him, images of Ollie's body coming to mind. The note said to park in front of Eric's but there was a pizza place and a fish and chip shop, both owned by the same family. One was directly in front of him whilst the other was located at the rear. Which one did they mean? While he was deciding, he heard a mobile phone ringing. He looked around the car park, but the sound seemed to be coming from closer to him. There was still no one visible nearby and no movement from any of the buildings.

He switched off the engine and the ringing sound was louder. It was coming from inside the car, but not the cabin. He got out, hearing the muffled ring tone coming from the boot. He leaned back into the car, popping the boot release. As soon as the lid lifted, the volume increased. He went to the rear, seeing a ringing phone lying on a canvas bag. It was a basic mobile, old school, not a smart phone. He picked it up and answered the call.

"Hello?"

"Open the canvas bag." He glanced around, saw nobody, then clamped the phone between his shoulder and the side of his head. Inside the canvas bag was a piece of black material, which he found was actually a bag with a string tie. Besides that was a set of zip cuffs. They were similar to cable or zip ties, only the plastic was much thicker and far less easy to break. "Okay, what do you want me to do with this?" he said.

"First, you will place your hands into the cuffs."

"How do I—"

"Tighten them with your teeth."

He inclined his head, not liking this at all. A flutter of fear made its presence known in his chest, but he did as requested. He put the mobile down inside the boot space, slipped his hands through the loops, and tightened them with his teeth as instructed. He then retrieved the mobile. "Done."

"Now put the bag over your head, pull the string tight around your neck—"

"And how am I going to drive?"

"That is not your problem. Put on the bag, tighten it around your neck, and get into the boot."

"In the boot?" he asked. "Are you mental? I'm not doing that."

"If you don't, I will send you Alexa's head in the mail, and you can explain to her how you wouldn't get into the—"

"All right, all right… I'll get in the boot," he said, putting the phone down again. He pulled the makeshift hood over his head, tightened the cord and slowly climbed over the lip and into the boot. It was a tight fit, and he had to adopt the foetal position to get in. With his cuffed hands against his chest, he silently hoped the microphone was still working. "Where are we going?" he asked, the mobile cradled in his hands in front of his face. He was worried he wouldn't be able to hear the reply but, in any event, an answer wasn't forthcoming.

His face covered, it was difficult to track the passage of time, but he couldn't have lain there long before he felt the boot lid move and the gas struts hiss as the lid slammed down above him. It was already dark, but now he'd been plunged into the pitch black.

"You'd better be watching," he whispered, praying the surveillance team were still in sight and could hear him.

CHAPTER TWENTY-FIVE

THE CAR REVERSED BRIEFLY BEFORE ABRUPTLY STOPPING and then accelerating away. He heard the gravel crunching beneath the wheels and then the car stopped. He felt them pull away again, turning to the left. The road surface bounced him around in the boot but he was fairly sure they had to be on the main coastal road, but not for long. The car slowed and then quickly turned right. In his mind's eye, he tried to imagine where they were going.

They must be heading away from the sea, because turning left would have taken them towards the marshes, beach and the sea. He felt his weight pulling him to the rear of the space, and so he figured they were heading uphill. The car made another sharp turn, probably ninety degrees. He wanted to give a running commentary but there was always the chance the mobile phone was still connected. He had no way of telling due to the hood he was wearing. The last thing he wanted to do was to give away the police team. He'd have to trust they were following.

The car made another turn, and he'd lost his bearings. They were inland from the coast and on a fairly open road, probably a little-used one. The roads in this area were fairly quiet most of the time, used primarily by locals in the know trying to navigate around the bottlenecks on the busier roads. Aside from the tyre noise, the odd squeak or thump as they passed over uneven surfaces, he heard nothing. It was hot inside the boot compartment, especially under the hood, and claustrophobia was setting in.

He tried to moderate his breathing and keep calm. Panicking would do little to help him or Alexa. The car slowed again, eventually coming to a stop but the hum of the engine was still audible. He thought he heard the sound of a passing lorry nearby, the car rocking slightly due to the turbulence which confirmed his suspicion. Were they stopping here? The car pulled out and turned left. No, they were at a junction.

The longer the drive went on, the more scenarios came to mind. Were they taking him out of the area? If so, that threw up issues. The surveillance team might not know where they are and could lose him. Having thrown the mobile phone into the sea, if they lost the communication link to the microphone, and lost them on unfamiliar roads, then he faced a real problem. Seemingly, whoever was behind the wheel was responsible for two murders and a kidnapping. The death of one more person likely wouldn't faze them at all.

He pushed those thoughts aside. He hadn't been in the car very long even though it felt like a long time, but they couldn't have gone very far. Feeling the car slowing again, he tried to picture the conditions outside. He thought he heard other cars, so they were still in a relatively busy area, which he found reassuring. As busy as rural Norfolk could be, at any rate.

They were driving slowly now, negotiating a bend and then he felt repeated bumps and the uneven surface below the car. The tyre noise changed as well, becoming quieter. His guess was they'd left the main road and were now driving along an unmade track. They could be anywhere. The car came to a stop, on a steep slope judging by the feeling of his weight distribution. Perhaps it was a grass verge. There were certainly no inclines like this that he could recall in the area. Not that he was at all confident about where he was.

The driver's door opened, and he sensed, rather than heard, someone walk down the side of the car, pausing at the rear. He heard the button depress and the mechanism release, shafts of light falling upon his hooded face. Trying his best to peer through the material all he could see were shapes and shadows.

Firm hands grasped his jacket and he was hauled unceremoniously out of the compartment. He did his best to aid the process, it was in his own best interests after all, but hooded and cuffed, he was little use. Lifting his legs out, he set them down but so much time spent in that position had made them numb and he slumped down to the floor.

He was lifted back up roughly, and he tried to shrug off the hold someone had on him but the response was a grunt and he was shoved back against the car, driving his lower back into the edge where the rear quarter panel met the back of the car. He yelped but received no sympathy. If they wanted to speak to him, then they'd say something.

He heard the boot slammed shut, and he was hauled forward, sensing the man step behind and shove him firmly. He stumbled forward, silently cursing the fact he'd left the mobile in the boot. It wasn't his, but it was a communication device and right now, he had nothing. Unable to see the ground before him, he stumbled several times on the undulating surface. It was pitted with what felt like deep ruts. It must be a farm track of some kind.

He stumbled again, falling face first, but managing to get his cuffed hands up to help break his fall. Air exploded from his lungs and he cursed as he hit the ground. Again, he felt large hands reach under his armpits and pick him up. Steadying himself, he was pushed forward again, only this time a hand gripped his upper arm, keeping him steady. Even so, he took smaller steps.

They were walking in a straight line, as far as he could tell. Doubts were surfacing in his mind though. They wanted the mobile phone belonging to the dead man in the Range Rover. So, why didn't they ask him for it or simply take it? Why were they intent on leading him somewhere, and to what end?

The nature of the breeze changed, and underfoot the ground also seemed to shift. He'd imagined them walking along a track, pitted and uneven but with long grass in places. He could feel it brushing against his ankles. Now though, the ground was firmer underfoot, and yet he was walking on loose material. He heard bird calls above, recognising them as warning calls to others. The breeze appeared to whistle, and so he assumed they'd entered some woods, hence the change in both terrain and accompanying noises.

They walked up an incline and he stumbled again, catching his foot on an obstacle in front of him. An exposed tree root, perhaps? He didn't fall, managing to keep upright. They kept moving, and his breathing was becoming laboured beneath the hood. The ground levelled off and he felt the breeze again. They were still close to the trees because he could hear the birds along with the movement of the branches on the breeze.

The hand left his arm and he kept walking. After a few moments he could no longer hear or sense anyone alongside him and he tentatively stopped, half expecting a nudge, push or something even worse. But nothing came. He decided to wait until he was instructed otherwise. Judging the passage of time was difficult, but he must have been standing there for a few minutes before he heard something unnatural.

A whirring hum came to ear, initially sounding distant but drawing closer, disrupted by the breeze intermittently as the sound was carried away from him.

"What is that?" he asked, but there was no reply. Taking a chance, he reached up to the base of the hood, loosening the tie. When no one objected, he pulled it off, blinking at the glare of the daylight. He was in a clearing, perhaps a hundred yards wide, maybe more. The clearing was almost entirely encircled by trees with a chalk cliff face rising up to his right. It towered perhaps seventy or eighty feet above him with trees along the ridge and bushes growing from outcrops in parts of the face.

There had been repeated collapses over time and the debris of each was in front of him. He glanced around, and he was definitely alone. There were several picnic benches dotted around the clearing. It looked familiar but he couldn't put a name to it having completely lost his bearings. The humming grew louder, and he looked skyward searching for the source.

Moments later, he caught sight of an object. It was small, mobile, and flying high above the trees. He shielded his eyes from the glare. They were still adjusting after leaving the darkness. He focussed on it as it began to descend towards him. It was a drone. He made out the four flickering rotors at each corner, the humming increasing in tempo as it got closer. It was descending directly towards him.

The drone touched down about six feet away from him, and he looked nervously around but seeing and hearing no one, he slowly walked over to it. Attached to the body of the drone was a small, netted cradle. Dropping to his haunches, he inspected it. Only when he reached out did a radio crackle into life.

"Put the mobile phone into the cradle," a voice said. It sounded like the same one from the telephone conversation but this line was different, distorted somehow. The quality was lesser, maybe.

"Where's Alexa?" he asked, checking the tree line again and seeing no one.

"If you want to see her again, put the mobile into the cradle."

He took the mobile from his pocket, weighing it in his palm. He hesitated. "How do I know you'll keep your word?"

"Have you kept to your end of the bargain?"

He stood, biting his lower lip and looking up at the trees atop the chalk face. Someone could be watching him from above and he would have no idea.

"I have."

"Put the mobile phone into the cradle." The tone was firmer this time. He could hear the aggression, but there was also something else. He couldn't describe it but he felt there was something else not being said. He had no choice. He had to follow the instructions. He knelt down, slipped the mobile into the netting, checking it was unlikely to fall out, and stood up. The rotors began to turn once more, the pitch increasing as the drone slowly lifted off the ground. It hovered in front of him, and he stared at the camera lens.

"Where's Alexa?" There was no reply. "Hey!" he shouted as the drone rose further into the air and made to turn away from him. "I kept up my end of the deal. Where's Alexa?" He saw the camera swivel towards him and the drone held its position. He heard movement to his right and just as he turned something flashed across his vision and he leapt back.

The body hit the ground with a dull thud. He was so taken aback that he didn't manage a scream. He simply stood, open-mouthed, staring at the figure, dried blood smeared across a battered, almost unrecognisable face.

"No, Detective Constable Collet," the voice said. "You didn't keep to your end of the bargain."

Eric spun around in time to see the drone rise up and away from him at speed, setting off over the trees on the ridge above him. "Where is she?" he yelled, watching the drone get smaller until it disappeared from view completely.

He turned back to the body. It had fallen, or been thrown, from the cliff face above. He approached it slowly, but it was clear they were dead. There was no life in the eyes, or in one eye at least, because the other wasn't present. The socket was empty, the skin around it ripped away. The solitary eye was wide open and staring up towards the heavens. Both legs were lying at odd angles, evidently broken, and the head lay strangely in relation to the rest of the body.

Eric had seen enough death to know when someone died in pain. It was an expression etched into the face at the moment of death, the last fleeting glimpse of life depicted for all to see.

Mark Nolan died horrifically.

CHAPTER TWENTY-SIX

ERIC CROSSED the clearing to the nearest picnic table. It was solidly constructed and using a rough edge of a leg support, he struggled to work free the zip cuffs. They were thick, a heavy grade plastic, and it took a great deal of effort for Eric to grind his way through. Cable ties could be broken with a moment of forceful action, but these were far superior. Eventually, after a couple of minutes of strenuous sawing, his hands were free. The plastic had dug into the skin, and he was bleeding but it was superficial.

Walking back to where he'd been, Eric stood over the body of Mark Nolan, his mind reeling as to how he could have come to be lying dead at his feet. He had gaffer tape wrapped around his head, covering his mouth and looping repeatedly around the base of his skull. He felt nauseous looking at the face. His cheeks were swollen above the tape, the skin blackened and cut in multiple places. Eric could tell he'd experienced a vicious beating before contemplating what it must have been like for Nolan to have his eye removed.

"What on earth could you tell someone with your mouth taped up?" Eric said quietly.

A bird called from the tree line and Eric turned to look in that direction. He'd already spoken into the concealed microphone taped to his chest beneath his shirt. No one could answer and he couldn't tell them where he was. Why hadn't the surveillance team arrived? The only answer was that they'd lost him. A passing sense of dread, followed by relief struck him. By rights, he should be dead now, perhaps lying beside Mark Nolan.

He saw a plume of smoke drifting into the air above the trees in the distance. Something was burning and the breeze was carrying an acrid smell in his direction. He'd experienced similar before, back when he was a uniformed constable attending road traffic accidents. A car was on fire, and Eric found it plausible that it was the same vehicle that had brought him here. Wherever here was.

He was startled by movement coming out of the woods and he looked that way, adopting a defensive stance. A little girl, no older than eight or nine, came into view. She stopped when she saw him, a dog ran out beside her and it, too, looked at Eric warily. He smiled and she returned it but as soon as she caught sight of the body at Eric's feet, she screamed.

"No, wait," Eric said as she turned tail and fled back into the woods. "Where am I?" Eric asked forlornly, but she was already gone. Eric heaved a sigh. A man came out from the trees, the girl hiding in his shadow. He didn't enter the clearing but remained some distance from Eric. The look on his face depicted shock. No doubt hadn't believed his daughter – presumably she was his daughter – but now he was observing Eric suspiciously. That suspicion turned to fear when he also saw the body.

"I'm a policeman," Eric said, holding his hands up before him to assuage the man's concerns. He still didn't move. If anything, he looked ready to run. "I don't suppose you have a phone on you I could borrow?"

"Do you have any identification on you?" the man called. Eric didn't. He was supposed to be Finn Harper, after all.

"I... really don't, no." He pursed his lips. "Feel free to call 999 though and tell them where we are. You'll be doing me a favour if you do."

The man took out a mobile phone, but his eyes remained on Eric. If he so much as flinched, Eric figured the man would be off and running. He couldn't blame him.

TOM STOOD alongside Eric as the paramedic bandaged his bleeding wrist. An ambulance had come as far as it could along the access path, but the crew had been forced to walk the remainder of the way. They were in a clearing on Ringstead Downs, a nature reserve just south of the village of Ringstead, very popular with local families and dog walkers for the open meadows, wooded areas and general seclusion and tranquillity it offered.

The Downs were an ideal location, just as the choice of the pier in Hunstanton and Drove Orchards had been. Tom would have to tip his hat to whoever planned this little episode on such short notice. They'd executed it perfectly. He was lucky that he hadn't lost one of his officers, a thought reinforced as he cast an eye over Mark Nolan's body as it was wrapped in a body bag and sealed for transport to Doctor Paxton's morgue.

"So... you lost the signal?" Eric asked. Tom winced, nervously looking at him. Cassie was standing off to Eric's left. She'd arrived with a look of wide-eyed fear for Eric's safety, but that had been replaced soon enough with a scowl that hadn't left her face for almost an hour. Tom nodded.

"When you reached the pier, we had to hold back to avoid being seen. We had Finn's mobile GPS on our tracker, but that dropped off—"

"They made me throw it into the sea," Eric said.

"That'll do it," Cassie said drily. "Every time."

"When did you lose audio?"

"We had you all the way up to Drove Orchards," Tom said. "Again, with only one way in and out, it was impossible to maintain line of sight." Eric nodded. "But we still had audio, although when you were talking on the phone, we could only hear what you were saying. We realised you were getting into the boot, and we assumed they were going to show themselves, and we planned to intercept or to follow, but…"

"That's when the signal went down," Cassie said. "We lost the comms."

Danny approached and he must have heard the last of the conversation because he held an evidence bag aloft for all of them to see.

"This will be the cause," he said. Tom gestured for him to explain. "It survived the fire," he said, referring to the white BMW Eric had been transported in. It had been set alight, as Eric had suspected, shortly after he'd arrived at Ringstead Downs. "It was fixed to the underside of the vehicle," Danny said, "which is why it wasn't consumed by the flames. Fire burns upwards, after all."

"What is it?" Tom asked, taking the bag from Danny and inspecting it.

"Best guess, it's a signal blocker of some description. It will have interrupted the signal between Eric's microphone and the receivers we had with us."

"They called me on a mobile phone," Eric said, frowning.

"You can switch them on and off as you please," Danny said. "Our receivers are only good for a few hundred metres, after that we were looking for a needle in a haystack. That's why we couldn't find you, Eric. We had no idea where to start looking once we lost sight of you. I reckon this guy was prepared for us. He must have been playing it safe, just in case Finn Harper had come to us or something." He shrugged. "I couldn't imagine they'd think the likes of Finn Harper would need signal blockers—"

"No, that was definitely for our benefit," Eric said, "They knew we were here all along. They were one step ahead at every stage."

"How can you be sure it's they?" Tom asked.

"When I was speaking through the drone to the guy in charge, I assume he was in charge, the drone was in flight."

"So, what about it?" Danny asked.

"Have you ever operated a drone?" Eric asked. Danny shook his head.

"No, but I've seen them fly."

"You have two toggle switches," Eric explained. One controls pitch and the other, elevation. You need two hands to fly it. One if it just goes straight up or is hovering but, either way," Eric pointed to the departing body bag containing Mark Nolan on the other side of the clearing, "you'd also need two hands to throw him off the cliff above us." They all looked up to where Mark Nolan came from. "I know his mouth was taped up but he didn't make a sound when he came down. The blood flow from hitting the ground was also minimal."

"He was dead before he did his high-dive," Cassie said solemnly.

"That's my point," Eric said. "You can't pilot the drone and throw him down towards me. That means there has to be two people."

"Even so," Tom said, "the guy on the end of the phone

didn't show any sign of knowing Finn was with us at the station when he called him."

"That's what they wanted us to think," Eric said, "lulling us into a false notion of superiority."

Danny scoffed. "You're being paranoid, Eric. There's no way they made us—"

"No, they knew from the start," Eric said.

"What?" Tom asked. "They guessed you were a policeman?"

Eric looked at him. "They knew I wasn't Finn Harper. "And he called me by name... by name and title."

"How is that possible?" Cassie asked. Eric shook his head.

"I can only think they had us marked from the beginning. They led me on a merry dance," Eric said, looking around the clearing. The forensic team were sweeping the area, analysing both where the body was found and from where it had fallen. "Everything we set up, all of our plans. It was all for nothing. They set it up perfectly."

"And they got what they wanted," Tom said, taking a deep breath, watching Mark Nolan being loaded onto a gurney for transport. "If you're right, Eric, that marks them out as a professional team. We're not dealing with an enthusiastic amateur."

"I agree," Eric said. "They knew who we were, what our response was likely to be... and they counteracted it brilliantly."

"What can you tell us about them?" Tom asked.

Eric frowned. "Not much. I only heard one voice, over the mobile and then through a speaker on the drone."

"What about the person who locked you in the boot and drove the car over here?" Tom asked. Eric shook his head.

"He... didn't say a word. As I say, the only voice I heard

was by way of the phone and the drone. I think it was a man who walked me into the clearing. His hands were large, and he was strong. He had to pick me up a couple of times and stop me from falling again." Eric was concentrating, evidently trying to recall the details but Tom figured they would be more guesswork and feeling rather than fact, seeing as there wasn't a lot a blind man can describe other than through sound, touch and smell. Little that would stand up in court or grant an arrest warrant anyway.

"What else?" Tom asked him.

"Big, as I said, strong. I had the feeling he was much bigger than me—"

"Everyone is bigger than you," Danny said, looking down when Tom glanced sternly at him.

"I never had the thought he was ever off balance, even when he was keeping me from falling. I'd wager he is as big as you, sir," Eric said to Tom. "He wasn't one for chit-chat, didn't say a word. He left me when we got to the clearing. I didn't hear him go, but I… sort of sensed he'd stepped away. After a while, I removed the hood and found I was alone. He looked at Tom. "I'm sorry, sir. You know the rest."

Tom nodded. Whoever these people were, Eric was right. They were one step ahead of the police at every turn. Somehow, his team needed to gain ground, and quickly. Tom didn't know what the motivation was for these murderous actions, and it didn't seem like they were intent on stopping either. The idea that they knew the police were onto them, and not only continued with their scheme, but were seemingly unfazed by escalating matters.

Another death. Another murder. Only this time, it was carried out right under their noses. But where did Mark Nolan fit into all of this? He turned to face the team. An air of resignation hung around them.

"Mark Nolan," Tom said, drawing their attention. "Let's work through this, because I think we're missing something, something key."

"Where does he fit in?" Cassie asked. Tom nodded.

"Any thoughts, let's hear them."

Danny's forehead furrowed. "Nolan is Alexa's cousin, so there's the connection."

"Why kill him?" Tom asked. "And while we're on the subject, how did he come into their orbit? Alexa was already missing before we made the familial connection."

"He did a bunk when I went round to their house," Eric said, "to Lisa and Mark Nolan's house, I mean. It was like he knew then that we'd made that link and he left."

"Where did he go?" Tom asked. No one knew the answer to that. The next they saw of him was when he landed at Eric's feet.

"Crazy thought," Cassie said. Tom encouraged her to continue. "What if… Nolan knew where Alexa was."

"That's a reach," Tom said.

"I know, sir, but hear me out. We were told she might go to her cousin if she was in trouble, right?" Tom nodded. The grandparents had said that. "Well, let's say she knew she was in trouble… finding a body in the back of the car, gangsters trying to run you off the road, plus the accident with Lisa…" Cassie was thinking aloud, working through it.

"She got out of the car," Danny said. "After the collision with Lisa Nolan's car, Finn said that Alexa got out and wanted to check on the driver. What if she recognised Lisa, or the car, at least?"

"She might wish to follow up with Mark," Eric said, extending the theory. "That'd make sense."

"And," Cassie continued, "if she went to him, explained the situation, maybe he offered to help her."

"How might he help her?" Tom asked no one in particular. "If she wanted to hide, especially after Finn was picked up by us and Ollie disappeared – assuming she was aware of that fact – then she would want to lay low."

"So Mark helps his cousin by getting her somewhere to stay, keeping her out of sight," Eric said. "Then I turn up asking questions…"

"And he does a bunk," Cassie said.

"Why though?" Danny asked. "Why not stay at home and…" he shook his head, "style it out?"

"He would go to her," Eric said. "He would go to Alexa and warn her or try to move her on. Let's say he has her stashed at a place tied to him. If we were onto their relationship, then it stands to reason we would find her. If he stuck around, then he might not get the chance to warn her."

"Wait," Danny said, sounding puzzled, "are we saying these guys *don't* have Alexa?"

"I think they have her," Tom said. "The fact they took Nolan and killed him suggests they had them both. The question is, how did they get to her, and to Mark for that matter?"

"Oh God," Eric whispered. Tom looked at him, concerned. Eric's face had gone pale. He glanced at Tom, and he thought Eric might be about to cry. "Don't you see, sir. It's my fault."

"Why is it your fault?" Tom asked.

"They knew we had Finn Harper," Eric said. "They'd already kidnapped Ollie Chalk, and likely tortured as much information out of him as they could before they killed him. They would know about Alexa, and they would know about Finn."

"How does that make it your fault?" Cassie asked.

"They could only have known about Mark Nolan through us," Eric said. "They've been shadowing our investigation this whole time." His eyes drifted around the team. "I led them straight to Mark Nolan... and he led them to Alexa."

"Then it's not your fault, Eric," Tom said. "It's all of ours... and mostly my responsibility."

CHAPTER TWENTY-SEVEN

"Brace yourself," Cassie whispered to Tom as he approached the door. He winced, receiving the confirmation from her of what he was already anticipating. He knocked.

"Come in!"

Tom took a deep breath and opened the door. Tamara met his arrival with a steely gaze. He felt like a schoolboy summoned to the headmaster's office, not that that had ever happened to him, but he imagined this was what it was like. Admonishment was the least he deserved.

"Hello, boss," he said, flatly.

Tamara, lips pursed, pointed to the chair on his side of her desk. Tom sat down.

"Well?" she asked. "What happened?"

He grimaced. "I messed up."

"That's an understatement," she said. "A massive understatement."

"I know, I'm sorry."

Tamara heaved a sigh. He felt guilty then. Tamara, always so calm and methodical, looked tired. She was under an inordinate amount of stress at the moment, and he'd added to it.

She must have been expecting him to do the polar opposite. She took a deep breath, lips pursed.

"I've not had a chance to speak to him. Is Eric okay?"

Tom inclined his head. "Yes, I think so. He didn't realise he was alone until after he was confident he was safe."

"That's a blessing at least," Tamara said, glancing out through her office window momentarily. "I… thought you had this under control."

That comment stung more than it would have if she'd spent the last couple of minutes tearing strips off him. "I thought so too."

"So, what happened?"

"They are good," Tom said quietly. "No, better than that. They knew we were there, and what our plans would be. As well as how to run countermeasures."

Tamara's eyes narrowed. "What are you telling me?"

"That they are professionals," he said thoughtfully. "Experienced in what they were doing, not amateurs. And they know how we work, procedures, protocols… what tech we have access to."

"Your average criminal can watch the television—"

"No, it's more than that," Tom said. "How they went about carrying out their plan. It was like… they knew we were there the whole time, and they didn't care."

"Arrogant."

"No, confident," Tom said, frowning. "The confidence that only comes with skill and experience." Tamara sat back in her chair, making a tent with her fingers beneath her nose.

"How long do you think it will take for them to realise you switched the mobile phones with a dud?"

Tom arched his eyebrows. "If they have the access code then… they'll already know. If not…"

"You know what they're likely to do to Alexa when they find out you screwed them, don't you?"

Tom nodded solemnly. "Yes."

"Geez, Tom," she said, shaking her head. "This is a nightmare."

"I know, and it's my fault—"

"I appreciate the whole *fall on your own sword* bit, but I signed off on it," she said. "The responsibility lands on me." She put her head back and looked to the ceiling. "This will just about do it."

Tom saw the resigned expression in her face. She wasn't sleeping. He could tell. "What's going on?"

"Oh, don't worry about it," she said, waving away the question. "I'll handle it."

"What aren't you telling me?" Tom asked. Tamara lowered her gaze to meet his eye.

"Major Crimes is a very high-profile unit," she said. "High profile teams are not supposed to fail, or they're not supposed to make anyone else look bad, at any rate."

"The people in charge of them, you mean," Tom said, drily.

"Yes, that's who I mean." She was pensive but Tom waited patiently. He sensed she wanted to tell him more and wondered why she was as tight-lipped as she was. Tamara relented. "Someone needs to take the hit… for the debacle of the last case—"

"Which should be Major Crimes—"

Tamara sighed deeply. "That's what *should* happen, and everyone knows it. But they haven't even started the case review yet… and it's become political already."

"I was never very good at politics," Tom bemoaned.

"No, and keeping out of it was probably very astute, Tom," she said, pinching the bridge of her nose between thumb and forefinger.

"So, what's going on?" he asked.

Tamara shook her head. "The thing about politics is that it's less about what you actually do and more related to the perception of what it is you are doing."

"Okay," Tom said, "you've lost me. What are you talking about?"

"How it looks to the outside – to the average person – doesn't have to reflect the reality." She rubbed her forehead, grimacing. "Before they've even interviewed anyone involved, they already seem to have formed a plan of attack."

"And why do I sense you're about to tell me they're going after the wrong people?" Tom asked. Tamara smiled, holding a flat palm up to her left.

"On the one hand we have the high-profile unit, Major Crimes, with all those seeking promotion, high flyers, on big name-making cases whereas," she held up another hand, "we have a regional CID team—"

"I don't like the sound of where this is going at all," Tom said.

"A regional CID team who threw a massive spanner in the works of a multi-million-pound investigation—"

"Run by – at best – a corrupt senior officer who was willingly complicit in what would have been the murder of a serving detective," Tom said, referencing Cassie's abduction. "Not to mention members of the public!"

Tamara nodded. "I don't disagree, Tom, but that is exactly why they don't want to go down that road." She drew breath, exhaling heavily. "No one wants the truth or, at least, they don't want it in the public realm."

"You can't keep that sort of thing quiet," Tom said. "Not these days."

Tamara snorted a laugh. "You would think."

"The inquiry—"

"The result of which has already been determined," she said. Tom bristled but she held up a hand to placate him. "Someone once said that you should never begin an inquiry that you don't already know the outcome of. It avoids surprises. Awkward ones."

"That's plain wrong," Tom said, but he heard the defeat in his own voice. He wasn't naive, nor was he inexperienced.

Tom had seen multiple officers promoted, over-promoted, into roles where they were either ineffectual or purely incompetent. It wasn't always down to disrespecting meritocracy and leaning into patronage though. If someone does well, then it stands to reason they will be promoted. The problems come when that person reaches the point where they stop being effective and successful and begin to fail. At this point they are already in the role they are unsuited for. They will usually go no further – also not a rule cast in stone – but it is not easy to remove them from that position.

"I haven't helped, have I?" Tom asked.

"No, Tom," Tamara said, smiling apologetically, "you haven't. If we don't find a resolution… and by that, I mean find Alexa, and bring her home safely, then…"

He nodded. "I understand." He had no idea what he could do to rectify this. By the look on Tamara's face, she knew it too.

"Tell me what you're thinking," she said.

"We believe Alexa, Finn and Ollie Chalk happened upon the Range Rover and took it for a bit of a laugh. It was an opportunistic theft."

"Which gave them a lot more than they bargained for," Tamara said. "So, you believe Finn's story? They had nothing to do with the abductors before?"

"I don't believe they did, no." Tom's brow creased in thought. "They have zero connections – or any common areas where their lives converge – with Martin Odiham. I can see no reason why they would harm him and therefore I think it's reasonable to take Finn at his word."

"So, these men killed Martin Odiham at All Saints Church in West Acre," Tamara said. "Why?"

"Well, we can only see a link between the deceased, whose body was in the Range Rover, and the church. Where the others fit in, I don't know."

"You don't know of their motivations?"

Tom shook his head. "I can see why they would abduct Ollie Chalk, to extract information from him regarding the other two."

"To what end?"

"They wanted something."

"The mobile phone?" Tamara asked.

"Yes," Tom said, "but what's on the mobile is what I'm finding curious. Is it the digital record of conversations, where he and maybe they have all been? Mobiles log so much information these days, GPS data and so on, and that's before using it as a storage device." He shrugged. "There could be a gold mine of incriminating information on there."

"But it's encrypted," Tamara said. "And we know from previous cases that the manufacturer isn't keen on helping the likes of us to access it."

"Yes. We need to get into that device, but I don't see how we can at the moment. I'm wondering why they hadn't already taken the mobile from the body prior to the car being stolen at West Acre Ford."

"An oversight?" Tamara asked. "Maybe they would have but wanted to find a dump site first."

"Maybe," Tom said, sounding unconvinced.

"You don't think so though."

"No, I don't. That would be a mistake and they're too

good. I don't think they've made an error yet, and they've certainly exploited all of ours. All of mine," he said disheartened.

"Care to speculate on what their motivation is?"

Tom scratched absently at his head. He really didn't know. On the surface, this appeared to be a very well-trained team. On another day, he might think they were carrying out an investigation of their own, much like he was only they were managing to stay one step ahead of him.

"I can only think that whatever is on that device is worth them killing for. And I mean killing unrelated people. That's risky, very risky." Tom smiled ruefully, drawing Tamara's attention. "Maybe we will find the motive for Odiham's murder on that phone and, in turn, that will lead us to who wanted him dead."

"You think it was a professional hit?"

"Yes," Tom said. "These people don't act randomly, as far as I can see. They are acting with purpose. Chalk was abducted and tortured to lead them to Finn Harper and Alexa. There was a reason for that. Likewise, Mark Nolan was taken along with his cousin, Alexa, and then tortured purely to elicit information from her. Again, this is speculation, but it fits. What we're missing is why all of this began?"

"Martin Odiham," Tamara said. "Back to square one, Tom. Why did they target him?"

Tom nodded. The phone of Tamara's desk rang, and she answered it. Tom was lost in thought.

"No, I'm too busy to speak with him. Take a message and tell him I'll call him back," Tamara said, putting the phone down. Tom read her fatigued expression.

"Problem?"

"Oh, just—"

Someone knocked on the door and Tamara glanced

towards it, irritated. "Yes?" she called. The door cracked open and her secretary poked her head around the door. "What is it, Susan?"

"It's Assistant Chief Constable Stephens—"

"Yes, Susan. I *said* I don't have time to take his call at the moment."

"Yes, I know but he's not on the phone, Ma'am. He's… here."

"Here?" Tamara asked. "As in—"

"He's outside your office, Ma'am," Susan said, glancing nervously over her shoulder. Tom sat forward in his seat. Tamara stood up and Susan moved aside. Assistant Chief Constable Gary Stephens walked into the room; his cap tucked under his right arm. He glanced at Tom, as he rose from his chair, offering him a curt nod by way of greeting. He then strode across to meet Tamara as she came out from behind her desk.

"Sir," she said, taking his offered hand.

"Tamara, what in blazes is going on in your team?" Stephens asked, dispensing with all but the most basic of pleasantries.

"Sir?" The assistant chief constable glanced at Tom, and the look left little to be desired.

"You have a great deal of unrest here, in your idyllic stretch of the county," he said. "And it will not do, Tamara. It will not do at all."

Tom looked at Tamara, inclining his head towards the door. "Should I—"

"Make yourself scarce, DI Janssen?" Stephens said. "Probably for the best, don't you think?"

"Thanks, Tom," Tamara said, forcing a smile. "Please update me later."

"I will, Ma'am," Tom said, nodding stiffly towards the

ACC. "Sir." Stephens returned Tom's acknowledgement with another curt nod and Tom was very pleased to leave the office, fearing for what Tamara was going to have to deal with. Inwardly, he apologised for his contribution in what was going to be an unpleasant conversation for her.

Tom closed the door behind him, exhaling as he met Susan's eye. She was back behind her desk but Tom could see she was thinking the same as he was. He raised his eyebrows as he walked across the outer office and into the corridor. His mobile rang just as he stepped out. It was Eric.

"What do you have for me, Eric?"

"Alexa Willis, sir," Eric said, stopping Tom in his tracks, fearing what Eric was about to tell him. "She's alive, sir. She's pretty banged up, by all accounts, but she's alive." Tom realised he'd been holding his breath, and he let it out in one go.

"They let her go?"

"Seems so, sir. Someone found her, down on the promenade," Eric said. "Dave Marshall is with her now, and the ambulance has just left the building to go down there."

"I'm on my way!" Tom said, breaking into a run.

CHAPTER TWENTY-EIGHT

Tom pulled into the car park serving the leisure centre on the sea front in Hunstanton. The tide was in, the waves crashing against the sea wall, but they weren't cresting the promenade itself. At least not for now. An ambulance was parked beside one of the entrances to the promenade and the flood defence barriers were open, so the high tide was not expected to cause a problem today.

Gulls cawed, wheeling above him in the air. Several swooped low over the new arrival, one landing on the sea wall and observing him just in case he proved likely to drop food nearby. The bird almost seemed disappointed when Tom walked between the police car and the ambulance onto the sea front.

PC Marshall spotted Tom's approach, breaking away from the two medics who were alongside a young woman, presently sitting on a bench, a thermal blanket wrapped around her while they examined her.

"Hello, sir," Marshall said, nodding an accompanying greeting. He looked back at Alexa, inclining his head. "She's been through an ordeal."

"How is she?" Tom asked.

"All things considered, she's doing all right, sir. The para-medics reckon she's a bit malnourished and she's in a bit of shock but other than that, she's in good shape." Tom found that intriguing, seeing as everyone else who'd come into contact with these people were found murdered, and brutally so in two of the three cases. "They want to take her into the hospital for a proper check-up," Marshall said, "but I figured you'd want them to hang on before they take her down to King's Lynn."

Tom nodded, the constable turning and leading him back to the trio. The medics greeted Tom with a polite nod, but he didn't know either of them. Alexa offered him a haunted look, her eyes wide and fearful.

"I'm Tom," he said, deliberately keeping the conversation informal. The last thing he wanted was to put her on her guard by announcing his rank.

"Hello," Alexa replied quietly, maintaining eye contact for the minimum time possible before looking down at her feet. Her eyes shifted to the paramedic who was down on one knee in front of her, giving her treatment. She smiled at Alexa before rising.

"We'll want to get her down to the hospital soon, if that's all right with you?" the paramedic asked.

"Of course," Tom said. "I only need a couple of minutes right now." The medic nodded, closed her emergency kit bag and stepped away. Alexa tensed as Tom sat down on the bench beside her. He was sure she was looking at him from the corner of her eye, her head slightly bowed. Tom looked out across the water, the waves churning the sea floor, turning the water a dark brown. "I often come down here when I want a bit of time to myself," he said. Her head tilted slightly towards him.

"Do you?"

"Yes, the sea has an untamed beauty to it, don't you think?"

She shrugged. "If you say so."

"You disagree?" he asked, but there was no hint of accusation in his tone.

"I don't know," she said, sniffing and drawing the thermal blanket a bit tighter around her. "I prefer it at night-time."

"The lights on the promenade?" Tom asked.

"Yes, and the ships passing on the horizon. When the clouds clear you get to see moonlight reflected off the waves… and you can see the white caps all the way out."

"Have you ever seen the Northern Lights from here?" Tom asked. She shook her head. "No, me neither. I always wake up in the morning to hear on the news I missed it."

"Me too," she said, sniffing again. "Apparently there's a website which tracks it and can let you know when it's going to happen."

"I could use that," Tom said, with a smile. "Do you know the address?"

"No," she said.

"I'd probably forget to check the website and still miss it anyway," Tom said and Alexa's lips curled into a hint of a smile. "How are you feeling?"

She shrugged again. "Okay, I guess."

"Where have you been?" Tom asked. Alexa stared out across The Wash. Spray from the waves striking the sea wall rose up in front of them and Tom could taste the salt on the air.

"I was at Mark's for a while," she said, "and then… I don't know where I was after that."

"Your cousin, Mark Nolan's?"

She nodded. "He has a caravan," she said, looking to their

left in the direction of the amusement park further along the sea front. There were several caravan holiday parks beyond there.

"How did you come to be staying at Mark's?"

Alexa didn't seem too bothered about answering questions which suggested to Tom that she had been through a rough time and more than likely felt she'd survived that and so what else could someone really do to her now?

"After that night," she said, looking directly at Tom with focussed eyes for the first time since he arrived, "the night we took the Range Rover, we dumped the car…"

"At Snettisham Sailing Club," Tom said.

"Yeah, that's right." Her forehead creased and she was pensive. Tom wondered whether he'd need to give her a nudge but he needn't have worried. She looked at him, possibly gauging his depth of knowledge. "You know about that night?"

"We've spoken with Finn Harper," Tom said, "in great detail."

She laughed but it was humourless. "I'm sure he was forthcoming."

"It took a while," Tom said. She inclined her head. "I suggest you be honest with me, and don't worry about what you think he may or may not have told us. We're going to piece it all together anyway."

"Those guys… the ones who chased us away from West Acre Ford," she said, her eyes darting to Tom's again. He nodded, indicating he was aware of it. "After we gave them the slip – through the woods on the Sandringham Estate – we hit that car, Mark's car."

Tom nodded. "Lisa is okay, and so is the baby," Tom said, seeing the concern in her expression.

"Mark told me she was too," Alexa said. "Thankfully. I don't know what I'd have done if they'd been really hurt."

"You got out of the car, didn't you?" Tom asked.

"I did, yes," she said. "Not that I knew who was in the car, but we'd just driven them off the road. It was only when I got out that I recognised the car." She looked at him nervously. "I wanted to help, I did, but… Ollie and Finn were yelling at me to get back in. They thought those guys would show up at any minute and… and… they were panicking. I was too, if I'm honest."

"So you got back into the car," Tom said.

"Yes, and we drove away. I tried to call an ambulance, but Ollie snatched my phone, and yelled at me for being so stupid!" Her eyes glazed over. "Ollie… he's dead, isn't he?"

Tom nodded. "Yes, I'm sorry." Her head dipped again, and he saw tears falling. "How did they find you, these men?"

"Right away," she said, blinking away the tears. "We left the car at the sailing club, and we made our way back up to town, splitting up on the promenade before we reached the town, Hunstanton I mean." Closing her eyes, perhaps mentally recalling what happened in her mind, she shook her head. "I was almost home… and I thought someone was following me. I was on edge after everything that happened and I thought it was my imagination, paranoia or something."

"Was someone following you?"

She nodded. "I didn't want to take a chance, and so I ran as fast as I could. Then I heard footsteps running after me. It was dark and I didn't look round but… who else would be out running at that time of night? It creeped me out."

"Who was it do you think?"

"It was one of them," she said, "from the car, from earlier."

"How do you think they found you?"

"When their car rammed us, every time it rammed us," she

said out of the corner of her mouth, "I was looking over at the car. I was in the back seat, and I could see the driver, clear as day, deliberately trying to knock us off the road."

"Would you recognise him again?" Tom asked hopefully.

"No!" she said, but Tom sensed this was a lie. She was frightened, and he couldn't blame her. "But he saw me, and I guess there weren't many others out and about in town matching my description either."

Tom considered that. She was right, but to stumble across her path so soon having already dumped the car did appear to be a real slice of luck. "What happened then?"

"Like I said, I ran away." She smiled at Tom. "I know this town like the back of my hand. They didn't."

"You lost them?"

"Yes, but because they'd found me so soon, I couldn't go home, back to my grandparents." She frowned. "I didn't know what to do and... I was worried about Lisa, and so I called Mark." She laughed bitterly. "Not that he answered. He must have been at the hospital by then. I knew Mark had this caravan that he uses for... that he uses on the sea front. I know where he keeps the spare key as well, and so I went there. I just wanted to keep my head down until things blew over a bit."

"Who were the men chasing you?"

She shook her head firmly. "I have no idea, I swear. We took the car, the Range Rover, but it was just for a bit of a laugh. We'd been smoking some weed... having a laugh." She turned her gaze back out over the water. "I wish we'd stuck to that plan."

"Why didn't you go to Ollie's?"

"I thought about it... but then I thought that it might not be safe either and, besides, Ollie told us, me and Finn, to lie low and keep away from each other. He knows about stuff like this—"

"Stuff like what?"

She shrugged. "He knows people," she said, "dodgy types. The sort you don't mess with, and these guys were serious. Ollie said…" she hesitated, drawing a deep breath, "we should keep away from each other. We didn't know what was going on, and he said we should be careful."

"You believed him?" Tom asked.

"What do you mean?"

"I mean, are you sure you could trust him?"

"Why wouldn't I?"

Tom splayed his hands wide. "How can you be sure that he didn't know what was going on?"

Alexa glared at him. "He wouldn't be involved in anything like this…"

"You said it yourself, Ollie knew some dodgy people," Tom said. "He moved in criminal circles—"

"We had nothing to do with it, with *any of it*," she said earnestly. "None of us."

"Is it not at all possible that any of this might be related to Ollie?" Tom asked.

"No," she said flatly, although her tone quavered as if she was more uncertain than she was trying to portray.

"They took Ollie," Tom said, "the same night, we think." Alexa averted her eyes from his gaze. For all the tough, hardened edges she'd developed over the course of her short life, right now, in Tom's mind at least, she came across like the little girl who'd lost her mother. "How do you think they found him, or you for that matter?"

"I… I don't know."

Tom believed her response, it seemed authentic. "So… you went to Mark's caravan." She nodded. "Then what?"

"Mark called me that night," she said, her expression fixed in concentration. "Around four in the morning, I think. I was still awake, wide awake. I couldn't sleep at all. He told me about Lisa being involved in an accident and that he was at the hospital."

"Did you tell him you were in the car?"

"No," she said, shaking her head. "Not at that time, I didn't. I said… I said I was in trouble, and I needed his help, that someone was after me." She looked at Tom, her eyes gleaming. "They killed him," she said, her voice cracking. "He only wanted to help me… and they killed him right in front of me…"

Tom gave her a moment to settle. He needed more from her before he could let her go down to the hospital.

"Why did they kill him, Alexa?"

"They… wanted me to tell them what I knew."

"And," Tom said calmly, "what is it that you knew?"

She shook her head, tears falling gently down her cheeks. "I didn't know anything. I didn't know what they wanted to hear. They hurt Mark in front of me. He didn't know anything about… I didn't know anything, but they kept hurting him anyway."

"Mark came to see you at the caravan, right?"

She nodded. "And then… this… man came in right after. It was only minutes later."

"They followed Mark, and he led them to you—"

"He would never have done it on purpose," she said. "He tried to tell him to get lost, and it all kicked off," she whispered. "Mark was beaten up so badly. Then, they took us, both Mark and me, from the caravan."

"Where did you go?"

She shook her head. "I had a bag or something over my

head. I couldn't see. I think it was in a lock-up garage or something. It was cold, a bit damp but secure, you know?"

"How many of them were there, do you remember?" Tom asked.

"I-I… I don't know," she said, uncertain. "One guy came into the caravan after Mark… and I… only saw him again when… when Mark was… before he died."

"You'll be able to describe him to me, won't you?" Tom asked sternly. Alexa was almost about to shake her head but something in Tom's expression must have made her think differently. She nodded. "Good. I'll have someone come down to the hospital and maybe once you've been given the all clear, we can have a sketch artist sit with you."

"O-Okay," she said.

"What was it you were being asked for?"

She seemed confused, but not at the question and possibly more at the memory. "They wanted to know where he was?"

"Where who was?"

She shook her head. "I don't know. I didn't know who he was talking about. At first, I thought it was the guy in the back of the Range Rover, but that was all over the news by then. I saw it on the television, so they must have known by then. I thought – like you – that maybe they meant Ollie, but they…"

"What?" Tom asked.

"They had pictures of what they'd done to Ollie. They showed us, me and Mark, told us that was what was coming our way if we didn't tell them what they wanted to know. I swore I had no idea what they wanted, and Mark didn't either. They knew it too, because they didn't ask Mark any questions. They just… hurt him to get me to speak." Her voice tailed off.

"You keep saying *they* but you only remember one man," Tom said. Alexa tilted her head to one side.

"I only saw one man, it's true… but there were others. There had to be. I heard them."

"You're sure?"

She thought hard. "I think so."

"They let you go," Tom said. "Why?"

Alexa was lost in thought for a moment. Then she looked directly into Tom's eyes. "I don't know. I told them everything I could think of, especially after Mark…"

"After he died?" Tom asked softly. She nodded, wringing her hands in her lap. "What did you tell them?"

"Only who was in the car, me, Ollie and Finn," she said. When uttering Finn's name she lowered her gaze. "They wanted the mobile phone that the guy in the back was carrying," she said, lifting her head once more. "The dead man in the back of the Range Rover. Ollie told us we had to leave everything in the car, and we were to take nothing with us, but Finn might have ignored him." She shrugged. "I don't know. But Ollie didn't have it and I sure as hell didn't either."

"Why were they so sure you hadn't left the mobile in the car?" Tom asked.

"The man, the driver, told me that he knew one of us took it. He was adamant and he wanted it back."

"Why?"

"I don't know," she said apologetically. "He never told me, I swear."

"When did you know you were being released?" Tom asked, looking to his right where PC Marshall and the paramedics were waiting patiently.

"I didn't," Alexa said. "I'd been sitting in a chair, tied to it," she said, as Tom glanced at her wrists which bore the hallmarks of having been tightly bound, "with a blindfold on for, it felt like days, but was probably hours. Then someone came and untied me, picked me up and dragged me outside because I couldn't walk, my legs were numb. I could feel the change in temperature and the feeling of the breeze on my skin. I thought I was going to be taken someplace and killed. No one said a word. I was bundled into a van – I know what the back of a van feels like – and then driven around."

"For how long?"

"It felt like twenty minutes or so, maybe a bit more or less, it's hard to tell."

"Then?"

"The doors creaked open, and I was pulled out and dumped on the ground," she said, looking around them. "Right here. I dared not pull my blindfold off just in case. I was so scared. There was this nice old man who was walking his dog who found me, and he untied me. Then he called you, I suppose."

Tom arched his eyebrows. For all the details she could remember, the only thing he'd gleaned that was remotely useful would be a description of the one tormentor she'd seen. It wasn't much, but it was at least something. He thanked her and rose from the bench. Alexa remained staring out over the water, lost in thought.

Tom joined PC Marshall, indicating to the medics that he was through. One of them returned to Alexa whilst the other went towards the ambulance, presumably to let the control room know they were heading to the hospital. Tom took Marshall aside.

"I want a police presence with her everywhere she goes until I say otherwise," Tom said. The constable nodded. "She is not to be left alone, do you understand?"

"Crystal clear, sir. I'll follow them down to the hospital."

"Good. I'll speak to the station and sort out some cover for when you come off shift. When do you finish?"

"I'm on shift, two till ten today, sir."

"You don't leave until someone—"

"Comes to replace me," Marshall said. "Got it, sir."

Tom looked around. "The dog walker, where is he?"

"Sorry… who, sir?"

"The man who found Alexa and called us, where is he?"

Marshall shook his head. "There was no one here when I arrived, sir. She was all alone."

Tom heaved a sigh. That was another witness who could have seen something significant. He glanced towards Alexa who was now being helped into the back of the ambulance. He couldn't help but wonder how much of her narrative was truthful. None of the players in this case seemed to be on the level, only offering up information when they had no other choice, and he felt no closer to understanding what any of this was about.

CHAPTER TWENTY-NINE

Tom was so deep in thought, sitting in his office, that he didn't hear Cassie knock on the door. He glanced up at her as she entered. He raised his eyebrows towards her, sensing she had news.

"What is it, Cassie?"

"I've just collated all the information we got back from Interpol," she said, "regarding the passports we found in the apartment our mystery man was staying in." Tom was interested, directing her to the chair in front of his desk. Cassie took it.

"It has made for interesting reading," Cassie said, her eyes scanning the notebook in her hand. "Each of the IDs he was holding are legitimate. They're all real people in their respective countries." She frowned. "All are in the correct age range for our man, more or less, with only the Hungarian one suggesting he is much older than we believe him to be."

"So… he stole real identities?" Tom asked.

"Definitely real people, yes," Cassie said. "Two of them are deceased; one through a heart attack late last year and the second in a car accident two years ago. What is interesting is that none of these people currently holds a passport."

"There's no danger of it being flagged as stolen or suspected of duplication then," Tom said.

"That was my thinking too," Cassie said. "However, they are not authentic."

"They are still forged?"

"Yes, according to my contact at Interpol anyway. He says they're good – better than good – but wouldn't pass through any border scanner in a developed nation. The more sophisticated systems would flag them." Cassie checked her notes again. "My contact says if he avoided airports in… say, the USA, the UK or Germany for example, then he'd probably get through."

"But he's here in the UK, though. How did he get in?"

"I'll get to that, sir," Cassie said. "Don't worry."

"Go on."

"The quality of the passports is such that they would probably pass inspection in the country of origin. If they needed to be reevaluated or time expired, he could probably get them reissued at an embassy abroad for example. In the actual state of issue, they'd probably be discovered for what they are. Facilities are less advanced overseas. That's a universal rule."

"How did he get in here then?" Tom asked. "Please don't tell me he came in on a dinghy."

Cassie shook her head. "The ferry terminals are less stringent, particularly when it comes to foot passengers. However, when I ran all the aliases through Border Control, one passport came up." Cassie looked at her notes. "Goran Ilić. A Serbian national who came to the UK four months ago. He arrived in the UK at Heathrow via a flight from Schiphol, Amsterdam."

"Four months," Tom said, cupping his chin with thumb and forefinger. "What's he been doing here?"

"No idea, sir."

"Can I deduce that his passport—"

"Is genuine?" Cassie asked. Tom nodded. "I think so, sir. Ilić has a substantial criminal record in his home country."

"Okay, what do we know about him?"

"According to Interpol, Ilić is a muscle man tied to Serbian organised crime. He's served several prison terms for violence, usually around extortion and also had an arrest a couple of years ago as part of a multi-European operation to counteract money laundering."

"Sounds like a decent man," Tom said. "What's he doing in the UK?"

"That, I can't say, sir," Cassie said. "After he was arrested and questioned in the money laundering probe, he dropped off the face of the earth. This is the first time he's shown up on anyone's radar since then. Interpol found it very interesting that he was here in the UK," she said, then shrugged. "Less so when I told them he'd been shot dead and left in the back of a Range Rover."

Tom sat back, thinking. "Does he have any ties to known figures here?"

Cassie shook her head. "None that I can see, but that doesn't mean he has none. Intelligence suggested that when his employers were arrested, and their network dismantled there was something of a power vacuum and a bit of a tussle between surviving members of the organisation. The fact that Ilić disappeared was indicative of him backing the wrong side. There was a thought that he'd fallen foul of whoever asserted control."

"That he left the country suggests that is possible too."

"Yes, I agree," Cassie said. "He either left before something

254 J M DALGLIESH

happened to him or he just took it upon himself to take himself out of the line of fire."

"To do what?"

Cassie exhaled heavily. "His type only know one way to make a living, and that's to go into business themselves or—"

"Get hired by someone else to do the same," Tom said. "If he came to the UK then it's likely he was asked to or hired to."

"The question is for what purpose?" Cassie asked.

Tom thought on it. "You don't need to import hired muscle from Serbia, not if you're already in that field."

"No, we have enough people dabbling in testosterone replacement therapy in this country as it is," Cassie said. "You only need to open social media pages to see that."

Tom heaved a sigh. "What did you say he was involved in? Extortion and…"

"Money laundering," Cassie said. Tom couldn't see how that played any role in their case. He glanced at his mobile seeing a text message come through. He opened it. "Problem?" Cassie asked, possibly seeing his expression change.

"Oh… Saffy has a gymnastics thing tonight," he said. "I think it's some assessment for an event coming up in a few weeks."

"Good for her," Cassie said, "but I always figured she'd be on a rugby team."

Tom tilted his head to one side. "I don't doubt it." He winced. "I said I'd be there tonight."

"She'll understand," Cassie said.

Tom nodded. "I hope so, it's just she's been struggling a bit recently."

"Oh, shame," Cassie said. "Do you think hanging out with her fun Aunt Cassie would help?"

Tom cocked his head. "I don't doubt she'd love it… but you put ideas in her head."

"I'm supposed to," Cassie said, indignant. "She gets enough sensible stuff from you as it is…" Cassie quickly added, "Sir."

"Right, bearing all this in mind, we need to find a link between Ilić and Odiham, or anyone else he's likely to have come across. He started with Odiham at All Saints Church, then he went over and ransacked his home. Why? Why focus on Odiham and why is he here? Norfolk is a beautiful spot but it's not usually a draw for Serbian gangsters in my experience. Remind me what Martin Odiham did for a living before he retired?"

"He worked as a senior manager for an insurance firm," Cassie said. "He headed up their loss adjustment division. You know, the ones who come out and tell you your stuff wasn't worth as much as you think it was and then down value your payout."

"You're far too cynical for one so young," Tom said.

"It comes with the warrant card," she said, "and the northern mindset."

"I thought you were all pretty happy people in the northeast?"

"Oh, we are. Then we move south, and you lot rub off on us."

Tom grinned. "We still haven't got to the bottom of how Ilić – and I think that is his real name – wound up in the back of that vehicle."

"Or who stole it from Jason and Natasha Law," Cassie said.

"Assuming it was stolen," Tom said. Cassie looked at him quizzically. He shrugged. "I know… it's a reach, but what do we know about the Laws… I mean, really know?"

"They are dull as hell, sir," Cassie said, stifling a laugh. "To be fair, Jason Law has just about enough sense to want to bash Danny's brains in – which I can understand – but he and his wife are hardly going to take on a Serbian gangster are they?"

Tom smiled, momentarily arching his eyebrows. "No, that's true. What else do we have?"

"Finn Harper and Alexa," Cassie said. "Their mate Ollie was up to no good. I reckon there's a lot more to their involvement than they are telling us. I'm only buying the wrong place, wrong time scenario for the car theft but when they started being hunted down." She smiled but it was inauthentic. "Come on. These guys are scumbags—"

"Low level, petty stuff," Tom said. "A bit of dealing."

"People get killed over drug debts though, sir. For a few thousand pounds sometimes."

"But dead people don't pay," Tom said. "And Oliver Chalk is definitely not going to pay." He scratched the side of his head. "Besides, guys who sell a few pills and a bit of weed out of a squat on the seafront don't usually incur the wrath of a Serbian gangster either."

"What do you want us to do?" Cassie asked.

"Back to the beginning," Tom said. "Every person who has graced this case, their backgrounds, work, friendships… everything. We're missing something, and it's starting to irritate me now." Cassie didn't object or mount a complaint. He could see she was thinking the same as he was. "Somewhere in all of this is one little detail that will open everything up as soon as we find it. It's like looking for a needle in a haystack, though."

"More like looking for a piece of hay in a stack of needles," Cassie said, glumly rising from her seat. "Oh, I nearly forgot. Doctor Death was looking for you earlier."

"Paxton?" Tom asked.

"The very same," Cassie replied. "He wouldn't tell me

why though. I think he's still smarting from the last time I took him down with my verbal ju-jitsu."

"Which time?" Tom asked. Cassie grinned as she left the office. Tom picked up his phone and dialled Paxton's number. "You rang?"

"Hello, Tom," Dr Paxton said, and Tom heard him rearranging things on his desk as he searched for something. "Thanks for calling me back. It's a good job you called as I was just about to leave for the day."

"You have me on tenterhooks," Tom said.

"As usual, Tom, as usual. I've had the analysis back from the amalgam used in the fillings of the poor soul you gave to me."

"Let me guess," Tom said, "continental European in origin, common in the east, predominantly in countries on the other side of the Iron Curtain." He sat back in his chair and took a breath. "How am I doing?"

"Well, I think I feel like I'm an analogue watch in a digital age, Tom."

Tom smiled. "I'm close then?"

"If you are any more accurate with the next utterance that comes out of your mouth then I may well take retirement at the end of this call," Paxton said.

"At the risk of pushing you out to pasture," Tom said, "are you going to say the dental work was done in Serbia?"

Paxton scoffed, "I'm good, Tom... but I'm not a magician. Whatever makes you think I could know that?"

"Then you'll not be leaving us anytime soon, because I have nothing further."

"Excellent, then I shall continue." Paxton cleared his throat. "You are right, the make-up of the amalgam matches what was commonly used in Eastern Europe. However, having spoken to a colleague who is far more experienced in the field of dentistry than I am, I would say the quality of the finish is not high. We noted substantial wear, cracking of the fillings and, generally, the preparatory work was not carried out particularly well."

"A poor dentist?" Tom asked.

"No, not in our opinion. It's more likely that we are looking at dentistry completed to a basic standard. The deceased had more recent work completed which was far higher quality, but this older work is what I am referring to. My best guess, it was likely completed in an institutional framework."

"Military?" Tom asked.

"Something like that, yes," Paxton said. "The work was rudimentary in nature, certainly lending itself to a military setting or perhaps a penal one."

"We believe he spent time in prison," Tom said, recalling Ilić's history.

"In which country, Serbia?" Paxton asked. Tom confirmed it. "I'm not sure how good the provision of dental services was in the former Yugoslavia, but it is certainly in the realm of what would be offered in the military."

Tom paused for a moment, taking in the information. "You mentioned the newer work. What do you make of that?"

"Good quality, I would say," Paxton told him. "I think he's earning better money these days. It's not a great deal of information, I'll grant you, but I hope it's a little bit helpful."

"Thanks very much," Tom said. "Honestly, I don't know whether it helps at all."

"Well, do let me know if you have any questions, Tom. Good night."

"Good night," Tom said, taking the receiver away from his

mouth. He held it aloft in his hand momentarily, the kernel of a pertinent thought teasing him at the back of his mind, but he couldn't quite bring it to the fore. He placed the receiver down, irritated. Tom put his head in his hands, slowly running them back through his hair. Someone knocked on the door. He looked up.

"I'm about to head home," Eric said. Tom nodded. "Unless you have something else you want me to do tonight?"

Tom shook his head. Eric made to leave but Tom called him back. "Eric!"

"Sir?"

"I just wanted to say – about earlier – that I'm sorry," Tom said. Eric cocked his head.

"What for, sir?"

Tom was pensive. "We lost you today, and for a time we had no idea where you were and no control over what could have happened to you. And that's on me—"

"That's okay," Eric said. "It's just one of those things."

"No," Tom said firmly. "You are my responsibility, and I let you down. I won't let it happen again."

Eric met Tom's eye, and he nodded, then turned to leave. Tom sat back in his seat, exhaling as he looked to the ceiling. Maybe things would look clearer in the morning. He switched off his desk lamp and stood up, pulling his jacket off the back of his chair.

"Time to go home," he said quietly to himself. A message flashed up on his mobile and he read it. It was an invitation – one that he couldn't choose to ignore – to interview in two days' time. It was his turn to be grilled over the events that nearly cost Cassie her life in their previous case. A cold thought struck him. Had these people chosen to take Eric's life, he would have been powerless to stop them.

Leaving his office and passing out through the ops room, he found himself wondering why they'd allowed Eric to leave unharmed and how they were so bold with their approach. Confidence or arrogance? Perhaps it was neither. It could simply be the perfect execution of their skill set.

CHAPTER THIRTY

TOM PULLED into the driveway of his home, seeing the interior of the house in darkness. He remembered that Saffy had her gymnastics assessment and, somewhat belatedly, he checked his watch momentarily considering driving down to the sports hall to try and catch the tail end of the session. Realising it was far too late and they'd probably pass one another on the way, he switched off the engine and got out.

As he reached the front door he glanced at the window to his right, half expecting to see Russell, Saffy's terrier, leap up onto the windowsill of the living room window, observing his arrival. Strangely, Russell was nowhere to be seen, but the dog was getting older, and he was certainly less sprightly of late than usual. They didn't know how old the dog was, having inherited him from a man sent to prison a few of years ago.

Sliding the key into the lock, Tom's mobile rang. He opened the door and walked into the house. It was an unknown number.

"Tom Janssen," he said, closing the door behind him with his heel and slipping his coat off with the mobile tucked between the side of his head and his shoulder.

"Mr Janssen, it's Claire calling," she said, and Tom didn't recognise the name or the voice.

"Claire?"

"From Elite Gymnastics? I'm Saffy's coach down in—"

"Yes, of course," he said. "I'm sorry, I'm just getting in from work. Is everything okay?"

"That's what I was about to ask you," she said. "Saffy didn't show up for this evening's session and we were scheduled to choose the team for the upcoming—"

"She's not there?" Tom looked around. The house was in complete darkness, and he switched on the hallway light. There was still no sign of Russell. "She was due to attend," Tom said, moving along the hall towards the kitchen.

"That's why I'm calling, because Alice said she would definitely be here. I had a confirmation note from the team app only this morning."

"Yes, I couldn't make it but her mum…"

Tom stopped at the entrance to the kitchen.

"Mr Janssen," Claire said. "Are you still there?"

"I… er… I'll call you back," Tom said, hanging up . Claire said something but Tom had already lowered the mobile from his face.

At the far end of the kitchen, sitting in the darkness, Tom could see Alice. Her hands were in her lap and she stared straight ahead. Saffy was opposite her mother, also with her hands cupped in front of her. There was another person there too. He sat beside Saffy, one arm loosely around her shoulder. His free hand lay flat on the surface of the table. Beside it was a handgun.

Tom stood stock still. Alice looked up at him and even in the limited light, he could see the anguish in her expression. She'd been crying, dark rings around her eyes where the little make-up she wore had run. Saffy was terrified. He could see her visibly shaking.

"Good evening, Tom," the man said. His tone was amicable. "May I call you Tom, or should we keep it formal, DCI Janssen, acting, of course?" Tom's eyes flicked to Alice and then Saffy and he forced a smile, taking a step into the kitchen. He saw the man respond by slowly lifting his hand from the table and resting it on the gun's handle.

"Whichever you feel more comfortable with," Tom said.

He saw the white of the man's teeth as his lips parted and he smiled. "Let's keep it informal, shall we, Tom? After all, I feel like I know you so well."

"Then you have me at a disadvantage," Tom said evenly. He tried to read the man sitting in his kitchen. He was in his fifties, Tom thought. He was well-dressed, wearing a suit beneath a long overcoat. It was good quality too, Tom knew the difference. His hair was dark, shot through with grey and he sported a well-manicured beard.

"I will probably keep it that way, Tom," he said. "I'm sure you'll understand." Tom made another forward step and this time his fingers curled around the grip and gently lifted the gun from the table, but he made no effort to bring it to bear on anyone, let alone Tom. Even so, he stayed where he was, leaning his back against the kitchen counter and casually looking around.

He couldn't see anyone through the double doors separating the dining area from the living room, and the rear garden was shrouded by the overhanging trees that ran inside the boundary wall. This man could be alone, or he could have accomplices nearby, Tom was uncertain. Although Tom deemed his cursory looks to be subtle, they didn't go unnoticed.

"You have no need to be concerned, Tom."

"Well, I'll be the judge of that," Tom said, fixing his eye on the intruder. "It is often considered polite to call first before making a house visit."

The man smiled. "Under normal circumstances, I would agree, but this is far from normal."

"Agreed."

The man glanced sideways at Saffy, who looked up at him, her eyes tearing. He smiled at her and she returned it, although Tom knew she was forcing it. He took the gun and put it inside his coat, out of sight, then looked back at Tom.

"I think we can continue this conversation without…" he removed his hand from inside his coat, leaving the gun inside the folds, "all of the accompanying theatrics." He fixed Tom with a cold stare. "Do you agree?"

"I should think so," Tom said. He studied the man, first calculating the distance between them, and then his chances of getting to him before he could pull the weapon concealed inside his coat. Could he close the distance between them, subdue him and do so with an acceptable level of risk to Saffy and Alice? Possibly. He would like nothing more than to tear him limb from limb, having first removed his wife and daughter from danger, obviously.

"I do know what you are thinking, Tom," the man said. "I strongly advise against it though."

"What's that?"

"Whatever you are contemplating." he said, smiling at Tom. "We have been several steps ahead of you at every stage, as I think you know. Do you believe I would make this move if I wasn't absolutely certain how it was going to play out?"

"Even the best of us miscalculate from time to time," Tom said evenly.

"You should not blame yourself for what happened with Eric," he said. Alice's head snapped sideways to look at Tom, fearful. "It is okay," the man said, addressing Alice directly. "Your young detective constable friend is safe and well. As are his beautiful wife, Becca, and their son, George. He's a bit of a handful," he said, grinning as if he was an old family friend, "or so I am led to believe."

"You've been doing your homework, I see," Tom said.

"I know you. I know all of you." He offered Tom an earnest look. "How is Cassie getting on after what happened to her recently? It must be difficult, working in such a high-pressure environment... going home to stay in your boss's spare bedroom. I wonder if she's still pining for Lauren?"

"Who are you?" Tom asked. The man smiled, drawing a deep breath.

"I'm not likely to give you my real name, am I?" he said, frowning. "But, if it helps to ease the tension between us, then you can call me..." the corners of his mouth turned down and he tilted his head to one side, "Simon. I've always liked Simon as a name. It's not pretentious, but it speaks of honesty, reliability. Yes, call me Simon."

"Okay, Simon," Tom said. "What do you want?"

"Direct, aren't you?"

"I sense you're not a man to play games," Tom said.

"No, everything I do has a purpose." He shrugged. "Otherwise, there's no point. I don't like to waste my time."

"Neither do I," Tom said. "What do you want."

"I want the same thing as you do, Tom," he said, smiling warmly.

"I doubt that," Tom said, "but please go on."

Simon chuckled. "You don't believe me... but that's okay. I can work with that." He glanced down at Saffy. "How about a show of faith?" He removed his arm from around Saffy's shoulder and tapped her with his fingers. "Why don't you go and play in your bedroom, Saffy."

Alice flinched, drawing Simon's attention. He smiled at the girl.

"Go on, off you go." Saffy looked at her mum and then at Tom but Simon gently nudged her with his forearm. She slowly got up from the table, probably wondering if it was some kind of a trick. Simon nodded to her. "Go and play in your room for a bit. Let the grown-ups talk."

"I'll be up in a bit," Alice said, trying to reassure her daughter. Saffy hesitated but when Alice smiled weakly at her, she moved around the table and hurried from the room. Alice made to rise but Simon took the handgun from within his coat and pointed it at Alice. Tom instinctively stepped forward, only to be chastised.

"Stay where you are, Tom," he said, but his eyes remained on Alice, looking down the barrel of the weapon. "And I didn't say you could leave, Alice."

"What do you want from us?" she hissed at him, but Simon was unfazed and ignored the question. He slowly turned his face towards Tom.

"You and I aren't so dissimilar, you know, Tom."

"At the risk of annoying you," Tom said quietly, "which isn't something I care to do with you pointing that thing at my wife…"

Simon relented, putting his hand down on the table, still holding the handgun but at least it was no longer trained on Alice. "Speak freely," Simon said.

"I don't see what we have in common."

"That's only because you don't understand my motivation, Tom." Simon used the barrel to encourage Tom to join them at the table. He slowly crossed the kitchen and took a seat beside Alice who reached out beneath the table to put her hand in his. He squeezed it reassuringly. "You see, both of us are seeking the same thing."

"Which is?" Tom asked.

"Justice, Tom. Justice." Simon arched his eyebrows. "We simply diverge when it comes to the punishment side of things."

"That's not my role—"

"Which is why you need people like me, Tom." Simon sat forward, excited. "You see, I simplify all of this," he said, spinning his hand in the air, wielding the gun as if he was using it to conduct an orchestra.

"You've lost me, I'm sorry."

Simon laughed. "I tried very hard not to do things this way, Tom. You have to believe me. I didn't want all of this… it's so… messy." He winced. "You do believe that, don't you, Tom?"

Tom heaved a sigh. "I'd believe it more if I knew what you were going on about, that's for sure."

Simon sat forward, folding his arms and resting his elbows on the table. He was incredibly casual. He was within arm's reach now, but his confidence suggested to Tom that all of this was still happening as Simon figured it would play out. Saffy was safe. He needed to get Alice safe too, and then he could focus on Simon.

"What I want…" Simon said, tapping the end of the barrel on the table in front of him, "is the same person you want. I want the man who killed my associate."

Tom narrowed his eyes. "Your associate?"

"Are you deaf?" Simon said flatly. "Or are you an idiot?"

"I'm neither."

"Then you must think I am an idiot."

Tom inclined his head, remaining calm. "I think nothing of the sort when a man has a gun on me."

Simon glanced at the weapon, nodding knowingly. "That's fair enough." He put the gun back into his coat. "I think we both know that you're not going to do anything silly, are you Tom? My associates would take a dim view of it," he said, meeting Tom's gaze, "and I think we both know that."

Tom's eyes scanned the darkness outside, seeking any sign of who might be out there watching them.

"Why don't you tell me why you're here?"

"I have been on the hunt for justice for a very long time, Tom." He scratched his head. "Looking to right a wrong. You might say… it's been almost all-consuming. And I say almost because I've still managed to make something of myself, but you know… that feeling, when you have an itch that you just can't scratch. It irritates you and as time passes it becomes all you can think about."

"Yes, I can imagine. What's the cause of yours?" Tom asked.

"Vengeance that goes unpunished leaves a stain that nothing can clean," Simon said, his tone was cold, matter of fact. "And for a long time I thought I would have to live with that and then, one day, word reaches me." He held his hand up before them, pinching his thumb and forefinger together. "It's just a snippet of information. A lead, you would call it, that brought me here to Norfolk. Years… I've been waiting years and so I put my best guy on it. He did the leg work because too many times I've been chasing around," he waved his hands in the air theatrically, "going from here to there and back again… wasting my time."

"But you're here," Tom said.

"Because this was different. This was solid, substantial," he said, his eyes lighting up. "He found what I was looking for."

"Ilić?" Tom asked, and Alice glanced sideways at him, but Tom only had eyes for Simon, who nodded. "He… found something?"

"Yes, he did, but," Simon said holding a pointed finger in

the air, "before he could tell me what I wanted to hear, someone saw fit to murder him."

Alice gasped.

"And that's why you want his mobile phone," Tom said. "Because you're hoping it will tell you what you want to know."

Simon sat back and smiled at Tom, nodding slowly. "You see, I was right about you. You're a smart man, Tom." He drummed his hands on the table in front of him. "Smart enough not to give me the mobile as we agreed."

"You knew we were there," Tom said. "And you knew we'd switched Finn Harper for Eric."

Simon scoffed. "Of course I did!" He splayed his hands wide. "But it was worth a shot."

"You played it very well, I have to say," Tom said with genuine admiration. "You got away cleanly."

"I rather hoped you'd be overconfident and use the real mobile phone though," Simon said. "But you were smarter."

"If you knew, why did you release Alexa?"

Simon shook his head. "I told you; I don't do anything unless it has a purpose. I had no reason to harm the girl. She didn't have what I needed, and she couldn't help me to retrieve it—"

"Then why did you kill Ollie?" Tom asked. "And her cousin, Mark, for that matter?"

"Those actions had purpose, Tom," he said, fixing Tom with a steely gaze. "And everything I do has purpose."

"Why are you here?" Tom asked.

"Because I want you to know something."

"What's that?"

Simon stared at him and Tom felt he was looking into the eyes of pure evil. For all of his amiability, this man was a ruthless killer, likely sociopathic, and incredibly dangerous.

"I want you to know that I can reach you anywhere, at any time," Simon said, "and I can hurt you in ways you can only imagine in your worst nightmares."

Tom saw a tear fall from Alice's eye, and he squeezed her hand to support her.

"To what end?" Tom asked.

"You said I wasn't one for playing games, Tom." Simon smiled. "But we are going to play a game, you and me. Let's call it a game of *Simon Says*." His eyes seemed to gleam as he met Tom's gaze. "Simon says *you* are going to lead me to the person I am looking for."

"Is that right?" Tom asked.

"Yes. You just don't know it yet."

"I won't do that," Tom said.

"I don't think you understand the rules of this game, Tom," Simon said with a sideways smile.

"If you know me as well as you say you do," Tom said, "then you know I'll never do that."

"We'll see, Tom, we'll see," Simon said, rising from his chair. He leaned forward, balled fists resting on the table, looking down upon them both. "You'd better be quick though, because I'm not known for my patience."

He backed away from the table and without turning away from Tom, he opened the left side French door out onto the rear garden. Russell bounded through, turning on Simon, his lip curling as he snarled at him.

"Cute dog you have there," Simon said, looking from Russell to Tom. "It's a lovely family you have, Tom. A beautiful wife, a daughter and a cute dog." His expression turned menacing. "It would be a shame for anything to happen to them."

He turned and stepped out into the darkness, disappearing into the gloom. Tom got up and hurried around to the door, waving for Alice to move out of sight. She left the table and hunkered down beside the kitchen cabinets out of view of the windows. They both heard footsteps, and Saffy came into the kitchen from the hallway where she'd obviously chosen to stay. Alice beckoned her over and Saffy leapt into her mother's embrace. Tom stood against the wall beside the French doors, peering out into the darkness, trying to see if anyone was still out there.

"Who was that man?" Saffy asked. Tom came to kneel beside them both. He placed a supportive hand on Saffy's back, gently rubbing it whilst he met Alice's eye.

"Don't worry about him, Saffy. You'll never see him again."

"He was scary."

Tom did his best to offer her a warm smile. "That was what he wanted you to think. Luckily, people aren't as scary as they try to make out."

"Are you scared?" she asked. Tom touched her cheek affectionately. "Are you?"

"No. He was just sending me a message, that's all."

"Why didn't he just phone you?"

Tom laughed. "That would have been much better, wouldn't it?" He looked at Alice. "Pack a bag, we're leaving."

"Where are we going?" Saffy asked as her mum nodded.

"Just away for a couple of days, darling," Alice said, tightening her arm around her daughter.

CHAPTER THIRTY-ONE

Tom kept close to the wall beside the window overlooking the driveway. They lived on a quiet road and most of the neighbours had already settled in for the evening. Nothing stirred near the house. He went to the front door, meeting Alice and Saffy at the foot of the stairs. Alice had hastily packed two small bags with essentials, toiletries, and a couple of changes of clothing for them.

Saffy had her favourite soft toy clutched close to her chest. She looked fearful. Despite Tom and Alice's best efforts to present this as a normal event, Saffy wasn't daft, and she knew full well it was anything but normal.

Tom cracked open the door, holding a hand up behind him to indicate for them to wait. He edged out, looking up and down the street but he couldn't see anything untoward. There were no unfamiliar cars or people loitering where they shouldn't be. If there was anything that would strike him as odd, he was confident he'd see it.

Moving swiftly to his car, he carried out a cursory check around the wheel arches and on the sills underneath, just in case someone had stuck a tracker to the car. He found nothing. He unlocked the car and opened the doors to the passenger side. Beckoning to Alice, she emerged from the house, leading Saffy to the car and buckling her into the rear seat. Tom closed the door, keeping a watchful eye on the immediate vicinity but it all stayed quiet. Alice got in and closed the door. Tom went back to the house. Russell was sitting on the entrance mat watching him. Tom inclined his head towards the car and made a clicking sound with his tongue against the roof of his mouth and Russell leapt up, scurrying outside to the car.

Tom locked the house up and went around to the driver's side, opening the rear passenger door for the waiting terrier who leapt onto the back seat beside Saffy. He sat bolt upright, ears pricked, alert. The dog was also on edge, probably picking up on their anxiety. With one last sweeping look around them, Tom was satisfied they weren't under observation, and he got in.

He started the car and reversed out of the drive. He checked his mirrors to see if any other car moved off at the same time, but he couldn't see any signs of being followed. In a city or large town, he knew how to run counter surveillance because it was easy. In a built-up area, all he would have to do is to make frequent right turns – making four in quick succession – and then look to see who was behind him. If the same vehicles were present, then there was every chance you were being followed.

Police procedure was to use multiple vehicles, thereby mitigating that problem, and he was confident that these people wouldn't have the resources to covertly follow him properly. In any event, most Norfolk roads were unsuitable for such countermeasures being far too rural. To make four consecutive turns might encompass a fifteen-mile round trip, and so it just wasn't feasible. However, the nature of the roads also made tailing somebody incredibly difficult as well for the same reasons.

Despite these concerns, Tom took a circuitous route to his planned destination. Travelling along the coast road, Tom turned off onto Beach Road, just before they arrived at Holme, a coastal village backing onto the Holme Dunes nature reserve. He made his way along the road, the light from the village itself glowing across the fields nearby as they bypassed it.

A small holiday park was located to their left, but Tom pressed on following the road around to the right when it reached the extent of the golf club. Skirting the edge of the reserve now, Tom kept looking in his rearview mirror, but he was confident they were not being followed.

Broadwater Road culminated in a visitor centre a short walk from the dunes, but Tom wasn't going that far. There were a handful of residences lining the road and Tom pulled into a narrow driveway of one house. The exterior lights were on and there was another car already parked in front of the house.

Tom brought the car to a stop and quickly got out. Russell leapt over the centre console, onto Tom's recently vacated seat and followed him out onto the gravel drive. Alice got Saffy out, gathering the little girl up in her arms. Tom shepherded them to the front door which opened as they approached. Cassie greeted them with a broad smile which almost masked her concern.

"Hello," she said, reaching out and gently pinching Saffy's cheek.

"Hello, Aunty Cass," Saffy said. Alice nodded a greeting and Cassie moved aside to let them enter.

"Go on inside," Cassie said. "I've lit the wood burner and there are some snacks out on the table."

"Thanks, Cassie," Alice said, moving past her. Cassie smiled at Alice, then stepped out, coming alongside Tom who was anxiously staring back into the darkness, listening for sounds of a vehicle which may have turned off its headlights and was trying to approach with stealth.

"Any sign?" she asked quietly.

"No, I don't think anyone was following us," he said, keeping his eyes on the direction they'd just come from. "They don't need to follow us. They know where to find me."

"Yeah well," Cassie said. "If they want to swing by, I'll be ready."

Tom looked at her and then noticed she had a shotgun at her side. "Where did you get that?" he asked, glancing nervously towards the house.

"This is Norfolk," Cassie said, shrugging. "Every other man has at least one."

Tom wanted to give her a lecture on gun safety, particularly with a child in the house, but this wasn't the time. Besides, if he didn't trust Cassie then he wouldn't have called her. Tom gestured towards the house and having first collected the bags Alice packed from the car, he led them into the house.

Saffy was already curled up on the sofa in front of the fire watching cartoons Alice must have found streaming on the television. Alice was making herself busy, and Tom knew she wasn't able to settle. Not yet, anyway.

"How long do you have this place?" Cassie asked.

"Pretty much as long as we need it," he said, catching Alice's eye. "But hopefully we'll only need it for a day or two," Tom said, silently grateful to his friend for lending him their holiday home at such short notice. It was an ideal location for him to stash his family. There was only one road in and out and behind them were the marshes and the sand dunes. Beyond that, the North Sea. "Have you spoken to Eric and Danny?"

Cassie nodded. "I have. Eric is sending Becca and George to stay with family for a few days."

"And Danny?"

Cassie scoffed. "He hasn't got anyone he cares about or who care about him, so he's not overly concerned." Tom arched his eyebrows and Cassie relented. "He's all right. He's going to bunk in at Eric's house for the time being, once Becca is safely away."

"Good. What did you say to Tamara?"

Cassie winced. "Nothing. I just slipped out. I don't feel good about that, though, sir." She shook her head. "Surely, we need to be calling all the big guns in on this. They've threatened—"

Tom steered her away from the reception room, back into the hall, conscious of Alice and Saffy overhearing. Saffy had her mother's ability to appear as if she wasn't paying attention only to be taking in every detail and Aunt Cassie sporting a shotgun as an accessory would certainly be enough to have her listening.

"I understand your concern, but if we set off all the alarms, then we'll drive these people underground and then who knows when or where they'll resurface."

"I get that," Cassie said, "but this is exactly the sort of stunt that will get us into serious bother if—"

"It all goes wrong," Tom said. He glanced into the living room, seeing Alice look his way. "I know, and it's on me if it does."

"And it'll be one of us who gets it in the neck, sir."

"I'll take the responsibility," Tom said.

"I'm not talking about the senior brass," Cassie said. "I couldn't care less what they think." She checked no one else was within earshot, craning her neck to see through into the living room. "I mean these people, the ones we are hunting or should I say, the ones who are hunting us, are pretty frightening."

Tom took a moment, thinking hard. He was taking a gamble, that was true, but it was calculated. Simon had told him he didn't do anything unless it served a purpose. That had to also include revealing himself to Tom. This meant either he didn't care about being identified or he was incredibly confident that he would never be identified. The releasing of Alexa had proven that he wouldn't kill indiscriminately, but he'd set enough of a precedent for Tom to know that things could change very quickly.

"I think they played their best hand," Tom said. "Coming to see me like this, making the threats he did, is not the brash act that we might see it as."

"I don't follow, sir," Cassie said.

"They could have sat back and waited. They've been shadowing our investigation... possibly all the way, and you'd think they could have continued to do so."

"Bide their time until we led them to what they wanted you mean?"

Tom nodded. "But something made them feel the necessity to intervene."

"What?"

Tom laughed. "I wish I knew, but Simon – the man I told you about – didn't come to see me just to make a threat. He will have known the weight of resources we could bring to bear upon him for threatening police officers and their families."

"Then why do it?" Cassie asked. "There has to be a reason."

"There is," Tom said, frowning. He rubbed at his face,

feeling the weariness that follows a period of intense drama. His family was safe, at least for now. "We just have to figure it out, that's all."

"Oh good, sir," Cassie said, drily. "That's all. What are we going to do?"

"I'm going back to the station," he said. "I'm going to take a look at the files again from scratch."

"You think we missed something?"

"I do," Tom said. "All of the cloak-and-dagger stuff is designed to focus my mind, I'm sure of it."

Alice appeared at the end of the hall and Cassie alerted Tom by flitting her eyes towards her and back again. Tom turned, seeing Alice and walked over to her, looping his arm around her waist and pulling her to him.

"I have to go into work for a bit," he said. An alarmed expression crossed her face. "I'll not be long, I promise."

"I want you to stay here," she said.

"And I want that too, but if we are going to head home sooner rather than later, then I need to figure this out." He looked back at Cassie. "Cassie will take care of you, too." Alice's gaze passed to Cassie and then she saw the shotgun by her side. "Stay indoors and try to keep away from the windows," Tom said. "And that goes for Saffy too."

"Tom, this is crazy —"

"You're both safe, I promise."

"You've got the dream team on point," Cassie said, grinning broadly. Alice seemed unconvinced. Tom drew Alice's gaze back to him.

"It'll be all right. I'll call in every hour and you can always phone me if you need to," he said. Alice looked away, her lips pursed.

"You promise that this will be all right," Alice said.

"It will."

"No! You *promise me*," she said sternly.

"I promise," Tom said firmly.

"Daddy never breaks his promises," Saffy said from behind them and all eyes turned towards her, standing at the threshold of the living room. "He never does."

"That's right, munchkin," Tom said, smiling at her, detaching himself from Alice and moving to Saffy, scooping her up into his arms. She held to him tightly. "And I'm not going to start now."

CHAPTER THIRTY-TWO

TOM ENTERED THE STATION, bypassing the custody suite and heading for the CID ops room. The lights inside the station were on their night-time setting, reduced to thirty percent to allow the cleaners to go about their business but much of the station was in darkness and relatively silent. Only the custody suite was staffed with emergency calls routed through the central control room. Two uniformed officers, on their break, were sitting in the canteen and neither saw him as he walked past.

Entering ops, he switched on the main lights and blinked as the tubes flickered into life. He'd been planning what he would do from the moment he left Alice and Saffy with Cassie near Holme, the conversation with Simon playing on his mind. *What was his motivation for the visit?* He was sure that it stretched beyond a threat. There were other ways he could have delivered that without adding the personal touch.

Tom approached the information boards, casting an eye over them. The process always followed the same course. To begin with, the timeline started with the first victim, in this case Martin Odiham. The ties to the deceased, people they spent time with, associates and family, their movements, financial and criminal history, all followed from there. Everything they could find out about the victim's life, all of it gathered in one place to build a wider picture. Somewhere in that wealth of information would lie the answer to their death.

In Tom's mind, however, this time it was different. They had too much information, and it was having the opposite effect. The answer lay in a simplified approach. He began by taking down the photographs of the three car thieves: Finn, Ollie Chalk and Alexa. Mark Nolan's picture followed. These people were all in the wrong place at the wrong time. In piecing this together, they were complications, rather than solutions. Despite a variety of nefarious connections, none of them had any proven link with Ilić.

Once Tom was finished, he was almost back to square one. He had a victim, Martin Odiham, at All Saints Church. He had another victim, Ilić, and a vehicle, the Range Rover owned by Jason Law. If he was to take Simon at his word – which Tom was loath to do, but right now it seemed logical – then they were both hunting the same person; the killer of Ilić. Up until now, they'd assumed the killer of this man was likely to be Simon and his associates for an undiscovered motive. The notion that they were in fact chasing the same figure was quite a revelation.

With the notable caveat that if, of course, it was true.

Tom sat down at a nearby desk, turning on the computer. He logged into his files. There was no discernible link between Martin Odiham and his killer either. Nor was there any motive for his murder and then the subsequent ransacking of his cottage.

"What were you looking for?" Tom asked quietly, and then a thought struck him. "Or what was it you found?"

He re-examined the forensic report from Odiham's cottage,

but nothing leapt out at him. He sat back, staring up at the information boards, looking much as they had when they first got the investigation underway. There wasn't much there. Martin Odiham, Ilić and the Laws. The trace evidence on Ilić's body led them to a cold case, over thirty years old but, again, this had no clear links to the present day. Tom opened that archive folder on the screen.

The original paperwork was hard copy but there had been a programme of digitisation underway to aid cold-case reviews and this was one of those which had been updated. The crime scene photographs of the deceased man were graphic. He'd been beaten to death in his kitchen. The details surrounding his wife, who was still missing, were scarce.

They were a middle-class couple, unassuming by all accounts. There were no personal images of them in the files. Just their basic details; names and addresses, job descriptions and known associates. There was no evidence of criminality or motives for the murder that the investigating officers found. This was also the conclusion of both cold-case review teams who examined the case in later years. The case was still open but there were no leads to follow.

Tom sat back. The only link between them was that Ilić undoubtedly murdered Odiham, and he was subsequently found dead in the car belonging to the Laws. He opened the forensic report on the examination of the Range Rover. He scanned the summary at the end. The only fingerprints found inside the vehicle, beyond those matching Ollie Chalk, Finn Harper and Alexa Willis, were those of Jason and Natasha Law.

There was evidence that the vehicle interior had been wiped down but there were still fingerprints found, but nothing proving Ilić had been inside the vehicle other than where his body was found, in the boot, wrapped in tarpaulin.

"If you eliminate the impossible then whatever is left," Tom whispered to himself, "no matter how improbable, must be the truth."

He sat forward and switched off the monitor. He checked the time as he rose from his seat. He'd promised to check in with Cassie every hour either by text or phone call. He dialled her number. She answered swiftly.

"Sir?" she said.

"Everything all right?"

"Yes, no change," Cassie said. "Alice has taken Saffy to bed. They are going to sleep in together. The little one is scared, and Alice is putting a brave face on it, but they're okay. Don't worry."

"And you?"

"I'm all right. Eric and Danny are making their way over here and we're going to run shifts, just in case."

"Eric got Becca away safely?"

"Yeah, she and George are holed up. We're all well. How's it going with you?"

"I'm just thinking…"

"Just thinking?"

"When Eric was given the runaround, remember, when he was playing the role of Finn Harper?"

"Yeah."

"What was with the blindfold and leading him around, only to leave him alone again in Ringstead?"

Cassie was silent for a moment. "Just to waste our time, maybe?"

"That's what I thought at first too, but… these people strike me as efficient, methodical."

"Yes, that figures. So… why would they do it?"

"Why indeed. I'm… heading out for a bit to check something."

"Anything you want to share, sir?"

"Not right now," he said, moving to the window over-looking the car park at the front of the station. The road was quiet, the businesses opposite were all locked up as well.

"You know you'll have company," Cassie said, "if you're heading out, I mean."

Tom nodded. "Yes, I'm counting on it."

"Should one of us come to you—"

"No, I know what I'm doing."

ONLY A HANDFUL of lights were visible in houses as Tom drove into Great Bircham. Pulling up outside the Laws' farmhouse, Tom could see Natasha moving around in the kitchen through a small side window. He got out of the car, greeted only by the sound of the breeze passing through the nearby trees.

He made his way down the side of the house, approaching the conservatory at the rear. The interior lights were on and he was able to observe from the shadows, safe in the knowledge that he couldn't be seen. Natasha was alone, clearing things away while steam rose from the kettle on the counter to her right. Tom walked up to the conserva-tory and gently rapped his knuckles on the glass, startling Natasha.

She tentatively approached the door, eyeing Tom warily but he was certain she recognised him. He was illuminated by the light coming from the interior. She unlocked the door and smiled nervously at him.

"Detective Inspector," she said. "This is a surprise."

"Hello, Natasha. I apologise for the lateness of the visit, but may I come inside?"

"Yes, of course," she said, stepping back and Tom held the

door to stop it from closing on him, passing through and then closing it.

"I was just making Jason a nightcap," she said, the kettle clicking off in the background. "Can I offer you a cup of tea—" she frowned, looking up at the clock. "It is a bit late for tea or coffee, isn't it? Jason and I tend to have a herbal tea or something at this time, to help us sleep. I have decaffeinated, if you'd like?"

"A decaffeinated tea would be lovely, thank you," Tom said, glancing around them. Natasha moved to the cupboard and set about arranging another cup and saucer for Tom.

"What brings you out here at this hour, Mr Janssen?" she asked, moving to another cupboard where Tom saw a variety of coloured boxes, each containing flavoured or herbal teas. She reached up to the top shelf and pulled down a larger box, containing several smaller ones, sifting through the collection to make her selection. Once she'd chosen the bags, she put the box back on the shelf and closed the cupboard.

"I've been reviewing our progress," Tom said, absently looking around the kitchen whilst Natasha busied herself pouring water into the cups.

"How is it going?" she asked him without looking up.

"There has been a development," Tom said, "and it is rather surprising, I have to say."

"Oh?" she said, glancing at him. "That sounds intriguing."

"It is," Tom said.

"Care to share it?" she asked. "Or is it confidential?"

"Not really," he said, leaning against the counter. "You see, we've been struggling to tie our victims and suspects together. No matter how hard we looked or how deep we went into their lives, they just don't fit."

"That sounds like a conundrum," she said.

"Which brings me back here, to you and Jason."

"To us?" Natasha said, turning to face him, the steam rising from the cups as the tea brewed. "I can't think why." Tom was about to speak but Natasha held up a hand. "Let me take Jason his tea, and then you can tell me what's on your mind."

"Where is Jason?" Tom asked.

"He's in his bed," she said. "His health has taken a bit of a downturn this past week."

"I'm sorry to hear that."

She shrugged. "As I said before, he has good days and bad ones. The bad are becoming more frequent though."

Natasha passed Tom a cup and saucer, gesturing towards the milk and sugar she'd set out beside the kettle. He thanked her and she picked up Jason's cup and left the kitchen. He heard the squeak of the treads as she slowly climbed the stairs.

Tom added a splash of milk and then peered out of the kitchen window, surveying the garden. He couldn't see any movement, but he was acutely aware he was at a disadvantage now he was indoors. He walked into the adjoining conservatory, cup and saucer in hand. He didn't feel at all threatened. Glancing up at the ceiling, Tom heard movement in the room above the kitchen.

He didn't have to wait long before he heard Natasha coming back downstairs. She smiled at him as she entered the kitchen, picking up her cup and bringing it with her to join him. She gestured for them to sit down, and she took a seat opposite him with her back to the French doors. She lifted her teacup with both hands, blowing steam from the surface and watching Tom over the lip, before sipping at the brew.

"I suppose I shouldn't be surprised, not really," Natasha said. Tom cocked his head.

"About what?"

"That you're here," she said. "You struck me as a very

bright man when you first came to visit. And your young detective constable, what was his name?"

"Danny."

"Yes, Danny." She smiled sweetly, lifting her cup again and wincing as she drank. "A fine young man. I thought he coped well with… well, Jason." She smiled apologetically. "I'm so sorry about the way Jason attacked him, but… you see, he mistook you for two more of them. He thought I was in danger."

"You expected us to come back then?"

She nodded. "Yes. It was only a matter of time." A sound came from upstairs, a dull thud, but Natasha seemed unconcerned. "After all, the doddery old pensioner routine will only last as long as the facts allow, won't it?"

"Yes, I think that's fair," Tom said, sipping his own tea.

"What was it that made you suspect our involvement? How did you know?"

"To be honest with you," Tom said, sitting forward and resting his elbows on his knees, "I still don't understand." He fixed her with a stern look. "But when I stripped everything away, the only conclusion I could draw was that Ilić came here on the night he died."

"Ilić?" she said. "Is that the man's name?"

"Yes, Goran Ilić. You didn't know him?"

Natasha shook her head. "I've never seen him before, and I doubt Jason knew him either. He was far too young to have been in our sphere back then."

"Why was he looking for you?" Tom asked. Natasha smiled, but Tom could tell she was considering what she would and would not say. "I might not know what this is all about – yet – but I assure you, I will soon enough. You may as well tell me."

Natasha sighed. "I don't doubt it." She grimaced, placing a

hand against the centre of her chest. Tom noticed and she waved his concern away. "It's perfectly natural. Volatile stomach acid is not a problem for the young, Mr Janssen." She appeared to settle herself, taking a sip of tea to soothe her throat.

"Why did he come here?" Tom asked again. Natasha was momentarily reticent and then she relented.

"I suppose it doesn't matter any more," she said suddenly. "There isn't a great deal of time left, so who really cares."

"I do," Tom said. "Three people are dead and—"

"There will be more than that, I can assure you," she said, glancing at Tom in resignation, "once all of this plays out." She gasped, sucking air through her teeth. Tom leaned forward.

"Natasha, are you—"

"I'm fine," she said, holding up a placating hand. "It's completely natural, I assure you." She lifted her head and took a deep breath. "Besides, if… what did you say his name was, the man who came here?"

"Ilić," Tom said.

"Yes, well once he came here… it was clear that others were sure to follow."

"Undoubtedly," Tom said. "I know his associates are here already. They've been running amok locally."

"I know. I figured as much."

"Well, you should be aware that these are very dangerous men. And if I can figure out your involvement then it's only a matter of time until they do. The best thing you can do right now is level with me."

"To what end?"

"I can protect you."

She laughed bitterly. A small carriage clock on a shelf in the kitchen chimed, signalling the top of the hour, and she looked at it. "Time," Natasha said, nodding gently with a half-smile on her face, "eventually runs out, for all of us."

"What did Ilić want of you?"

"We are nothing to him," Natasha said. "He's only a foot soldier."

"A heavyweight for hire," Tom said, "or so Interpol tells us."

"Yes, that figures."

"Where is the shotgun?" Tom asked, keen to ensure it was secured sooner rather than later. "Or did you dispose of it after he died?"

Natasha pointed towards the kitchen. "On top of the row of wall cabinets."

Tom rose from his seat, setting his cup and saucer down on a small table beside his chair. He walked into the kitchen, gathered a chair from the dining table as he passed, setting it down in front of the cabinets. He climbed up and retrieved a double-barrelled shotgun, along with a box of cartridges, from the narrow space behind the pelmet.

Stepping back down, he broke the barrel and ensured the weapon was empty before putting it down on the dining table. There were only four cartridges in the box. He put those shells in his coat pocket, and returned to the conservatory where Natasha was calmly drinking her tea, deep in thought.

CHAPTER THIRTY-THREE

TOM FOUND this whole scenario quite surreal. Taking his seat opposite Natasha again, he fixed his eye on her but her expression was blank, distant.

"He came here to meet us," she said. Then she inclined her head, focussing her gaze on Tom once more. "Well, to meet me. You see, I took it upon myself to make the arrangements at any rate."

Tom was intrigued. "You... wanted to meet him?"

"Not him exactly." She frowned. "We've been away for so long, out in the cold, so to speak, Detective Janssen." Her expression took on a faraway look. "After all these years... it's odd to have to face your own mortality – once it was clear how fragile Jason was becoming – and then to have to make a decision."

"What decision?"

She heaved a sigh, grimacing slightly. "I wanted to go home," she said, lifting her eyes to meet his. She seemed genuinely saddened by the comment. "I never would have thought I would feel that way, not after so long. I thought I'd closed the door on that part of my life but, as I've grown older, it's felt more important to me to go back."

"Why can't you go home?" Tom asked.

She smiled, arching her eyebrows. "Politics. People come and go, policies change… governments change and then – sometimes in the blink of an eye – everything is different. When that happens, you have to adapt to the new way of things." She shook her head. "Jason and I… we saw the way things were going in the motherland. There was a great deal of change already underway… Germany reunited… the old order was falling apart around us."

"You are talking about the eighties?" Tom asked.

"The eighties, nineties… it all began in the seventies," she said, tilting her head to one side. "The invasion of Afghanistan was the beginning of the end, only none of us realised at that point. Our country was already in its death throes, even then. A decade later, it was all progressing on one path, and Jason," she said, smiling warmly, "he saw the direction of travel. Our allies across Eastern Europe were tumbling, the wall fell in Berlin. Budgets were already being cut, money… appropriated… by those who shouldn't have had access to it." She sighed. "Believe me, the country we served so diligently was lost to us. History, and I mean the last thirty years, has proved that he was right. An empire, the Great Bear, reduced to a mangy bruin managed by a coward who rules for his own gain and for those lieutenants around him."

"You're speaking of Russia," Tom said. He glanced upwards, as if he could see Jason in his bed upstairs through the ceiling. "That means… the two of you were—"

"We aren't Cold War spies with covert listening devices… carrying out bag drops and the like," she said, with a smirk. "Not exactly, anyway. Not all of it is like what you see in the films, you know."

"Then what are you?"

She pursed her lips. "We were data gatherers... delivery personnel, if you like. We moved information from one place to another, cultivated relationships," she said, seemingly nostalgic about their past. "They were good times. We were all doing it. It was the natural order of things, a shell game that everyone played."

"Until?"

She shrugged. "Things changed. We knew it was coming," she said. "Jason could see us being returned home, to a country we no longer recognised. To an uncertain future."

"I thought you said that you loved your country?"

"Oh, I do," she said, her eyes glistening. "I really do but, you see, I love Jason more. And if we went back then we would not be together. It wouldn't be allowed."

"Why not?"

"Great Britain is famous for its class structure, is it not?"

Tom nodded.

"Things are not so dissimilar at home. Jason – Anatolii – is descended from a very noble family and I am... well, less so. Anatolii's family, as it turned out, fell afoul of the power struggles that played out after the turn of the century when everything changed again, back home." She shrugged. "Our union would never have been acceptable. For us to leave here would have seen the end of our time together, and that was unacceptable to us both. We were to be together. That was our plan, whatever it took."

"You could have asked for asylum." Tom said and she snorted with derision. "It's been done before and since."

"And you think we would have been safe?" she said, shaking her head. "Tell that to Litvinenko or the Skripals for that matter. How safe do they feel? One of them is dead, so forgive me for not having confidence in the security of your country."

"Who was the man you murdered in 1991?"

She remained tight-lipped, averting her eyes from Tom's. "It is of no consequence," she said.

"I disagree. A man lost his life—"

"And if he had not, then we would never have been free," she retorted. "And do not think for a second that this man was not ruthless. He was cut from the old cloth. He cared not for anything other than his ideology, and people suffered as a result."

"And what of you?"

"What about me?" she asked.

"What is your ideology?"

She was reflective for a moment. Then she stared at Tom.

"I believe views change. People change. For those who can afford an ideology, then it is a great thing to hold onto. But to give yourself to one vision of how things should be only leads you to dismiss the benefits of another way of doing things. And that is a negative."

"You sound like someone who's lost their faith," Tom said. She nodded.

"That's the thing about dying," she said. "If nothing else, it offers you clarity."

"Who did you reach out to?" Tom asked. "I presume you contacted someone, testing the water about returning home for your final days."

"I did," she said. "With Jason the way he is, I thought it might be time." She winced, adjusting her seating position but it appeared not to make her any more comfortable. "But it was naive of me." She laughed. "There's no fool like an old fool, is there?"

"You set up a meeting," Tom said.

"Yes, I arranged to meet at the church, at All Saints. I know it is left open… and although people come and go, it's not often used for worship anymore. It's close to here, but not on our doorstep."

"And they sent Ilić," Tom said.

"And as soon as I saw him," Natasha said, "I knew."

"Knew what?"

"Two things. Firstly, that he wasn't one of ours… in the service I mean. I don't know how it wound up being that man who came for us, but he is not from the FSB or their military equivalent. He was a private contractor, very basic with his craft. Believe me, I would know."

"And the other thing?"

"That he wasn't there to help facilitate our journey home."

"Did you speak with him?"

She shook her head. "He was expecting Jason, not me. I was sitting in the pews and I left as soon as he arrived. On some level, I think he realised, but not in time."

"And Martin?"

"The warden?" she asked and Tom nodded. "I… feel badly about that. Ilić… must have mistaken him for Jason."

Tom exhaled, shaking his head. He'd been correct. Martin Odiham was in the wrong place at the wrong time. A stroke of bad luck which ultimately cost him his life.

"How did he find you?" Tom asked. Natasha slowly got up, bracing herself on the dining table before crossing to a drawer in a nearby sideboard. She opened it and took something out. Shuffling back to the table, she passed it to Tom. He noted she didn't seem to be moving as freely as before and took time to retake her seat. Tom studied the photograph she'd handed to him.

He recognised the outside of All Saints Church. Although, the grounds were rather overgrown and the trees lining the entrance path were huge, growing together overhead, and

Tom recalled them having been cut back as long ago as he could remember. He flipped the photo over and read the date on the back. It was entitled *the restoration team*. He looked at the people in the shot. Although their hair and clothing were very different, and they were younger, he could make out Natasha.

"Is this Jason, at the back?" he asked. She nodded.

"The church needed work, and what better way for us to build friendships and become part of the community than to help raise funds, offer our time," she said. "We were retired after all."

"You knew Martin then?"

"A little," she said, "but we soon realised it was better for us not to get too close to people, to anyone. Just in case."

"Ilić recognised you from the photograph?" Tom asked.

"Yes, Martin had this picture at his home. Stupid of us really, Jason and I, to allow ourselves to be photographed. It is an occupational hazard, but I suppose we got careless after a while."

"Who killed him? Ilić, I mean?"

"Oh, that was me," she said in a calm, matter-of-fact tone. "I don't feel bad about that one. It was him or us." She frowned. "I only wish I had been better at disposing of the body. Had they… not taken the car, then all of this could have been avoided."

Tom was about to challenge her, but Natasha gasped again, only this time Tom immediately got up as she doubled over in pain, clutching her stomach. Tom came around to her, dropping to his haunches beside her.

"Natasha? Are you okay?" he asked, seeing the pain in her expression. "What can I do?"

She looked sideways at him, and he could see a sheen of

perspiration on her forehead, her face had drained of all colour. She smiled weakly, offering him the slightest shake of the head.

"Not much, I'm afraid," she said. She tried to right herself, and Tom was needed to help her to sit upright. Her breathing was laboured now and she seemed to still be in a degree of pain. "It's funny," she said, her forehead furrowing. "You never know what it will feel like when it happens. I hoped…" she sucked in a deep breath, "that it wouldn't hurt this much."

Tom followed her gaze towards her cup and peered into it. There were only dregs of the herbal tea left inside the cup, and he picked up the cup, smelling the contents. It had a strange odour to it, with a hint of almonds. He set the cup down and looked at Natasha.

"What have you taken?" he asked, but she was no longer able to focus on him, her breathing shallow.

"I would have loved to see my home… one last time." Her head pitched to one side and Tom reached out, catching her face by the cheek with his palm. He gently rested her against the back of the chair. He felt her neck for a pulse with two fingers, but she'd already gone.

Tom bit his lip, then looked at his own tea. It was clear she hadn't poisoned his cup because he felt absolutely fine. He looked up at the ceiling and rose, hurrying out of the conservatory, through the kitchen and into the hall, breaking into a run that took him up the stairs. On the landing, he checked every room until he opened the bedroom door to find Jason, sitting up in his bed, propped up on numerous pillows.

Tom entered the room slowly, taking in the man's appearance. His eyes were closed, his mouth hanging open to one side. It was as if he was frozen in situ, stifling a yawn. An empty saucer was in his lap, a teacup lay on its side on the rug beside the bed. What was left of the contents had spilled onto the bedspread as he dropped it, seeping into the material.

Tom checked for a pulse, but he knew it was fruitless. Natasha had ensured that the two of them would stay together, if not in this life then in the next.

CHAPTER THIRTY-FOUR

HE WATCHED as the detective came out of the house. Shivering against the chill in the air, he stepped back further into the shadows, confident that he was invisible to the naked eye. Unless the detective shone his headlights straight at him, he would remain invisible. Tom Janssen walked to his car and got in, starting the engine and turning the car around. He waited in the shadows until the car reached the end of the driveway, disappearing amongst the trees, and listened as it turned out onto the main road, accelerating away.

Emerging from his hideaway, he rolled his shoulders. He wasn't used to this, standing still, observing, for this length of time. It was worth it though. The risk of revealing himself to the policeman had worked, steering him in the right direction to lead him here.

A dog barked in the night. The neighbouring properties weren't close enough to cause a problem but, just in case, he took the gun from inside his coat and quickly attached the suppressor, screwing it into place. Seeing his breath visible, he covered the open ground between the barn and the house.

Coming alongside the conservatory, he put his back to the wall and tentatively peered around the corner.

Keeping his wits about him, conscious of what had befallen the man he'd hired, he cast an eye over the interior. The policeman had gone in through the conservatory door. Perhaps it was still unlocked. Darya – or Natasha as she called herself now – was sitting in a chair with her back to him. There was no sign of Anatolii.

He tried the door handle, and it moved. He depressed the handle and teased the door open. The hinges were well-greased and didn't make a sound. All the while, he kept his eye on Darya, but she didn't flinch. She might be asleep. He eased inside, glancing to left and right, but saw no threat. Creeping up behind her, he could see her reflection in the glass opposite her. Her eyes were closed, and they would be forever. He raised the barrel of the gun, aiming at the back of her head. His father's face came to mind as he squeezed the trigger.

There was a gentle pffft sound and her head lolled forward before she slumped to one side.

Satisfied, he turned his attention to finding Anatolii. His death would be much slower. He listened intently, but there was no sound in the house. The structure of the conservatory creaked as a gust of wind struck it but other than that there was silence. Moving slowly but purposefully through the interior, he checked the sitting and drawing rooms, but they were empty.

The upstairs was in darkness as he made his way up, eyes trained on the landing just in case Anatolii heard his approach. The bedroom doors off the landing were all closed and he silently cursed as every step seemed to announce his arrival, squeaking and groaning under his weight.

The door handles were all old, and he found himself

hoping that his quarry was either asleep or ignorant of the danger he was in. They'd seen off that fool Ilić, who'd massively underestimated who he was dealing with. He wasn't the first, certainly, but he would be the last. This would end tonight.

Having made steady progress, there was only one room left untried. He took a deep breath, steadying himself as he reached for the door handle, his fingers curling around it. He hesitated for a moment, his ear close to the door, but there were no sounds emanating from within. All he could hear were the creaks and groans of an old farmhouse which appeared to have a life of its own. He eased the door open.

Anatolii lay in his bed, sitting upright, an open book in his lap. He was asleep and hadn't stirred as the door creaked open. The surge of adrenalin was such a rush, like a drug, and he had to quell it as he moved into the room, coming to stand at the foot of the bed. Something didn't feel right though. The reading lamp on the bedside table was off, but he still had the book in his hands.

Inching forward, keen not to wake him, he moved to the side of the bed and switched on the lamp. Only then did he realise, stepping back, confused.

"You're too late!" a familiar voice said and he made to turn, intending to bring his gun to bear but he heard the tell-tale click of someone cocking the hammer of a shotgun. He glanced down at the gun in his hand, by his side. "I'm sure you're quick," Tom Janssen said, "but I doubt you're that quick. If your hand even twitches, I'll put you across the wall behind you, have no doubt."

"You are a policeman!" he said, his eyes meeting those of the detective. "There are rules for policemen."

"Not tonight. Not when you've threatened my family. Have no doubt, I'll drop you where you stand if I have to."

He smiled, genuinely appreciating his adversary. "Well done, Detective Janssen. You played this very well. I'm impressed."

"I wish I could say the same," the detective said, his eyes flitting to the deceased form of Anatolii, lying in bed. "I had help, in a manner of speaking."

"You did. I was somewhat careless, wasn't I? I let my excitement get the better of me, Detective Inspector. I've waited so long for this day."

"And who are you, to them?"

He slowly turned to face the policeman, careful to keep his hands in a non-threatening position, although he was keen to take any opportunity that might come his way. He knew what he was prepared to risk, but what he didn't know was the agility and mentality of his opponent. He'd studied Janssen, that's true, but you would never truly know what a man was capable of in a life and death situation until you witnessed him in one.

"I am here to deliver justice."

"You have a strange way of going about it."

"They murdered my father," he said, almost spitting the words. "And no one has ever seemed interested in pursuing justice for him."

"Thirty-odd years ago, priorities were very different."

"I suppose so, but not to me… or the few friends my father had."

"In that case it's not justice you're here for, but vengeance."

"Semantics," he said.

"Perhaps, but it is over, and you're too late."

"So I see." He looked at Anatolii. "Always taking the coward's way out. I told you you'd lead me to them, didn't I? You didn't believe me, but you did as I said."

"And now you're under arrest and you'll answer for what you've done here."

He grinned, shaking his head. How did a rural policeman get the upper hand on him? He had underestimated Darya and Anatolii, and now this man. When his father's former colleague got in touch with him to tip him off about their whereabouts, in his eagerness to find them, he'd allowed his emotions to get the better of him and he'd been too rash.

He'd lived here, in this country, since he was a teenager, building his life, but always with the lingering feeling that he had to avenge his father. One day. And now it was here, and he'd been cheated of it, just as he'd been cheated out of knowing his father as he grew from a teenager into a man.

"I don't think so."

"You don't?"

"No. You think my people won't come in here and take me away from you?" he said, nodding towards the shotgun. "You have two shots with that weapon. That's not enough to stop them all…" The detective smiled. A knowing smile. *How could he know?* "Is this amusing to you?"

"I have nothing to fear," the detective said. "You are alone here."

"One word, one shout and they will—"

"No one will come to rescue you. You've been clever, I'll give you that," the detective said. "But we both know you have been doing this by yourself. That's why you used all of the theatrics, walking Eric into that clearing in Ringstead without speaking, flying in the drone to collect the mobile phone and why you left him alone to give yourself time to get above him on the cliff face, ready to throw down Mark Nolan's body. All of it is an illusion, and it very nearly worked."

"How can you know, for certain, I mean?"

"Because you sat in my kitchen and looked me in the eye."

"And?"

"Reading people is my job. It's what I do, what I've always done. I couldn't take the risk attempting to disarm you while you held my family at gunpoint, but here, tonight, I've watched. I parked along the road and came back. You are alone, and you would not have come here by yourself if you did have associates with you. And that means you have always been alone throughout this. Government agencies don't send family members to avenge their father's death, nor do they hire low-level gangsters to do their dirty work. This is on you and you alone."

He still couldn't figure out how this man had got the better of him. He'd been one step ahead all the way along. Had Goran Ilić been what he'd expected, what he'd been told he was, instead of little more than a thug for hire then it wouldn't have come to this. That's what you get for trusting the judgement of others. Amateurish behaviour. Darya and Anatolii had seen to him quite effectively. If he'd communicated their whereabouts sooner, rather than approaching them himself, then this situation would never have happened. There would have been no need for the deaths of those others. Police involvement would have been minimal.

"Darya – Natasha – was already dead before I came inside, wasn't she?" The policeman nodded. "Well played," he said, smiling. "You did well, Detective Janssen. I underestimated you."

"I advise you not to do so again."

He sighed, glancing down at the pistol in his hand.

"Put down the gun!"

He shook his head. "No, I would rather not. How about one last round?"

"What?"

"*Simon says;* game over." He raised his hand, turning the gun towards the detective, knowing his opponent had the drop on him. To succeed, the policeman would have to hesitate. He saw the flash from the barrel, but never heard the sound of the subsequent blast or the force of the impact as his body was torn from his feet and hurled against the wall behind him.

CHAPTER THIRTY-FIVE

TOM CURSED, the distinct odour of a freshly discharged shotgun filling the room. The man lay against the far wall of the bedroom, his body slumped forward, head dangling down, his hands in his lap. Tom slowly edged towards him keeping the loaded shotgun pointed at him. He toed the gun, lying on the floor beside the leg, away from the body. He was dead, Tom was almost certain, but he wasn't going to take any chances.

"It didn't have to end this way," he said quietly.

One man's vengeance-fuelled killing spree was over. Alice and Saffy were safe, as were the rest of the team. Breaking the barrel of the shotgun, Tom knelt beside the dead man. He checked for a pulse but the wound in his chest had proven to be fatal, and it was simply a procedural check. Standing up, he took out his mobile and dialled Cassie's number.

"Boss," she said, and he could hear the tension in her tone. "Is everything all right?"

"It's over," Tom said softly, glancing between the still forms of Jason Law and his would-be assassin. "Tell the others they can stand down."

"It's over?"

"I'll need to square things away this end, but I'll be across as soon as I can. Are you able to stay with my family until I get back?"

"Aye, of course. Are you sure it's over?"

"Dead sure," Tom said, and hung up. He quickly typed out a text message to Alice. *You're safe. I'll call you later when I get the chance, but I don't know when it will be. I love you.*

TOM STOOD by himself in the driveway of the Laws' house, his hands thrust deep into the pockets of his overcoat. He was feeling the cold of the night air permeating through to his bones now. The darkness was punctuated by the flashing lights of multiple police cars sealing off access to the house. A forensic team were already inside, taking steps to prepare the scene for a full analysis. Hearing footsteps on the gravel drive approaching him, Tom turned to see Tamara Greave making her way over to join him. He smiled weakly as she came alongside.

"Everything is underway inside," she said. He already knew that, but she was using it to break the ice. Once she'd checked on his wellbeing, Tamara had steered clear of him after her arrival at the crime scene. She was furious. He knew her well enough to see through the façade of professionalism she wore so well.

"Good," he said in lieu of knowing what he should say. Tamara looked around. There were officers milling about but there were no onlookers loitering beyond the freshly erected police cordon, at least not yet. That would change once word spread and, in Norfolk, you could be certain word would indeed spread like wildfire.

"You know this is going to take some explaining?"

Tom nodded solemnly. "I'm sorry." The apology was heart-felt but sounded tame and rather pathetic when the situation was viewed in the round.

"Sorry," Tamara repeated. She heaved a deep sigh. "I don't think sorry is going to cut it, Tom."

"I know." He looked at her, tight-lipped. "But I mean it."

"You should have come to me as soon as—"

"I should have, but I couldn't."

"You put yourself and your family at great risk, Tom."

"If I'd called everyone in then he would have gone to ground," Tom argued. "Who knows when or where he'd have popped up—"

"Your visit here…" Tamara said, her words tailing off as she gritted her teeth, struggling to stay calm. "It forced Natasha's hand… and she took her own life as well as that of her husband's."

"If I could figure it out then it was only a matter of time until their hunter would too. She'd already made those plans. She as good as told me so—"

"And the whole *using them as bait to lure him in* trick," Tamara said, laughing bitterly. "You could have got yourself killed."

"But I didn't."

"No," Tamara snapped. "What you did *was* you set a trap for a murder suspect and then used the weapon from a previous murder to kill him!"

"That's not how it happened," Tom countered, but he could see her point of view.

"That's how it will be shaped by some," Tamara said. "How could you be so foolish?"

"It wasn't premeditated, I—"

Tamara held up a forceful hand, looking over her shoulder

briefly to check they weren't being overheard. "Don't say another word to me about it, Tom. Not here, not now." She drew breath, closing her eyes. She suddenly looked tired as if the weight of recent events were taking their toll. "I don't want to have to repeat what you say now to anyone else."

Tom nodded. "I'm sorry. The last thing I want to do is to cause you more grief."

"The sentiment is appreciated, Tom," she said, "but this has escalated into an officer involved shooting... and it's not in a controlled environment either." She pursed her lips. In any incident involving a firearms officer, there were protocols to follow, both prior to the incident and afterwards, especially where the death of an individual occurred. The difference in those scenarios was that they were planned operations, protocol had been followed. In this case, Tom was working alone without oversight. "I think you know what comes next, don't you?"

"I do, yes," Tom said. Tamara looked pained. He reached inside his jacket and took out his wallet. Holding the black leather in the palm of his hands, this seemed a significant moment. Tamara didn't ask. She didn't have to. Tom handed her the wallet containing his warrant card and constabulary crest. She took it silently, avoiding his eye.

"You are officially suspended, Tom, pending an investigation," she said, her voice cracking as she spoke. "On full pay, obviously." She looked up at him and he could see her eyes were glazed, reflecting the flashing lights illuminating the two of them. She struggled to swallow. "I'm..."

"It's okay, you have no choice."

Tamara nodded. "Go home, Tom... be with your family... and hold them close."

FREE BOOK GIVEAWAY

Visit the author's website at **www.jmdalgliesh.com** and sign up to the VIP Club and be the first to receive news and previews of forthcoming works.

Here you can download a FREE eBook novella exclusive to club members;

Life & Death - A Hidden Norfolk novella

———————

Never miss a new release.

No spam, ever, guaranteed. You can unsubscribe at any time.

The little bell above the door chimes again and I look up expectantly. It's just a little old man, the one who'd been sitting in the far corner who is now shuffling out into the street, drawing his coat around him whilst leaning on his walking stick. I can see he's struggling with the zipper of his coat. I think it's far too warm for a coat that heavy. Maybe that's one of the things that changes as you get older. You need more protection from the elements. That thought sparks something inside me and I remember last night. It's a warm feeling that tingles, creating a sense of longing, excitement and anticipation of the possibility of its repetition.

Looking up at the clock on the wall, I check my watch to see if they match. The lady behind the counter catches my eye. She saw me look up to check the time. She's thinking along the same lines as me. My cup is empty. The hot chocolate is long gone and even the remnants of the frothy whipped cream topping has hardened around the rim. I nursed it for as long as I dared, finishing it when it had already gone cold.

Glancing up towards the counter, she's giving me the stink eye. There are several people in the queue now and only one free table left, recently vacated by the little chap with the hunchback and walking stick. She wants me to leave. Fair enough, I guess. I've been here for three quarters of an hour, maybe longer. One hot chocolate with cream and mini-marsh-mallows is hardly going to pay the bills. I pretend not to see her looking but she's staring at me intensely now.

"Fine," I mutter, pushing back my chair. The legs scrape on the wooden floor and I see her smug, satisfied expression as she comes out from behind the counter, gathering up my cup and wiping down the table's surface before I've even stepped away.

She doesn't say anything and I hurry to the door, feeling like everyone's eyes are upon me. They all know. I've been there alone for ages and they all know I was waiting for some-one. He didn't show up. I know it. They all know it. I can feel my cheeks flushing as I push the door. It opens inwards and now I think they can all see I'm also an idiot, unable to read the big red letters on the sticker attached to the glass that reads *PULL*.

Once I'm safely out into the street, I chance a glance back inside but no one is looking at me. People are already taking their seats at my table. The sour-faced cow who owns the place is smiling warmly at them. She didn't smile like that at me. Am I invisible or so insignificant that I'm so easily forget-table? Catching my reflection in the window, I feel stupid. The lipstick I'm wearing is a brighter shade of red than is probably best suited to my skin tone and clashes with the frames of my glasses. I'm also wearing far too much foundation and my cheeks are aglow artificially with over application of my blusher. My embarrassment would probably be enough to achieve the same effect. I look like one of those Russian dolls with the painted cheeks.

I wanted to make a good impression. I wanted him to

think… I don't know what I wanted him to think. What was all of this about? It's me being silly, isn't it? When all is said and done, what is it that I have to offer him? I'm such a fool.

There's a lady sitting in the soft chair beside the window. Her husband has his back to me but she is watching me, studying me. I turn and hurry away, head down, picking up the pace and pretending that everything is happening exactly as planned.

A figure stumbles into me on the narrow pavement and instinctively I apologise, knowing I wasn't looking where I was going. I catch his eye and realisation dawns just as he takes a firm grip of my upper arm, steering me into an alleyway off the main road.

"I thought you weren't coming—"

"Shush!" he says, forcibly guiding me forwards.

"Hey!" I say as he pushes me off balance and further into the narrow passage between the old buildings. "You don't have to be so rough—"

"Shut up!" he says firmly, and something in his tone makes me do exactly that. I've always been cowed by authority and I lower my head. His demeanour changes, softening and with his hands gently, but firmly, placed on my shoulders, he turns me to face him, looking down into my eyes. He looks much more serious than usual. Sterner. Older. There's that flutter of anticipation in my chest again, along with the manifestation of the knot in my stomach at the same time.

"I thought you weren't coming," I say. "I would have waited inside if I'd—"

"Seriously, shut up," he says, his grip tightening on my bare shoulders, the skin exposed by my choice this morning to wear a sleeveless crop top.

"Sorry."

"Listen… it's not that I don't… want to see you…"

Why is he speaking to me like this? He's never spoken to me in this way before. I raise my eyes to meet his gaze. He has a hooded sweater on, and the hood is pulled up over his head. He glances back towards the street, people are passing the entrance but none are paying us any attention. *Is he ashamed to be seen with me?*

"I should never have let things get this far," he says, almost apologetically, but I sense there's something else motivating him beyond contrition. He's not had any complaints over the past few weeks. I can't see anything that should have changed things. But it has changed. All of it. I can see it in his expression.

"You're… breaking up with me?" The words catch in my throat, and I feel real pain as I say them out loud.

"We were never together," he says, coldly dismissive. "You know that."

"But I thought you said—"

"Forget what I said!" he hisses, startling me. "It never happened."

"But it did happen."

He forcibly squeezes my shoulders and it hurts. I mean, it really hurts. I protest but he pushes me against the wall, the coarseness of the brick scraping the skin of my shoulders.

"It shouldn't have—"

"But it did!" I counter, repeating myself. "You said you loved me—"

"I said all kinds of things! I should have known better. I didn't mean it, any of it." I can feel my eyes tearing and I want to speak but my mouth is dry. He relaxes his grip, if only a little, leaning forward and resting his forehead against mine. He lowers his voice, speaking softly, more like he does usually. "For what it's worth, I am sorry. I never meant to hurt you."

He makes to leave but I reach out, grasping the material of

his sweater and trying to pull him back. He shrugs off my hold with ease, increasing the length of his stride.

"No! Wait… please," I shout at him, trying to stop him from leaving me. Running after him, I grab his arm, hauling him back. He spins on his heel, lunges at me and, using both hands, shoves me away from him. I stumble backwards, tripping over my own feet and falling to the gound. He comes to stand over me, jabbing a finger towards me.

"Don't look at me, call me… and don't speak of this to anyone… ever," he says, glaring at me. "If you do… so help me girl, I'll make your life a living hell!"

"Please… don't leave me like this!"

But he is already at the end of the passage and, after furtively looking in both directions up and down the street, he moves to his right and disappears from view without looking back. I'm on my knees now, sobbing uncontrollably.

Why would he do this to me after everything we've done together, after everything that's been said. I don't understand. How can he be like this, so cold and uncompromising?

What have I done?

Enjoy this book? You could make a real difference.

Because reviews are critical to the success of an author's career, if you have enjoyed this novel, please do me a massive favour by entering one onto Amazon.

———

Type the following link into your internet search bar to go to the Amazon page and leave a review;

https://geni.us/JMD-watchandprey

———

If you prefer not to follow the link please visit the sales page where you purchased the title in order to leave a review.

Reviews increase visibility. Your help in leaving one would make a massive difference to this author and I would be very grateful.

ALSO BY THE AUTHOR

In the Misty Isle Series
A Long Time Dead
The Dead Man of Storr
The Talisker Dead
The Cuillin Dead

In the Hidden Norfolk Series
One Lost Soul
Bury Your Past
Bury Your Past
Kill Our Sins
Tell No Tales
Hear No Evil
The Dead Call
Kill Them Cold
A Dark Sin
To Die For
Fool Me Twice
The Raven Song
Angel of Death
Dead To Me
Blood Runs Cold
When Death Calls

Life and Death**
**FREE *ebook* - *visit* jmdalgliesh.com

Audiobooks

In the Dark Yorkshire Series
Read by Greg Patmore

Divided House
Blacklight
The Dogs in the Street
Blood Money
Fear the Past
The Sixth Precept

Collections
Dark Yorkshire Books 1-3
Dark Yorkshire Books 4-6

In the Misty Isle Series
Read by Angus King

A Long Time Dead
The Dead Man of Storr
The Talisker Dead
The Cuillin Dead

Printed in Great Britain
by Amazon

53348125R00192